As soon as Lovejoy saw the packet drop from the shopping bag, she grabbed it and ran. She wasn't sure what it was at first. All she knew was that it was colorful and pretty, a welcome relief from the grim brick and stone buildings, the jagged bomb ruins that hemmed in her poor London neighborhood. The package held flower seeds, blue cornflower. It also held the seeds of a dream. For from this small stolen start, Lovejoy was determined to build something beautiful, some place that was her own to tend and love. It would be a small street child's garden, yet one that would bring together people from all sides of Catford Street: Vincent, the failing restaurant-owner and Lovejoy's reluctant guardian; the rich Miss Chesney in the square, who had no time for the games of the "street sparrows"; and most importantly Tip, the leader of a rough street gang who at first had only scorn for Lovejoy's dream, but who would learn to make that dream his own.

"Rumer Godden's work needs no praise. Her place in the literary world is high and secure. But perhaps one may say that in none of her books are her profound understanding and light touch more skillfully combined than in this poignant, tender, and subtly strong 'Episode of Sparrows.'"
— *Christian Science Monitor*

"Only a Rumer Godden could make the simple tale of a forbidden garden pulse with suspense, could avoid the pitfalls of sentimentality, could breathe into such ordinary adults and ordinary children the quickness, the hope and the hopelessness of life itself."
— *New York Herald Tribune*

RUMER GODDEN

AN EPISODE
OF SPARROWS

A NOVEL

Puffin Books

PUFFIN BOOKS

Published by the Penguin Group

Viking Penguin Inc., 40 West 23rd Street, New York, New York 10010, U.S.A.

Penguin Books Ltd, 27 Wrights Lane, London W8 5TZ, England

Penguin Books Australia Ltd, Ringwood, Victoria, Australia

Penguin Books Canada Ltd, 2801 John Street, Markham, Ontario, Canada L3R 1B4

Penguin Books (N.Z.) Ltd, 182–190 Wairau Road, Auckland 10, New Zealand

Penguin Books Ltd, Registered Offices: Harmondsworth, Middlesex, England

First published in the United States of America by Viking Penguin Inc., 1955
Published in Puffin Books 1989

1 3 5 7 9 10 8 6 4 2

LIBRARY OF CONGRESS CATALOGING-IN-PUBLICATION DATA
Godden, Rumer, 1907-   An episode of sparrows.
Summary: In post-war London, two street-tough children
attempt to build a hidden garden, an act that awakens hidden courage
in the children and profoundly disrupts the neighborhood.
[1. Gardens—Fiction. 2. London (England)—Fiction]
I. Title.   PZ7.G54Ep 1989   [Fic]   88-30656
ISBN 0-14-034024-6

Printed in the United States of America
Set in Fairfield

"You are making a mountain out of a molehill," said Angela.

Olivia was suddenly inspired to answer, "A molehill can be a mountain to a sparrow."

This book is for my mother

I should like to thank Sir Norris Kenyon, J. P., B. Sc., L. C. C., a Chairman of the Metropolitan Juvenile Courts, and Mr. C. J. Collinge, Chief Clerk of the Courts, for valuable help and advice; also Inspector Rogers of Bow Street, for his assistance, and the Governors and Secretary of the *Arethusa* Training Ship, for permission to use its name.

I must also give thanks for very special help to Mr. Alex Gaudin of L'Escargot, whose father, once upon a time, had a little restaurant like Vincent's but not, of course, in Catford Street.   R. G.

AN EPISODE OF SPARROWS

CHAPTER I

THE Garden Committee had met to discuss the earth; not the whole earth, the terrestrial globe, but the bit of it that had been stolen from the Gardens in the Square.

The three members of the Committee were the big gun, as Lucas the gardener called Admiral Sir Peter Percy-Latham, who lived at Number Twenty-nine, the little gun, Mr. Donaldson, who had the ground-floor flat at Number Forty, and Miss Angela Chesney from Number Eleven. To Lucas, Angela was not a big or little gun, she was *the* gun; she ran the Committee, she ran the Gardens. "And she won't let us have wallflowers, says they're common. I like wallflowers," said the Admiral, but behind Angela's back; when she was present he deferred to her, as did Mr. Donaldson; Lucas looked only at her; it was like a court round the queen, thought Olivia. Olivia, Miss Chesney, was Angela's queer, dark, elder sister, who often attended her. They all stood looking at the holes, round pits of holes that had been made in the shrub bed at one end of the Gardens.

"It's the Street children," said Angela. She did not mean any street but the Street that ran behind the Square down to the river, Catford Street.

Mortimer Square, gracious and imposing, with its big houses, stood, like many other London squares, on the edge of a huddle of much poorer streets. That had always bothered Olivia. "It's too rich," she said, meaning the Square, "and too poor," meaning Catford Street. It was always Catford Street she saw in contrast to the Square, but nowadays neither was as rich or poor as Olivia thought. The Square had gone down, its big houses were mostly divided into flats, as could be seen when the lights went on at night; probably the only whole houses were the admiral's, the Miss Chesneys', and the one at the corner that was the strange embassy of one of the lesser South American States. Some of the houses had not been painted for years, some of them were even noisy—there was a dancing school at Number Three, though Angela had protested—while the poor streets had come up; Catford Street, for instance, though drab and shabby, with children playing in the street, an open-air market at the river end on Saturdays, and the Canal Works behind it, was proud and respectable. That did not prevent those same children from being a small plague in the Square, and "It's the Street children, I'm sure of it," said Angela.

"Looks as if an elephant had been standing in the bed," said the admiral, looking at the holes.

"Three elephants," said Olivia. "There are twelve holes." "Be quiet, Olivia," said Angela. "It isn't funny. Things are too expensive these days for it to be funny. First the shears, then all my beautiful irises!"

They were not Miss Angela's irises, but the admiral let it pass. "Band of hooligans," he said.

Mr. Donaldson said nothing but then he never did say anything, which was a disappointment; Angela had chosen him to sit on the committee because he worked for the Royal Horticultural Society. "That *should* be useful," said Angela, but so far nothing useful or otherwise had come from Mr. Donaldson, and it was Angela who said, in her quick, decisive way, "We shall have to get the police."

"Surely if it's children we can catch 'em ourselves," said the admiral. "It must be children, but what did they want it for?"

"They sell earth to the mews houses for window boxes," said Angela. "People shouldn't encourage it. If they want earth they can buy it at the Army and Navy Stores."

"But," said the admiral, looking at the holes, "*can* it be children? How did they cart it away?"

"They ought to have a medal for persistence," said Olivia. They all looked at her, and she blushed.

"Olivia, it's not funny, and it must be stopped," said Angela, and she pronounced, "Lucas must sleep in the shed."

The shed was at the far end of the Gardens, lonely and draughty and cold. Lucas shivered.

"Mr. Donaldson, do you agree?"

Mr. Donaldson nodded.

"Admiral?" She whipped them all in and it was settled.

"Supposing it's one of those gangs?" said Lucas. "They're big boys, some of them, and tough. They've got razors, I've seen them," quavered Lucas.

"I will give you a whistle," said Angela.

"There was a boy here, from the Street, sent to Borstal for using a knife. I don't like it," said Lucas.

"I think," said Olivia, "it's a little boy or girl."

"Nonsense," said Angela. "No little boy or girl could carry all that earth."

But Olivia knew they had; while the others were talking she had seen, under a bush, a footprint that no one had smoothed away. It was a very small footprint. Olivia had scuffed it out with her shoe.

CHAPTER II

CATFORD Street might have been any of the poorer streets in any city—a city that was old and had been bombed—but its flavour was of London; its stucco and its sooty brick, its scarlet buses, the scarlet post-office van, and the scarlet pillar box at the corner of Garden Row were London, as were its log-carts, the occasional great shire horses in the drays, the starlings, pigeons, and sparrows, the strange uncouth call of the rag-and-bone man, the many pubs, and the way the news-paper woman trustfully went away and left her papers, know-ing that the pennies and the halfpennies would be thrown down.

The ugly accents of the Street children were unmistakably English but the older people could have belonged anywhere; a great many had come from somewhere else—all tongues

7

were spoken in Catford Street, faces were all colours, but even the people who had been born there and lived and died in it were like any people anywhere. It was all perfectly ordinary; seen from above, from the back windows high up in some of the Square houses—Number Eleven, for instance, from the old schoolroom at the top of the house—Catford Street, with Motcombe Terrace and Garden Row—which had no gardens—running to left and right of it, made the shape of a big cross.

That was how Olivia, looking down from the old schoolroom windows, often saw it, spread out before her, yet hidden, teeming. At night it was a nest of lights, and it was always filled with sound, endless, myriad human sounds, while behind, booming from the river, came the sirens, tugs, and ships sounding almost equally big, reminding the Street, thought Olivia, of the world; and, falling down between the house walls, the sound of bells, reminding it, or failing to remind it, of heaven. The Anglican St. Botolph's Home of Compassion, with its black-and-white-habited nuns, was just behind the Square, and hidden somewhere among the houses was a convent of the Sisters of Charity; Olivia had never found out where it was but she had often seen the Sisters' blue gowns and big-winged cornettes going through the streets, and, as long as she could remember, the Angelus had rung from their convent three times a day. It used to be echoed by the big bell from the Catholic church in Catford Street, but that had been bombed and now there was only a tinny little bell from the makeshift hut that was used as a church.

Four times a day there was another sound; it came from the red brick building that took up a whole block, a school with high walls round it, topped with wire netting to keep in the balls that were bounced on the asphalt playgrounds; at twelve o'clock, at half-past three, and at recreation times the noise went up to the sky as first the infants, then the girls, and then the boys came out to play. It was like a vast, lively cheeping. It was this that first made the Miss Chesneys call the Street children "the sparrows."

When two people say the same word it can mean two different things. To Angela they were sparrows because they were cheeky, cocky, common as sparrows; to Olivia nothing was common; sparrows were sold for three farthings but not one should fall to the ground, though how that was possible she did not know, and apparently they fell all the time; Angela was always being summoned to cases of accident, illness, sorrow, or sudden death; it was paradoxical that it was Angela who worked indefatigably for the sparrows while the sensitive Olivia did nothing.

Angela tried to make her. "You might at least come on the Roll of Visitors," she said.

"To visit whom?"

"People, like the Street people, in their houses, and ask them questions."

But Olivia was appalled at the idea. "I?" she said, shrinking.

"Yes. Why not?"

Olivia thought of those swarming, vital houses and was appalled again. "I—I couldn't," she said. "They're too rich."

"They're well off, I know," said Angela, "all but a few—ridiculously well off; that doesn't stop them getting into messes." But Olivia was not thinking of money; to her they seemed rich in everything she had not, children and strength and life. It's odd, thought Olivia; half the time I'm troubled because I've scarcely anything at all, half the time because I have too much.

As a matter of fact, it was Angela who had real riches; she was the one who kept up the big house in the Square. "On my own I couldn't live like this," Olivia said often; she did not add that she would not. They had all been left their share of the Chesney and their mother's money—"Quite a tidy sum, even in these days," said Noel, their brother—but Angela, who had been a beautiful and very taking child, had inherited from a rich old bachelor godfather as well. "Be polite to Aunt Angela," Noel told his children and joked, "Besides being good as gold, she's solid gold."

If anyone were well named, Olivia thought often, it was her sister Angela. She looked like all the things that went with angels—a candle, a lily. Angela's figure was more like a tall boy's than a middle-aged woman's, she moved lightly and swiftly, her hair was still golden—no grey, though she's forty-five, thought Olivia with pride—and she had the Hewitt features (the Miss Chesneys' mother had been a Hewitt), straight, clear-cut features, with a slightly intense expression that reminded Olivia of the Burne-Jones pictures that had been fashionable when their mother was young.

Angela not only had good looks, she had good works. "By their fruits ye shall know them" was carved over the porch at St. Botolph's, the big church in the Square; for years none of them had gone into St. Botolph's—Mother had been well known as a rationalist—but now Angela, being thoroughly modern, had begun to go again and had made friends with the new young rector, Mr. Wix, whom she called David. "By their fruits . . ." That haunted Olivia because she had no fruits. If there should one day be a recording angel—and how funny, thought Olivia, if there should turn out to be one after all—while most people got three or four out of ten, and some, like Angela, full marks, Olivia could imagine him looking at her and saying, "No marks at all." How had that happened? Olivia did not know.

She had had the same chances as Noel and Angela. Then why was she so different? If she had felt well it might have been easier. Olivia's headaches were a family nuisance, and she was given to hot dark blushes that turned her face a mulberry colour—hideous, thought Olivia—and her attacks of indigestion were so sharp that she had grown a habit of pressing her hands suddenly against her chest—"Like a tragedy queen," said Angela. Sometimes Olivia wished she had a real illness, something for which a doctor could be called in; as it was, "You think you are going to have a headache, and you do," said Angela.

"Yes, I do," said Olivia wearily.

It was not only her health. "I was born inept and clumsy," said Olivia often. No one contradicted her.

It had been one of Mother's maxims that her children, the girls as well as the boy, must be qualified. Angela had been qualified at twenty-one; she was that still uncommon thing among women, a trained accountant, but Olivia had never qualified for anything. It was strange that she, who had not been able to stand against Mother for a moment, had been the one to defeat her in the end. Perhaps I always defeated her, thought Olivia, and that was why I irritated her so much. That faraway girl, the young Olivia, used to spend half her time banished to the schoolroom—which is perhaps why I'm so fond of it, thought Olivia now.

She had wanted to move up here when the house was converted and a flat made on the second floor for Noel's family to use when they were in town, the basement altered to make a home for old Hall and his wife. Hall had been the butler— "When we had butlers," said Angela lightly. Now they had old Ellen, who had been their nurse, and a procession of dailies, and Mrs. Hall came up to do the cooking. Angela and Olivia had moved their rooms down to the first floor, though Olivia still hankered after the schoolroom. "Olivia is senti-mental," said Angela. "She likes to go back into the school-room world." But up here in the schoolroom Olivia did not go back, she seemed to go a long, long way beyond any world.

Here, high over the Catford Street houses, she had a feeling of immensity, of power, as if—as if I could play God, thought

Olivia. She could look down over the Street, and the roofs of other streets, over thousands and thousands of chimneys from which the smoke went curling up; she could look away to faint spires of unknown churches, past the big bulk and flat roofs of the new council flats—no chimneys there—to the cranes and warehouses that showed where the river ran; across it, on the other bank, above other cranes, other warehouses, rose the great shape of the power station. As Olivia watched, the whole, all the world she could see, tilted against the sky; it was the passage of the clouds that made it seem as if the world moved, Olivia knew that very well, but she liked to think, as she had thought as a child, that it was the earth tilting, slowly tilting, as it turned on its axis in the sky. I, a pinprick, in this pinprick city, can feel the power of the earth, she thought, and, on the afternoon of the Garden Committee meeting, thinking that, the word "earth" made her pause; "earth," and again she remembered the footprint in the garden bed.

As if she had been Crusoe and the footprint a little Man Friday's, Olivia had followed it most of the day in her mind. All day she had wondered whose it was. But there must have been more than one child to carry all that earth, she thought. What were they doing? What did they want? thought Olivia.

"Want." It was like a match put suddenly to a . pile of tinder, old wood, cut long ago, lying for years, and drying so that it caught and flamed. What did I want? thought Olivia. So many things; the things all girls want, and it wrung her to think with what supreme confidence she had waited for them to come. "There is no reason," said Mother, "why a woman should not have a career and a home . . ." "When you have your own home . . ." she said often to Olivia and Angela. "When your children are grown up . . ." but those premises, thought Olivia, had rested on one thing, a man; and there had never been the vestige of a man for Olivia.

It was not the absence of a man that Olivia regretted so much, though she could have wished that both she and Angela had married—Angela was too fastidious—that blank in her life was not the worst; but I wish children were not so unknown to me, she thought, looking down on that hotbed of children, the Street. Olivia divined something in children—not in her nieces and nephews, Noel's children, who were precocious and spoiled—but in the children who were let alone, real children. Though she knew from Angela's dealings with them that they were blunt, even rude—as I am myself, thought Olivia—they seemed to her truer than grown-ups, unalloyed; watching them, she knew they were vital; if you were with them you would be alive, thought Olivia.

Angela was, in a way, Olivia's child; she was ten years younger, though she might have been ten years older in experience; and she needs me, Olivia thought in surprise, and she said aloud, because she was so surprised, "She makes mistakes." Olivia said that as if it were a miracle; but I wanted real children, she thought—and today that want was even sharper than before—children and to be rooted in the earth, not in manmade things, bricks and stones, but in the earth; and a confusion of things came into her mind, things of which she knew scarcely anything—dew, haystacks, compost, picking peas, and marrows, tangles of flowers, sweet williams, larkspur, marigolds, all the naïve cottage flowers that are seldom found in shops; and animals, thought Olivia, not pet dogs but real animals, calves and kids and chickens, and she remembered how she had once begged to keep a hedgehog in this very schoolroom.

I didn't want extraordinary things, she said, to go up the Amazon or dig for gold—if you do dig for gold—an ordinary little bit of life would have done for me; and she leaned far out from the window sill, as far as she could, for it was high, as if she wanted to see into all those countless thousands of

ordinary lives below. I wish I could have one chance, thought
Olivia, one real chance, the chance and the courage—she
could see she had been singularly lacking in courage—not to
have a life of my own, she thought—it was a little late for that,
she could see—but the chance to join in something real—real,
pleaded Olivia.

There was, of course, no answer. The house was quiet; at
this time of the afternoon the Halls were in their own sitting
room, far down in the basement; Ellen was out, gone for what
she called her "little potter." Angela was in the office with her
secretary, Miss Marshall.

After the war Angela had not gone back to her Clarges
Street firm; she had turned, as the *Times* had said in the
obituary notice of Mother, "her talents to voluntary work."
"I don't need a salary," Angela had said. "If I take it I keep
it from somebody who does, and these old charities are crying
out. They can't be run in a slipshod old-aunt fashion these
days; they must be organized and administered professionally."

There was certainly nothing amateur about Angela; she
had an office in what had been the morning room on the
ground floor; Miss Marshall worked in the old dining room,
which was now a waiting room; and the typist, Jeannie, had
the dark little room they had always called "the Slit."

Angela was secretary or auditor or member of so many different boards and committees that Olivia had long ago given
up trying to remember which was which; if she did remember, Angela called them by their initials, which confounded
Olivia again. Angela found time to run a literary club and
discussion group—"Just for refreshment," said Angela—and to
be Chairman of the Anglo-European Women's Initiative
Movement as well, the A. E. W. I. M. "That pays me,"
said Angela. "I get my trips abroad with all expenses." And
in her spare time—she still had spare time, Olivia marvelled—
she was writing a book, "On economics" said Olivia reverently.

It was only Olivia who was unoccupied and idle. This afternoon, for instance, there seemed no place for her, nothing she need do, and she stayed where she was. After a moment she began to think again of the stolen earth and the footprint, and again the questions began. Who were they? What did they want? How did it all begin?

CHAPTER III

IT HAD begun on a windy Saturday morning in March, in Catford Street, three months before.

The footsteps went up and down, down and up; in the High Street that ran across the top of Catford Street they made one sound that joined with the noise of traffic; in Catford Street itself the steps were separated; though they were continual, they were—people's, thought Sparkey, the newspaper woman's little boy. He knew what he meant; in the High the steps were a noise, a crowd; here he could identify them with his eyes shut—man, woman, child, child skipping, man with dog; man, woman, child—and from everyone who passed, there went up, though Sparkey was too young to know it, a little steam of thought, of plans and hopes and worries—in Catford Street it was mostly worries. "Is everyone un-happy?" the child Lovejoy was to ask Vincent in despair.

Vincent said, "Everyone," but after a moment, when he had thought, he added, "That doesn't prevent them from being happy."

Though Catford Street was in London it was a little like a village; to live in it, or the Terrace, or Garden Row, off it, or in any of the new flats that led off them, was to become familiar with its people; Sparkey, for instance, knew nearly everyone that passed, though he did not know their names. Sparkey had permission to sit on the steps of the house nearest the newspaper stand. He was delicate, one of those little boys who are all eyes and thin long legs; he was always catching chills, and his mother put a wad of papers under him to keep his bony little bottom off the stone and wrapped a copy of the *Evening News* round his legs; even then he was mottled with cold; his nose was as scarlet as his scarf and kept on running, so that he had to wipe it with his glove. He had objected to gloves. "Boys don't wear gloves!" he had said. "You will," said his mother. As he grew colder and the gloves grew dirtier his face was gradually smeared with black and damp and began to chap; his hair felt as if it were frozen to his head, but he would not move.

"Why don't you go and play?" asked his mother.

"I like to watch," said Sparkey.

The newspaper stand was at the end of the Street, where it joined the High by the traffic lights and the bus stop. It was the busiest corner, with the queue for the bus, people waiting to cross with the lights, more people coming to buy papers. When the bus came it stopped just by Sparkey and sent out visible fumes of warmth and smell from under its red sides; it looked as if it were a real big animal breathing. Sparkey watched the people file in; the bus looked comfortable with its paint, the pale steel of its handles, the glimpse of seats behind its glass. It started with a harsh grinding noise, the people were carried away, and Sparkey's mother rattled the coppers in the pocket of her big newspaper sling; she rattled them, thought Sparkey, because the conductor had rattled his in his bag. Sparkey liked the newspaper sling; it was crimson canvas, lettered DAILY MAIL, and looked cheerful over his mother's old coat. Every gleam of colour was cheerful in that plain street.

Some of the people in the bus queue had suitcases; of course, it was Saturday; Sparkey guessed they were going away for the weekend; some had babies and pale blue push-chairs that they lifted onto the bus. There was a girl in a black silk coat, her hair in a knot at the back of her head; she carried a small case, and her nails and her lips were bright red; Sparkey knew her and knew she was a dancer, going to rehearsal; he had heard her tell his mother. There were men with paper hats and green rosettes pinned to their coats; they had peaked, pale faces and their clothes were crumpled because they had been up all night; they were up from the provinces for a cup tie.

All down the Street women were scrubbing doorsteps ready for Sunday. There was a sound of barking and soon a man passed with two big dogs; Sparkey knew them; he had seen their kennels in the area of Number Sixty-nine; they barked when they were let out, which was not often; the fur had come off their elbows from lying on the area flags, and they stank.

There were plenty of animals in Catford Street; Sid, the log man, kept his pony Lucy behind the last house, in a shed by the canal; all the children in Catford Street knew Lucy and her little cart painted with hearts and roses. Besides Lucy and the dogs, there were budgerigars, canaries, and cats, many cats. In the very house where Sparkey sat on the steps, Mrs. Cleary and Miss Arnot kept fifteen cats; the two old ladies came creeping out every morning in old fur tippets and men's hats, their waists hung round with shopping bags to buy food for their cats; they bought fish-heads and horsemeat and then crept home again; presently the smell of the fish and meat cooking would seep out into the Street, and the cats that on fine days ornamented the window sills and the half-wall of the portico would get up and stretch and go mewing in to dinner.

People passed all the time. There were women with perambulators and children tagging along, holding to the handles; most of the women said "Hello" to Sparkey's mother; most of the children, as they came from the shops, were eating something, an ice or a lollipop; Sparkey looked at them and his mouth watered. Two girls came along with green coats, their hair tied with limp white ribbons; they were Yvette and Susie Romney and they had an orange lollipop to share between them; they took it in turns, three sucks each, each sharply watched by the other; in Catford Street one had to be sharp and strictly fair. Sparkey did not really look at them, though his eyes watched the lollipop. He was not interested in girls.

The children from St. Botolph's Home of Compassion came past: twenty-six little girls, walking two-by-two, with a nun at the end. Another kind of nun passed; her full blue cotton skirts made a sound that was like a quiet murmur of words, but her wooden beads rattled, and the sides of her starched white hat—Sparkey called it a hat—flapped, and her boots squeaked; the fringe of her shawl had bobbles that danced up and down as she walked. She was interesting, with the constant movement of her clothes, and Sparkey watched as she turned in at the broken church steps and went up them, out of sight.

The third house down from where Sparkey sat was the Priest's House, and next to it was where the Catholic church of Our Lady of Sion had been bombed. Now the church was only a hut standing in a rubble of broken pillars and masonry;

there was a notice board outside it, lettered in big letters, HELP TO BUILD OUR CHURCH AND SCHOOLS; above the letters was a wooden aeroplane rising slowly up the scale—£2,000, £3,000, £4,000; the aeroplane had stuck at that for a long time. "They need fifteen thousand pounds," said Sparkey's mother. "They'll never get that."

On Saturday morning the Catholic children went to Confession. There was no school, and the Street was full of children; some of them were shopping for their mothers, a great many had got on the bus for the children's show at the Victoria Cinema, some went down to the new Woolworth's in the Wilton Road, and some of the boys, with carts made out of packing cases and old perambulator wheels, took a sack down to the gasworks for coke, but most were just playing; there were little girls with doll perambulators, taggles of little girls; there were boys playing mysterious games with balls, or chalking on the pavement, and smaller boys with cowboy hats and cardboard chaps and metal pistols; they lurked round corners and shouted at one another. "Go and play with them," said Sparkey's mother again, but Sparkey was not interested in small boys; though he was only five, going on six, he was ambitious; he was waiting for Tip Malone.

Besides being ambitious, Sparkey was melodramatic; he frightened the other children. "Do you know what gravy is?" he would ask, hushed, and when they shook their heads he would say in a cold voice, "It's blood."

He would ask a small girl, "Do you see that man?"

The little girl would nod.

"If you met him at night he would take you away in a sack," said Sparkey.

"That's only old Mr. Isbister," the little girl would say uncertainly.

"That's what *you* think," said Sparkey.

"Perhaps it's being a newspaper child," Olivia was to say

when she had had some experience of Sparkey, but Angela objected. "A child that age can't read," she said. Sparkey could not read, but the lurid pieces of the paper seemed printed into him; not long ago one of the Catford Street boys, the boy that Lucas had told Angela about, had been caught by the police; he had slashed an old lady with a knife. "F'r her handbag," said Sparkey with relish. "He got sent away. That was Maxey Ford," said Sparkey. "He was in Tip Malone's gang."

"I don't believe it," said Sparkey's mother, but Sparkey was an authority on gangs. "Tip's a nicely brought-up boy," said Sparkey's mother.

"He isn't," said Sparkey indignantly.

Sparkey had thought Tip might have been sent to Confession, but there was no sign of him; Sparkey sighed.

Just as one day the grown-up Sparkey was to know the face of his girl, his beloved, every mark and line, so now he knew Tip's face, his face and all about him, his clothes, his voice, his doings, and his gang. The gang was not big but it was choice. "Jim Howes, Tony Zassi, Rory Isbister, Puggy, Ginger, and John Rowe," said Sparkey wistfully. Tip was the biggest—"Well, he's thirteen," said Sparkey with awe. Tip was heavy and tough and square and wore an old grey sweater and battered jeans. "Wish I had jeans!" sighed Sparkey.

No one knew how many Malones there were. "There can't be more than nine," Angela often said, but they were so big and loud-voiced that the Street seemed full of them. They lived in the basement and top-floor flats of Number Seventeen, and no one would stay long in the flats on the other floors, if they could possibly find anywhere else to go, because of the Malones racing up and down the stairs.

They were all as alike as peas, all strong and well set-up and astonishingly handsome with well-shaped limbs, straight backs, clear skins, and thick brown curly hair; "The stock must be good," Olivia was to say when she came to know them. They had the traditional blue eyes put in with smutty fingers—"Irish eyes," said Olivia.

"Irish blarney," said Angela. Angela, as usual, was right.

"Tip's got a bowie knife," said Sparkey longingly. "Every kind of knife."

"Who told you so?" asked his mother.

"He told Puggy Carpenter and Puggy told Jimmy and Jimmy told me." Sparkey's mother sniffed. "He's going to have a nair gun and he's got a space helmet and a bike with a dual brake control." Sparkey had faithfully learned all those difficult names. "He's going into the Navy, he'll be a sailor," said Sparkey as if he saw visions.

"It's not blarney exactly," said Olivia. "It's what they hope and believe is going to happen; it's a kind of faith."

Olivia was right too; there was something in the Malones that not even their poverty and untidiness and shabbiness could hide.

Mr. Malone, who drove a coal dray, was a big, bragging, blue-eyed man, but the one behind the whole family was Mrs. Malone; she looked, fittingly, like the pod they came from; she was big and bulging and flabby. "She looks used," said Olivia, whom nobody had used. Mrs. Malone was firmly behind her children: when they got into trouble, and they had plenty of trouble; when they had accidents, and they were always being run over, or falling off buses or onto their heads out of windows, or being taken to hospital in ambulances and returning in bandages or plaster. She was with them in their triumphs, and they took most of the prizes at school; with them in their enterprises, and they were always going off somewhere wonderful or doing something astounding; and she was with them, very often and personally, in their fights. Tip's nose had been broken in a fight. "He's a fighter," said Sparkey with pride.

It was not only because Tip had been with Maxey that

Sparkey worshipped him; there was something in Tip that warmed the cockles of a little boy; Sparkey could not put it into words but, "He once pulled a face at me," said Sparkey.

"Why don't you pull one back," said his mother, which showed how ignorant she was.

"I couldn't do that," said Sparkey, appalled. "But," he said reverently, "Tip knows me. P'rhaps one day I'll be in the gang."

"You can't be in a gang, you're not six," said Sparkey's mother, "and that's that." Sparkey shut his lips, and his eyes looked a long way beyond her. Soon his mother would not know what he did.

It was a strange thing that up to the age of seven children were noticeable in Catford Street; the babies in their well-kept perambulators and the little boys and girls in coat-and-legging sets were prominent, but after the age of seven the children seemed to disappear into anonymity, to be camouflaged by the stones and bricks they played in; as if they were really the sparrows the Miss Chesneys called them, they led a different life and scarcely anyone noticed them. At fourteen or fifteen they appeared again, the boys as big boys that had become somehow dangerous—or was it that there was too much about them in the papers?—the dirty little girls as smart young women with waved hair, bright coats, the same red nails and lipstick as the dancer in the bus queue; they wore slopping sling-back shoes and had shrill, ostentatious voices. The Street prickled with the doings of these boys and girls, as it had admired and petted the babies, but the children were unnoticed except by Sparkey; not even experienced mothers like Mrs. Malone knew all they did. "If the twelve apostles themselves came down and asked him, Tip couldn't help them," said Mrs. Malone about Maxey. "Tip never even spoke to him," she said indignantly. Sparkey knew that Tip had.

There was no Tip this Saturday morning. The first evening papers had come in and were beginning to be sold, and now the crowd of people in the Street grew thinner; Sparkey's mother would soon take him away for dinner, leaving her papers to sell themselves; the perambulators were coming back from the shops, and the handcarts from the gasworks with the sacks stuffed now with coke; Mrs. Cleary and Miss Arnot had gone, half an hour ago, into the house behind Sparkey, and now the smell of hot fish was coming out; the biggest cat, Istanbul, jumped suddenly off the portico wall, nearly on top of Sparkey, and walked in at the open door.

It was nearly twelve o'clock. Soon the clock from St. Botolph's in the Square would strike, and after that the Angelus. "He must have gone over the river to the park," said Sparkey. It was disappointing; there was nothing to do but look at the parcels.

Sparkey did not look at the heavy shopping bags; with their packets of cornflakes and tea and tinned peas, they were not interesting. He looked at the parcels belonging to the children and the big girls and boys. The girls walked together, talking and giggling, with their arms round one another; sometimes they walked backwards, showing off, and a knot of boys on the opposite pavement would whistle, rude, loud whistles. Sparkey knew what the girls had bought; his mother, who was still pretty, bought the same things, and he had seen them all on Woolworth's counters: a box of face powder, a spring flower in a pot wrapped with tissue paper, hair grips, ankle socks, sweets, a birthday card, tiny bottles of scent which they let each other smell as Sparkey watched.

Perhaps that was how he did not see the packet fall; someone must have dropped it; suddenly it was there on the pavement among the passing feet, an oblong cream-coloured packet, sealed like an envelope, splashed with brilliant blue.

Sparkey did not know what it was, but in a flash he had unpeeled the *Evening News,* darted down the steps, dodged among the people, and snatched it up. He nearly had his hand stepped on as a big girl almost fell over him, but he reached the packet and stood up with it in his hand; it was soiled with being trodden on but it was safe.

The blue splashes were pictures of flowers; Sparkey was only a little boy, and they caught his attention; instead of scurrying to the steps with what he had found, he stayed there in the open street to look. That was not wise. Somebody's hand came over his and twitched the packet away.

Sparkey clutched at the corner as it went, giving piercing yelps to his mother, but she was busy with a customer; another hand joined the first, and small iron fingers began to prise his away. "Leggo, or I'll pinch you," said a voice.

Anyone could have told Sparkey he had no chance; the face that looked down into his was a pale, small mask with pale, set lips; it had an obstinate nose and eyes that seemed to be sealed with their lids. All the little girls in Catford Street could be baffling; if they did not want someone to know something they dropped their lids; when they raised them again they would speak breathlessly and brightly, and it was anything but the truth; but this little girl's face was more than sly; it might have been carved in stone; when she swore at Sparkey and opened her eyes they were as grey and cold as pebbles. Her hair, which was very fine and mouse-coloured, was cut in a fringe and fell to her shoulders; when she bent her head it parted on the nape of her neck; Father Lambert saw that as he came out of the Priest's House; it was the only part of her that looked vulnerable, that small white exposed neck.

Sparkey knew her. She was Lovejoy, Lovejoy Mason from the restaurant.

"Nobody can be called Lovejoy," Angela was to say, but Lovejoy was.

"*Your* mother didn't give you a name like that," she was to say jealously to Tip.

"I don't think I want a name like that," said Tip.

What Vincent said was worse, but he did not know Lovejoy was listening. "No one who loved their child could give it a name like that," said Vincent.

Now Lovejoy and Sparkey began to threaten each other in the shorthand speech the Street children used. "Gimme," said Lovejoy.

"'Smine," shrieked Sparkey.

He had steel tips on his little shoes and he kicked at Lovejoy's shins. "You little varmint," called Father Lambert, while Sparkey's mother shouted, "You! Lovejoy! You leave Sparkey alone."

"Fancy a big girl fighting such a little boy!" said a woman; but Lovejoy was not fighting, she was, simply, taking. Before Father Lambert or Sparkey's mother could reach them Lovejoy gave Sparkey a blow in his small stomach that doubled him up, ripped the packet out of his hand, and ran.

CHAPTER IV

Lovejoy pelted down towards the river, then turned and dodged up Garden Row, past the iron gates of the canal dock and the blocks of the council flats with their lawns and concrete paths, down another side road until she found herself in just such another street as Catford Street, wide and shabby with drab, porticoed houses; she was out of breath but safe.

Older and more wary than Sparkey, she went into one of the porticoes, where no boy or girl could come up behind her, tweak her hair or jerk her elbow, and snatch as she had snatched. She had no idea what she had taken; she was simply a little marauder.

It would have surprised Lovejoy's mother, Mrs. Mason, to be told that Lovejoy never had any pocket money; Mrs. Mason was always going to give her some but, somehow, it was always spent. "I meant you to have an ice cream," she would say to Lovejoy in the teashop or café, "but look, I've only got sixpence for a coffee. Never mind. You can have the biscuit." Mrs. Mason paid Mrs. Combie now, to provide Lovejoy with the necessities of life, but she did not pay enough to provide anything else.

Now and again Lovejoy had a penny for washing up or running errands, but a penny did not go far. "I can't go without everything, forever," said Lovejoy.

"I don't know how she managed," Olivia was to say when she and Angela were told everything.

"Managed by stealing," said Angela.

Lovejoy did not steal big things, nor money; she knew that to take money was wicked; nobody had told her that ice creams and comics were money, and she was adept at taking a parcel out of a perambulator while she pretended to rock it, at making a small child look the other way and whipping a cornet out of its hand, at walking along by a shop counter, gazing innocently all the time at the assistant, and coming out with some sweets or a bundle of ribbon or a pencil-sharpener in her hand.

Now she looked at the packet, and her look changed to disgust. "Flowers. Seeds," she said and she almost threw the packet down the area. Then she saw there was printing on it and she began to read.

Lovejoy, to her continual disgrace, could hardly read. "She has changed schools too often and missed too much," the inspector had told Mrs. Combie severely. That was true. When Lovejoy and her mother first began to come to Catford Street between their bookings, Lovejoy had appeared and disappeared so often in school that the teacher asked her, "Are you a canal child?" Canal children sometimes came to school if their fathers' barge had to go into the dock for repairs. Lovejoy had said nothing but she had been mortally offended. "Do I look like a canal child?" she might have said.

"You think too much about how people look and much too much about clothes," said Mrs. Combie. Lovejoy did more than think about them; she had been trained in them as in a religion. "One must look smart"—that was her mother's creed, and Lovejoy was her mother's disciple. She had been the best-dressed child in Catford Street—"On top," Mrs. Combie said. "Her vests and pants were in tatters from the beginning"—but vests and pants did not show, and Lovejoy never wasted a thought on them. She had a grey flannel suit with a pleated skirt for school, white blouses, and a red beret; for best she had a black velvet dress, a black and white dog toothed checked coat, and a black velvet tam-o'-shanter with a long black tassel. Lovejoy's clothes were her stock in trade, her tools, and she took great care of them. When she came in from school or a walk or shopping, she would slip into her old pinafore dress and a plaid coat that she had worn so long that it was like her skin, and carefully put her good clothes away, hanging them up on her small-size hangers, sponging off marks with a bit of rag, and pressing the pleats and lapels with Mrs. Combie's iron; she washed her own blouses and white socks and gloves, and hung them in the window to dry; a clothes-hanger fitted with pegs was her most cherished possession, and she carefully hoarded the packet of soap flakes, the cleaning rags, and the pot of shoe cream for her red shoes that Mrs. Combie gave her. "She's not a child, she's an old woman," said Mrs. Combie's sister, Cassie. Cassie was a slattern, and Lovejoy's fastidiousness enraged her. "I suppose you think you're pretty?" she said.

"No," said Lovejoy certainly. She knew perfectly well she was not pretty; she had studied herself too often in the mirror to have any doubts about that; she had a certain fineness and lightness, dear little bones, thought Lovejoy, but her slant eyes and flat nose were not pretty; all the same, she did not

like Cassie any the better for saying it and she adopted a
way of looking Cassie up and down, taking in the trodden-
down heels of Cassie's shoes, the ladders in her stockings,
the place where the hem of her cheap tomato-coloured dress
had come undone; her eyes went over Cassie's hair, golden
but unwashed and bundled in a net, and the spots on her
chin. Cassie ate too many sweets and smoked too much. She
had stains on her fingers and teeth. Lovejoy saw the stains.

"What are you looking at?" Cassie would demand.

"Nothing," Lovejoy would say and would hum a little tune.

Lately clothes had been very difficult. "Too tight for you
under the arms, isn't it?" asked Cassie spitefully, looking at
the little grey suit.

"It isn't," said Lovejoy, but it was; and the scarlet shoes
were too small now, as were her school shoes; they hurt and
raised blisters; Lovejoy had five even blisters on the toes of
each foot, and the blisters were turning into corns. She had
had to tell Mrs. Combie about the school shoes, and Mrs.
Combie bought her a pair of plimsolls. *"Plimsolls,"* said Lovejoy in shame, and she set her teeth and bore the red shoes
if ever she went out of the Street. "When my mother comes
she'll buy me some new ones," she said, but it did not sound
very certain.

"Where *is* your mum?" Tip was to ask.

Like all the children, Lovejoy was often subjected to the
inquisition of the Street, pecking questions from sharp little
beaks.

"Where d'ya live?"

"Two hundred and three Catford Street."

"That's the rest'raunt. No one lives there."

"Mrs. Combie does," said Lovejoy.

"Is Mrs. Combie your mum?"

"No, she's *not*," said Lovejoy indignantly.

"Where is your mum?"

"She's away."

And then one of the children would cry, "Don't believe you've got a mum."

"I have"—but Lovejoy said it too fiercely, and they would know and cry, "There's something fishy about her mum."

"What is this Mrs. Mason, if I may ask?" said Cassie.

"She's a coloratura," said Mrs. Combie in the elegant, even voice which showed she did not know in the least what she meant. "A coloratura," said Mrs. Combie firmly. "Her stage name is Bertha Serita."

Cassie made a noise in her nose; it was between a hiss and a snort.

"Is there anything wrong in being a singer?" asked Mrs. Combie.

"*If* she is a singer," said Cassie.

"She's in the Blue Moons," said Mrs. Combie. "They're quite well known. You often see their picture in the paper. Look." And she went to the dresser and took out a cutting from a Bournemouth paper.

"Pierrots!" said Cassie, looking. "Pierrots on the beach!"

"The Blue Moons are on the pier too," said Mrs. Combie, "or in the Winter Garden. They're a concert party really, high class. They wear midnight-blue dresses, real silk net with silver ruffs. It looks lovely with her chestnut hair," said Mrs. Combie.

"Her hair's dyed," said Cassie.

"I know, but she's a beautiful woman," said Mrs. Combie, "though she is getting plump."

"Fat," said Cassie.

"Plump," said Mrs. Combie, "and she has a beautiful skin and colouring."

"Out of a box," said Cassie spitefully.

"Maybe, but it looks nice," said Mrs. Combie and she gave a little sigh as she remembered how her fingers had rasped on the blue skirts when she had gently touched them. "They have hats like tiny satin flowerpots with crescent moons. Saucy!" said Mrs. Combie, and a flush came on her sallow cheeks.

"But why doesn't your mother take you?" Tip was to ask Lovejoy. "She used to take you, didn't she?"

"That was when I was sweet," said Lovejoy. She told that to Vincent too. "I used to dance on the stage," she said. When they found out, at school, how Lovejoy danced, they had wanted to give her a part in the school pantomime, but like the children from the Home, who could not have parts either, there was no one who had time to see to her clothes. "I don't care," said Lovejoy, who cared bitterly. "I'm not like a norphan. You don't care," she told the other girls, "if you've danced on the stage.

"I used to do a kitten dance," she told Tip and Vincent. "I had a swansdown dress and little swansdown gloves; and I used to do a song with my mother. In it she was dead but she came back at night to see her child. I was the child," said Lovejoy. "I used to wear a white nightgown and say my prayers to her."

"Ugh!" said Vincent.

"It wasn't ugh," said Lovejoy. "People used to cry."

"But why did you stop?" asked Tip. "Why didn't you go on dancing?"

"My little teeth fell out," said Lovejoy.

To Tip, to all the children in Catford Street, the coming out of a first tooth was something to be proud of. "I got sixpence," said Tip, "and threepence for each one after." For most it was proud, but for Lovejoy it had been a tragedy.

"Did you say she could leave that child here?" Cassie asked Mrs. Combie in her loud aggressive voice.

"She has to be left somewhere," said Mrs. Combie helplessly.

Lovejoy had come willy-nilly to accept that. It could have been much worse; Mrs. Combie was kind, Vincent was very kind, but for Mrs. Combie there was really only Vincent and for Vincent there was only the restaurant. Lovejoy was a little extra tacked on.

She had never heard of a vortex but she knew there was a big hole, a pit, into which a child could be swept down, a darkness that sucked her down so that she ceased to be Lovejoy, or anyone at all, and was a speck in thousands of specks—"Millions," said Lovejoy, and then there was something called "no one."

She knew how easily that could happen because once she had been lost. I was only six then, thought Lovejoy; she was nearly eleven now but she had not forgotten it. She was lost and she was a speck and there was no one. It had been when her mother was out of work and they were moving restlessly about. At the police station they had asked Lovejoy questions.

"Where do you live?"

"We don't live anywhere."

"Where did you spend last night?"

"In London," said Lovejoy promptly.

"What place in London?"

"London," said Lovejoy.

"This is London," said the woman police constable gently.

"No, this isn't London," said Lovejoy certainly. "London was last night."

The constable tried again. "You don't know where you stayed?"

"We don't stay," said Lovejoy gravely. "We can't, because of the bill. They want us to pay it so we go somewhere else."

"Somewhere else?"

"Yes. That's where we were going," said Lovejoy.

Nowadays she was left behind; all she had of her mother, most of the time, was a pack of postcards she carried in the pocket of her coat. When her mother did come home—Catford Street had become home now—Lovejoy was kept away from school, though Mrs. Combie had told Mrs. Mason about the inspector. "What does she care? She isn't here when he comes," said Cassie.

Lovejoy was too useful to be spared; she washed and ironed her mother's clothes and brushed her mother's hair; she played the gramophone, ran out for a paper of chips, fetched in beer. Though Lovejoy's legs were strong they ached by the end of the day. "How do you expect to get on?" her teacher, Miss Cobb, would say when Lovejoy appeared in school again. Lovejoy, sadly, did not expect to.

She took a long time, now, to spell out the words on the packet. *Cornflower (Cyanus minor)*—she could not make anything of that—*double blue*. Double blue what? *Hardy annual, two and a half feet.* What's an annual? *Very showy for borders. In bloom from June to September. Sow in March or April*—That's now, thought Lovejoy—*in any good garden soil, raked fine. Cover the seeds lightly. When the seedlings come up, thin well.*

When she had managed to read through that, Lovejoy slit the packet open; she was careful not to break into the blue painted flowers—cornflowers, as she knew now. Inside was a small, very small, white envelope. Blooming cheats, thought Lovejoy, to put a little one into such a big one. She took out the small envelope and felt it; it was filled with something that felt like grains, but such tiny ones that, pinched together, they felt soft, like a tiny pillow, and yet they were grainy. She broke a corner of the envelope and shook it out into her hand; each seed looked like an insect with a white-looking body that had a white overskin, covering something dark, and, at one end, a minute fuzz of a head, golden colour.

Lovejoy tried to crack one with her teeth, but it was unexpectedly hard. She looked at it again. The seed is the dark part, she thought. She leaned against the pillar of the portico; a patch of sun had made it almost warm, and she felt warm too and, now that she was not out of breath from running, comfortable and interested. She looked at the dark part of the seed again; it was like knowing a person was there under a disguise, she thought. "Pooh, it isn't as big as a pin," she said—she meant the head of a pin. How could it grow into a flower, a double blue flower, two and a half feet high? "I don't believe it," said Lovejoy.

She nearly threw the packet away; but after a moment she put the seeds back into the envelope, put it in the packet, and tucked that into the pocket of her old plaid coat. Then, because she, like all the children, found it easier to jump and skip and hop than to walk, she began to skip home.

CHAPTER V

IF ANYONE observant had been walking or driving down Catford Street to the river, he might have seen a little restaurant; he would have had to be observant because it did not strike the eye; once seen, it was remarkable.

At the river end of the Street the houses were older than the Victorian ones farther up with their stucco and porticoes and railed-off areas. The river-end houses were built of small dark bricks; most of them had ugly shops built out to the pavement, but the house with the restaurant, flat-fronted and pleasing, had been put back as it was, and its door opened onto a small forecourt paved with cobbles. The restaurant had two half-lantern windows of rounded glass. "Twenty pounds each, those cost," said Mrs. Combie.

"Twenty-three," said Vincent proudly.

Under the windows, standing on the cobbles, were two

pyramid bay trees, their dark leaves fresh and clean. "He washes them," said Mrs. Combie.

"*Washes* them?" Cassie had never heard of trees being washed.

"With a spray," said Mrs. Combie. She was half bitter, half proud about those bay trees. "They get cut by the frost and that's the end of them," she said. "He spent seven pounds on those alone last year."

The little trees were astonishingly pretty; like the crimson sling Sparkey's mother wore, their colour stood out in the Street; their shapes were well clipped, the bands on their oak tubs were freshly painted. Between the windows was a plate-glass door with a polished brass handle; it looked inviting, and at night an apricot light shone onto the pavement from inside. On the brown oak panel across the house front, in dim gold letters, was written VINCENT'S. To anyone with accustomed eyes it looked a restaurant that might have been in Dover Street or St. James's, perhaps in Soho, but very few people who came down Catford Street had eyes like that.

It had been a restaurant before, the Victoria Dining Rooms. Then it had belonged to Mrs. Combie's father and had had an ordinary ugly window like the other shops—"Only we didn't know it was ugly," said Mrs. Combie yearningly. Then it had the ordinary electric lights, as in the other shops, glaring down, and long tables with green and white oilcloth slips, and a slate in the window on which was chalked:

Egg and chips	10d.
Sausage, bacon, tomato and chips	1/9
Bacon, egg and chips	1/6
Steak pie. 2 veg.	2/6
Cold meat and bubble	1/2
Good hot home-made dinners always ready from twelve o'clock.	
Pull up for car-men.	

Mrs. Combie had cooked the good hot home-made dinners; she had thought she was a good cook until she met Vincent, who said she did not know how to cook at all. "English cooking is uneatable," said Vincent. Mrs. Combie knew that was not true, plenty of people had eaten hers, but there was certainly something magical in Vincent's.

"He takes a duck," she told Cassie, "and puts it in an earthenware cocotte—"

"What's a nearthenware cocotte?"

"A deep oval pan," said Mrs. Combie, "made of earthenware. He puts the duck in whole, with butter—"

"Butter. For *cooking*?" said Cassie. "You mean lard." But Mrs. Combie was sure it was butter.

"He only half cooks the duck, it must be still red; in another pan he fries some button mushrooms—"

"With more butter, I suppose?" said Cassie sarcastically.

"More butter," said Mrs. Combie and sighed as she thought of the price. "Mushrooms and little onions and bacon cut into bits," she went on, "and herbs and seasoning; he lets them get nice and brown, then separately he makes a good brown sauce and puts in a glass of sherry."

"Sherry! Wine! What a wicked waste," said Cassie, impressed in spite of herself.

"Then he cuts up the duck, on a dish so as not to lose any blood—"

"Ugh!" said Cassie with a ladylike shudder.

"—and puts it back in the cocotte with the mushrooms and onions and bacon and pours the sauce over it all and shuts it up tightly and puts it in the oven."

"That's a nice expensive way of cooking," said Cassie. "Who does he think's going to pay to eat that?"

"People do," said Mrs. Combie.

"Not in Catford Street," said Cassie.

That was what nagged Mrs. Combie and would not go out of her mind. "I should have let him have his way and open somewhere else," she said. "Somewhere up West. But how could I?" she asked. "Even if we sold up here we shouldn't have had enough."

"You haven't enough here," said Cassie.

"We're on the river. The best people like the river," Vincent argued, but the river here was not the same as the river at Chelsea or farther up at Westminster, a polite stretch of river; here only a huddle of wharves and warehouses and sheds showed where it was, but Vincent would not give up hope. He used to come out every evening and stand at the edge of the cobbles, looking up and down the Street. "We must remember it's out of the way," said Vincent.

"Is it?" asked Mrs. Combie. As she had lived in Catford Street all her life—"Though we came from Cornwall once upon a time," said Mrs. Combie—it seemed to her right in the way.

The restaurant did not prosper; a few people drifted in from the block of flats along the river, and one or two came who looked, Mrs. Combie thought, as if they lived in the Square, but no one who, as Vincent said, really paid for a meal. "I told you. I should have started up West," said Vincent restlessly.

There was one regular client—Vincent liked to call them clients rather than customers—who came every Wednesday night and for lunch on Sundays. Mrs. Combie guessed that was when his housekeeper had her days off.

He was a thick, small man and his manners were strangely gross; he made loud noises when he ate, and spattered the tablecloth; his clothes were not spattered only because he tucked his napkin into his collar. "Why does he come?" asked Vincent irritably.

"I think he likes your cooking," said Mrs. Combie.

"Probably never has a decent meal in his own house," said Vincent.

"I think he lives in those flats along the river."

"All sorts of people live in them," said Vincent loftily.

His name, they discovered, was Mr. Manley. One night he asked if he could pay for his dinner by check. "He hasn't put an initial," said Mrs. Combie, looking lovingly at it. It was good to think of one pound, seven shillings, and ninepence going into the account.

"Thinks he's the only Manley in London," said Vincent. "Probably the bank will send it back." But the bank passed it through without comment.

Vincent was fastidious and he did not like serving Mr. Manley but he should have known better; Mr. Manley certainly knew what food should be and he spent more money than anyone else on the ungrateful Vincent.

He always had a plain dinner, one dish, a *chateaubriand* or *escalope de veau* or *tête de veau vinaigrette*, a salad, properly dressed—"I always thought dressing was salad cream," said Mrs. Combie—cheese, Stilton or Camembert, and a bottle of wine.

He never praised Vincent, merely nodded if things were right. Vincent resented that. "Real people, of course, don't flatter," he told Lovejoy, but Mr. Manley hardly came into that category. For Vincent there were two races of humans, people and real people, "People who are Somebodies," he told Lovejoy reverently.

What Mrs. Combie found most difficult of all to understand was that he wanted the restaurant to be expensive. She had always thought cheapness an asset but that, it seemed, was wrong, and it was wrong, puzzlingly wrong, to try and save money. "This kitchen's full of washing," Vincent often complained.

"I do it between three o'clock and six, George, when the

kitchen's empty; the stove is hot then and the things dry." If the washing were not hanging up it was being ironed. They had kept her father's big old-fashioned range, and, "I can heat the irons on the stove when it's hot, for *nothing*, George," said Mrs. Combie, but Vincent did not feel the charm of that. "It's squalid," he said, offended.

There was certainly a great deal of washing, but that, again, was Vincent, not Mrs. Combie; if the cloths and serviettes—he called them napkins—had a speck on them he would put them in the bag, and his shirts with their stiff fronts and collars were changed every day. "Send them to the laundry," he said in his lordly way.

"We can't afford the laundry, George."

"We must. Our linen must be white and glossy, starched, perfectly white and glossy. You can't get them like that."

"I will," said Mrs. Combie, but sometimes she failed. After a time, on Catford Street, the best washing turned grey, and then Vincent was almost mortally hurt. "I can't wear them like that," he would say, his nostrils pinched. "What is the use of trying to have things nice?"

"I'll try again, George," said Mrs. Combie.

There were many women like Mrs. Combie in Catford Street; from most of the houses an incense went up, an incense of faith and courage, and part of the courage was in the day-long battle for cleanliness. It was fought for the houses, but also against the houses; some of them, like the restaurant house, had stood a hundred years in soot and fog and dirt; they were ingrained with grime. Every morning Mrs. Combie washed her doorstep, scrubbed and whitened it, and immediately the feet coming in and out made it black again. Once a week she scrubbed down the three flights of stairs and turned out each room; she washed the curtains and cleaned the windows, and the smuts from the power station came in and blackened them all again, or, in the winter the fog came down, particularly here by the river, thick, grey-yellow fog, polluting everything. All up and down the Street the battle was fought and, usually, won. Out of those dark houses came babies with white clothes, starched white pillows, and pale pink and blue covers on their perambulators; the children playing in the Street were dirty, it was true, but if they were going out, to the shops or to school, they were clean from head to foot; the young men had glossy hair and boots, clean shirts, brushed suits; the girls came out in crisp cottons, white blouses, fresh collars and cuffs. Angela often talked to her committees about the amazing dirt in the Street; she did not know how amazingly clean it was. "The women look so old," said Olivia. That was natural; the cotton frocks, the perambulator covers, even the boys' glossy boots, did not have the wear and the tear the women had. Mrs. Combie was sallow because she went out of the house only to do some quick shopping; her back between her shoulders looked small and frail and stooped, and her hands were big and knotted. "Oh well," she said, "I never was pretty. Cassie was the pretty one," she said.

"You're much, much prettier than Cassie," said Lovejoy vehemently but added, "Cassie isn't pretty at all."

While Mrs. Combie wore slippers and a flowered overall, Vincent was always correctly dressed; he had dark trousers, a striped cotton jacket when he cleaned the restaurant or laid the tables, a white jacket for cooking, and for waiting a tail coat, white dress shirt, black butterfly bow tie, and a watch-chain that looked expensive, though Lovejoy knew it ended in a safety pin. He changed at lightning speed; everything he did was quick and neat. He worked frantically and sometimes he looked so thin, so tired, his skin so transparent —like Sparkey's, who, they said, would not live to grow up— that Mrs. Combie's heart turned over.

He was a fine pale little man with a little moustache that

looked like down, like two brown moths, thought Lovejoy, on his upper lip. He had grey eyes that could blaze with excitement; their pupils could grow small and dark if he were angry, which was often, and wide and bright if he were upset, which was more often; they were, if Mrs. Combie had only known it, a fanatic's eyes.

"You are really Mr. Combie?" Lovejoy asked him.

"No, I'm really Vincent," he said.

Lovejoy liked to be with Vincent. She used to watch him write the menus with a fine pen and mauve ink; he made such flourishes that hardly anyone could read what he had written. That disturbed Mrs. Combie.

"Shouldn't we put a card in the window to say what there is to eat and what it costs?" she asked.

"God forbid!" said Vincent.

Vincent liked to write an Italian menu. *"Risotto di Frutti di Mare,"* wrote Vincent. *"Costa di Manza al Vino Rosso."*

"Well really!" said Cassie the first time she saw one of these menus. "Really!"

"It isn't real," Mrs. Combie said hastily. "He only writes it."

"That's silly," said Cassie, but it was not silly. It was like a pianist exercising his fingers on a silent keyboard; it kept them in practice, and, with Lovejoy as an audience, it was as if the keyboard gave back a small sound.

"What is *Costa di Manza* . . . ?" she would ask.

"Rib of beef marinated in red wine." And Vincent would explain it to her.

"What is *Zabaione*?"

"A sweet made of eggs and sugar and Marsala."

"Have you got Marsala?" asked Lovejoy, who was versed in the ways of the house.

"Of course," said Vincent. "Anything that keeps we have got."

"What will you do if they ask for the beef?" asked Love-joy, troubled.

"I shall say, as I put the menu down, 'I'm sorry, the beef is all gone but the cutlets are very, very good.' Cutlets are quick, you see," said Vincent, "and if I say something is all gone, they will think we are popular."

The cutlets would be very, very good. Everything he served was good, even the ordinary dishes, the omelettes and steaks he cooked for the few customers he had; he dealt at the better-class shops in Mortimer Street off the High—Nichol the butcher's, Fenwick and Lay the poulterer's, and Driscoll the greengrocer's, the best and most expensive in the district.

"But there's good stuff on the barrows," said Mrs. Combie.

"Stuff's the right word for it," said Vincent.

He did not buy much, but every day he bought afresh, not only vegetables but meat or fish or poultry, and eggs and cream. "One day maybe we'll have our own farm," he told Mrs. Combie.

"Our own farm?" asked Mrs. Combie faintly. When she was frightened her voice seemed to reel away, and her breast palpitated.

"Why not?" said Vincent. "You don't know, Ettie," he would say, putting his arm round her shoulders, "you don't know the money there is in this; and not only money," he said, his voice solemn. "Men like Lombard and Romanos, and Vera, were famous all over the world. One day you may be proud, Ettie, of being married to Vincent."

"I am, George, I am," said Mrs. Combie. She would not have had him think otherwise, but meanwhile—and she sighed. There was so much she did not understand, so much that seemed necessary. "I saw some lovely looking salami in the Stores in the High for one-and-two," she told Vincent. "*English* salami." But Vincent shuddered.

"He only married you to get the restaurant," Cassie told Mrs. Combie. "And because you're soft."

"Yes, I married her because she's soft," said Vincent, and his eyes looked like an angry little dog's. "She has a soft voice, which you haven't. She feels soft." And he put his arm round Mrs. Combie and squeezed her; over Mrs. Combie's sallow, thin cheeks came her deep, pleased flush.

*   *   *

Lovejoy liked the restaurant, its quiet, and its good looks; good looks were the right word; the small mahogany cash desk, for instance, looked good, it was solid and its colour deep; the white damask cloths on the tables were so starched and white that they shone; they were laid with clean silver and glass, the napkins cocked; Vincent rolled them round his hand and tucked the ends in expertly in a second. There were specimen vases holding one or two flowers, roses, carnations, or camellias—Vincent picked them out himself. The light was rich and dim; there was electricity in the restaurant, though there was gas in the rest of the house. A brass shaded light stood on the desk, but in the centre of the ceiling was a chandelier of apricot-coloured stone. "Alabaster," said Vincent reverently. He had bought it at a country-house sale.

Lovejoy often looked at it; gilt babies, flying out from the alabaster centre bowl, held the lights, though the bowl itself glowed. The babies were naked and had wings; Lovejoy admired their round little limbs, complete even to gilt dimples and folds. "But they haven't any stomach buttons," she said, "no navels."

"They don't need navels," said Vincent. "They're cherubs, supernatural babies."

"Supernatural?"

"Things above, around, other than natural things," said Vincent; and, seeing that Lovejoy looked bewildered, he said, "Things we don't see."

"You mean not real?" asked the practical Lovejoy.

"Perhaps more real than real," said Vincent. "Things are more than just themselves." When Vincent thought, Lovejoy noticed, his forehead stood out in lumps; it was a big forehead for such a little man.

"No one knows, no one, what will come out of anything," he said. "'There are more things in heaven and earth, Horatio, than are dreamt of in your philosophy.'" And Vincent looked away, far over Lovejoy's head.

Mrs. Combie did not like it when Vincent called her Horatio or Brutus or any name but hers, Ettie; it made her feel as if she were not there. Lovejoy, as one accustomed to the antics of grown-ups, accepted it, but now one word struck her. She felt in her pocket for the edge of the packet of seeds she had nearly thrown away.

"Mr. Vincent," she said, "what is good garden earth?"

Strangely enough, Vincent could not answer this simple question.

CHAPTER VI

No one knew when Mrs. Mason would appear in Catford Street; a postcard or a telegram would come, and next day she would arrive; once she had come without telling anyone. It might be at any time, but in March or early April she always came. "She comes to see *me*," said Lovejoy, "before she goes where we're booked for Easter." Lovejoy still said "we." "It might be any day now," said Lovejoy.

Mrs. Combie spring-cleaned the house, and Lovejoy helped her; last of all they turned out the Masons' room, the first floor back. The walls were swept down, the linoleum scrubbed, the brown rugs washed, the fireplace black-leaded round the gas fire, the heavy curtains beaten and shaken, the armchair beaten too. On the armchair was a stain from some scent Mrs. Mason had spilled; the smell of it still lingered and

47

when Lovejoy was more than usually lonely she pressed her
nose against it and sniffed; as she sniffed she conjured up her
mother. The brass rails of the big bed were polished; soon
I won't be sleeping in it alone, thought Lovejoy, and she
thought of the big mound her mother would make in it, a
lazy mound but warm and soft to be against.

When everything in the room was clean, a fresh starched
tablecloth was put on the table, a clean white honeycomb
counterpane on the bed—Mrs. Combie did not know how
fashionable those had become—and a white crocheted runner
on the dressing-table, and it was ready. "Now don't you dirty
anything," said Mrs. Combie. She said it as a matter of
routine because Lovejoy was a child, but she knew Lovejoy
would not dirty anything; far from it; the room would be
dusted every day, the brass rubbed up, and Lovejoy would
hardly dare to sleep in the bed for fear of rumpling it.

Even in Catford Street there were signs of spring; spring
sun shone on the pavements, windows were opened, and front
doors were sometimes left wide; there was a strong smell of
spring greens cooking, of soap and dampness from spring
cleanings, of new paint. People bought bunches of primroses;
they were only threepence a bunch on the barrows in the
High, but the pale yellow of the flowers soon got sooty. The
smoke from the chimney pots eddied this way and that as
the breeze changed. Children, playing, left their coats open
and they seemed to have a new energy; they played hopping
games in squares and oblongs chalked on the pavement; they
skipped—skipping ropes were suddenly fashionable this year—
and some of the boys had scooters, painted scarlet. Cats lay
out on the sills, and Mrs. Cleary's and Miss Arnot's cats had
two litters of kittens. The birds were working, sparrows and
starlings flying with wisps of straw and fluff and feathers to
make into nests that no one ever saw. From the broken
masonry of the Catholic church came a continuous soft deep

coo, a pigeon brooding, and Father Lambert heard it as he went into his makeshift church below the aeroplane, which had not moved an inch. Young girls who had kept with other girls as if they were glued all winter, suddenly broke away and went with boys. Older girls announced their engagements; both Mr. Wix and Father Lambert had banns to announce.

Lovejoy's wardrobe was spring-cleaned too, at least as far as she was able; she let down the hem of her plaid coat, though it took her a long time; the hem looked a different colour from the other plaid but at least it was respectable; she cleaned the plimsolls with whitening, though she could guess what her mother would say when she saw them. "Never mind; she'll buy me some shoes," she said. She asked Mrs. Combie to wash her hair with her last remaining bit of green soap and brushed it for an extra five minutes every day, and every day she did her nails. "Anyone would think the queen was coming," mocked Cassie. Then one afternoon Lovejoy came in from school and found a letter on the mat.

Before she picked it up and turned it over she knew it was to say her mother was not coming. "She *never* writes, not a letter," said Lovejoy, looking at the writing on the envelope. Slowly she carried it to Mrs. Combie.

"Well, it's nice to change your plans and let other people know," said Cassie when Mrs. Combie had read the letter out. "I suppose you'll go on looking after that child?"

"She says they don't finish till the tenth and then go to Clifton for Easter," said Mrs. Combie, troubled. She appealed across the tea table to Vincent. "She says the time's too short for the fare. Well, Scarborough *is* a long way," said Mrs. Combie.

"If I had a little girl," said Vincent, "I'd come from John o'Groat's to see her."

Lovejoy had retreated to the shadow of the stairs. Vincent

had seen her standing out there in the side passage and had
meant to show he sympathized, but when Lovejoy heard what
he said she leaned her head against the banister knob and shut
her eyes; she shut them tightly, but two small fierce tears came
spurting out. Vincent saw the tears and turned his head away.

In the four years since the Masons had come to Catford
Street, Vincent had come to like and respect Lovejoy. Can
one respect a child? Yes, one can, thought Vincent. Respect
and like. "She's as hard as nails," Cassie said of Lovejoy;
Vincent knew she was not.

At first all that he had known of her was that Ettie's new
and abundant-looking lodger had a little girl of whom he
caught glimpses when she passed the restaurant on an errand
or on her way to school and back; a child in a plaid coat—
"Yes, I had it even then," said Lovejoy—so quiet he hardly
noticed her; after a while he noticed the quietness. "Ettie,
should a child be as silent and still as that?"

Mrs. Combie had not thought about it. "She's no trouble,"
she said uncertainly.

Vincent thought vaguely that a child ought to be a trouble.
"There's something wrong," he said. Then one afternoon he
had come out of the restaurant and found Lovejoy sitting on
the stairs.

It was three o'clock and the restaurant was closed; in any
case there had been no one in for lunch and the kitchen was
empty and tidy; this was the time Mrs. Combie did the washing or changed her slippers for shoes, took her purse and a
black oilskin bag, and slipped out to the house shops while
Vincent made up his accounts at the desk in the restaurant,
wrote the evening menus, and perhaps dozed off in the quiet.
It was uncommon for him to stir, but that day he had left an
account book in his room and came out to fetch it. He had
opened the glass door from the restaurant quietly and came

lightly up the first flight of the stairs and along the landing to the second flight; there he almost stepped on Lovejoy.

It was always twilight in that dark house, and Vincent had not seen much of her; there was only a glimmer of paleness from her hands and face, but he made out that she was sitting with her elbows on her knees, her chin on her hands; the way she sat was patient, patient and brooding. She looked small against the height of the stairs, and Vincent was moved in a way he was not usually moved with children. "Hello," he said.

She lifted her head and said, "Hello."

"What are you doing here?"

"Waiting."

"Is your mother out?"

"No, she's in." And she went back to her waiting in a way that prohibited further talk. Vincent went on upstairs.

He saw her there once again—on guard? thought Vincent. He knew there was a man there in the room and he knew that Lovejoy knew he had guessed it. "Who are these gentlemen who come and take your mother out?" he heard Cassie ask her.

"Gentlemen," said Lovejoy and walked away.

"I believe they go into her room," said Cassie.

"That they don't do." Mrs. Combie flared up.

"You don't know," said Cassie, "and Ettie, I think you don't want to know."

Vincent opened his mouth to say, "It's only twice," then shut it. Was it only twice? thought Vincent. Still, even if they were in the room I don't know they did anything wrong, he argued, and kept quiet, but he did not like it for the little girl. There were other things he did not like. Her mother sent her to the Crown; Vincent knew nothing about children, but he thought a child, especially a little girl, should not be sent even into an off-license. He watched Lovejoy more than

he knew; when her mother went out, which was almost every
night, Lovejoy waited up; she turned down the bed and put
a glass of orange juice beside it, and waited. Sometimes Vincent was moved to take her a glass of hot milk. "You go to
bed," he said. "She'll come." Sometimes, if he were there,
Lovejoy did go to bed, but Vincent knew that when Mrs.
Mason came in she would make a noise, and laugh and flash
on the light, while he had seen Lovejoy steal out of the room
in the mornings with her shoes in her hand so that she would
not wake her mother. "*She's* not the one who is hard," said
Vincent.

Now when Vincent had gone into the restaurant Lovejoy
came and stood by Mrs. Combie. "I should only be half fare,"
she said. "Couldn't I go to Scarborough and see her?"

"Dearie, she's staying with a friend," said Mrs. Combie.

"Friend in trousers," said Cassie.

Lovejoy had turned away to the sink, where they had been
peeling potatoes for the dinners. She picked up the potato
knife and threw it at Cassie.

"I couldn't blame the child," Mrs. Combie told Vincent.
"Cassie shouldn't have said that"; but, at the time, she did
blame Lovejoy sharply and sent her to bed.

Lovejoy lay in the double bed, trying not to look at the
room, its immaculateness, its starched covers, the vase she
had put ready for the left-over flowers from the restaurant
tables; Vincent had promised them to her. She had had no
tea and she was cold and presently she crept out of bed and
fetched her coat and huddled it round her. As she lay, she let
her fingers go over its warm wool roughness; it was familiar,
friendly, her own, and mysteriously it made her heart a little
less sore. Then her fingers met something stiff in the pocket;
it was the packet of cornflowers.

CHAPTER VII

"WHAT does corn look like?" Lovejoy asked Vincent. "It says it has blue flowers but—" "Fair waved the golden corn," they sang in the hymn at school. "The princess had corn-coloured hair," said the stories; Lovejoy had seen pictures of corn, of course, but they were not anything like the flowers on the packet.

"Corn hasn't any flowers," said Vincent.

"But—"

"It's a grain," said Vincent and he gave Lovejoy an explanation of how the seed grew and became wheat, "or rye, or barley or oats," said Vincent, and was changed into bread. "Bread is the staff of life," said Vincent, warming, "and it's more than that. It can be spiritual as well as material. It's a symbol." Then he saw Lovejoy was not listening.

"There are blue flowers on the packet, *printed*," she was saying to herself, and the obstinate, closed look came on her face. "I shall plant them and find out."

But before even one seed can be planted there has to be earth.

"What is good garden—?" she began, but she had asked Vincent that before. Vincent was quick to many things but he had forgotten about earth. It was not surprising; in Catford Street there was not a sign of earth, except in the bombed places; everything was man-made, "But under everything," Tip was to argue, "under everything's dirt." Tip called earth "dirt." "Under the houses and pavements and the road, there's dirt." That was true, and dirt, earth, has power, an astonishing power of life, of creating and sweetening; it can take anything, a body, an old tin, decay, rust, corruption, filth, and turn it into itself, and slowly make it life, green blades of grass and weeds. "These bombed sites," said Angela, "according to the Ministry of Works, grow one hundred and thirty-seven different kinds of weeds. It's amazing."

Olivia thought it was amazing too but not in Angela's way; as when speaking of sparrows, they saw two different things; Angela thought of the weeds, Olivia of the power of life.

When Lovejoy thought about the cornflowers, the seeds, she seemed to forget a little, a very little, about her mother. "I need to plant them," she might have said, but where? "Plant them in a box," said Mrs. Combie absently when Lovejoy asked her.

"I want a garden," said Lovejoy. If she had wanted the moon or a diamond tiara it would have been as easy to get in Catford Street.

There were, of course, back gardens to some of the Street houses; but they were dark, open cellars of gardens, spaces of dankness between sooty walls; coals were kept in them, handcarts and bicycles and mangles, washing was hung in them and they were full of bottles and tins. One or two had trees, but they were sooty, stunted trees that smelled of cat; Istanbul, for instance, thought every tree in the Street belonged to him. One back garden had a lilac bush, but it did not flower; even Lovejoy knew that nothing would be likely to flourish in those back yards, besides which each of them belonged to someone.

It was queer to think of people in Catford Street owning gardens. Lovejoy had lived there all these years but she had not seen what she saw now, the flowers—but they must always have been there, thought Lovejoy.

Now, in almost every window, she saw pots with plants growing in them; pots of red and pink flowers, of yellow ones, daffodils—she knew them—and hyacinths, as well as green things, ferns, palms, rubber plants; Sparkey's mother grew fuchsias in her flat window. Mrs. Cleary and Miss Arnot were unpopular, their cats spoiled the window boxes; some houses had window boxes as high as the fourth floor; they had not the profuseness of the Square window boxes but they made patches of unexpected colour up the Street. In the area of one of the houses a whole vegetable garden grew in boxes. Well, you have to use something like boxes down there, thought Lovejoy, an area's concrete all over. The plants, she had to admit, seemed to grow well in boxes. "What are those?" asked Lovejoy, peering down from the pavement and pointing to some small shiny-leaved plants.

"Broad beans," said the man who looked after them. "Don't you be throwing things down here."

"I'm not," said Lovejoy.

"Well, don't you," he said so belligerently that Lovejoy saw more clearly than ever that growing plants was difficult in Catford Street.

Another man, in another area, was setting little plants in half-barrels. It was a barrel garden; it even had barrels cut into seats. Lovejoy knew the man; he was Mr. Isbister, Rory Isbister's grandfather, a wrinkled, brown old man, who lived in the basement of Number Twenty-three. "What are those?" asked Lovejoy.

"Sweet peas," said Mr. Isbister.

He was not cross as the first man had been, and let Lovejoy talk to him. "I've got some seeds," she said.

"You'd better get busy," said Mr. Isbister. " 'S nearly April."

"Is April the time to sow?"

"March, April, for most things."

"Why?" asked Lovejoy.

"Because," said Mr. Isbister and grunted as he bent to tie a sweet pea to a little stick.

"Yes, but why?"

Mr. Isbister pushed his cap back on his head, leaving earth in his grizzled hair, and looked at her. Lovejoy was standing above him on the pavement. They were not at a good level for talking, but he answered her. When Mr. Isbister talked there were few words and long pauses. It was not at all like Vincent's eloquence but each word sank in. "Christmastime," said Mr. Isbister, "till round 'bout Febr'rary—" Pause.

"Yes," said Lovejoy encouragingly.

"Th'earth's like dead," said Mr. Isbister; another pause. "Round 'bout March"—pause—"begins t' work. April's working." Mr. Isbister looked up at the sky and frowned. "April's short month," he said, "must get after things"—pause. "Get busy," and he went back to his sweet peas.

But Lovejoy had not finished. "If you wanted to make a garden here, where would you do it?" she asked.

There was a silence, then, "Nowhere,' said Mr. Isbister. Lovejoy set her lips.

"When you do anything," Vincent had told her often, "people will advise you not to, they'll want to drag you down," and his eyes grew dark, thinking of Cassie. "Don't let them," cried Vincent. "*They—must—not.* You must refuse to let them. I am going to have a restaurant that I call a restaurant," said Vincent, "or I'll have nothing at all"; and, "I'll have a garden or nothing at all," said Lovejoy.

*   *   *

Every now and then, in the streets between the Square and the river, there was a gap, the bombed sites of which Olivia and Angela had spoken, though the children called them the bomb-ruins. Where once houses had been, or warehouses or shops, was a pit below the level of the street, a space that was sometimes a hundred or two hundred yards across, an open gap between the houses. After the war the bomb-ruins had been tidied up, the debris of the ruins removed, only rubble left that would do for making new foundations when new buildings went up. The workmen had left each one tidy, but soon they were all untidy again; people tipped rubbish in them, threw tins and scrap iron down in them; the boys used them as lavatories; most of the children were forbidden to go near them, and they were seemingly empty, but only seemingly. Lovejoy knew, as every child in Catford Street knew, that the bomb-ruins were the headquarters of the gangs.

Every boy in Catford Street who was big enough belonged to a gang. "But *you're* not six," Sparkey's mother told him. The gangs kept to themselves, though they fought one another at times, and they had partisan groups among the girls. By tacit consent, the girls kept out of the ruins; they were afraid of the eeriness of that waste ground. "Tramps go there," said Sparkey, "and thieves. There was a burglar dumped a safe there, an' one night a girl was killed, with a *stocking!*" said Sparkey, his eyes enormous. If a girl went in the ruins, she was not behaving like a girl; no book of etiquette had stricter rules of behaviour than the children of Catford Street.

and a girl who did not behave like a girl could be fought.
"It's y'own fault, y'asked for it," the boys used to say if they
had to fight the girls. "Come in here and we'll knock y'teeth
out," they said now to Lovejoy.

For Lovejoy was hovering. With the packet in her pocket,
she had been walking round and round the bomb-ruins; some,
bare and wide, she knew were no good; they were as public
as the streets, everyone could look in them; but there were
some where the rubble made hiding places, in which, picking
a way in and out, she could get where no one could see her—
places disused, derelict, given up, quite empty. "If it wasn't
for those blasted boys," said Lovejoy.

It was not only that they would have fought her; she knew
they could leave nothing alone. If they saw a tin, they must
kick it; a poster, they drew on it and tore it; a fly, they must
catch it. They took it out of one another too; if a boy were
near another boy, perfectly friendly, after a moment he would
kick or punch, and in a moment they would start scuffling,
twisting, and wrestling; they could not sit next to one another
in the bus without driving their elbows into or kicking one
another. There was no ill will, no malice, as there would
have been with girls. It was as if there were—a fizz in them,
thought Lovejoy. She did not know how else to describe that
bubbling, bottled-up energy. She had it herself, in spite of
her quietness, her self-containedness; often she felt more like
a boy than like a girl; sometimes she sat down on the boarding
steps of the bus if the conductor were upstairs, and, holding
on with one hand to the boarding rail, she would stick out
her legs low over the road to feel the air as the bus swept
round; all the old ladies screamed out that she would be
killed. Lovejoy put her tongue out at them and, before the
bus stopped, jumped off. Sometimes she walked on her hands
down the length of a block. She sucked gob-stoppers, keeping
the ball in her cheek, like any little hooligan; neither Vincent

nor her own mother would have recognized her. Lovejoy knew what it was like to be a boy but, thinking of the fragile loops of Mr. Isbister's sweet-pea seedlings, she drew her breath sharply. Isn't there anywhere those boys don't go? she thought. She seemed to have been carrying those seeds round for days.

"Have a box," said Mrs. Combie and Mr. Isbister.

"I won't have a box," said Lovejoy.

CHAPTER VIII

Just as a bird, after flying and fluttering and perching and looking, will suddenly build its nest in some exposed place so bare and noticeable that it seems that a cat must get at it or boys steal the eggs and tear it down, so Lovejoy, after days of searching for secret spots, suddenly chose an extraordinary place to plant her seeds.

There was one bomb-ruin where, as far as she knew, the boys did not go, where they had made no camps—they called anything they built on a bomb-ruin a camp. This site was too close to the seething High Street, almost at the top of Catford Street, opposite the newspaper stand; it was public, but left on it were pyramids of old bricks standing up and a few remnants of brick walls that must once have been cellar walls; among them, where two made an angle, she found a place.

It was sheltered, the walls made it feel secret, if she stooped or knelt on the ground no one could see her, and in it was a patch of earth that showed among the rubble.

It'll do, thought Lovejoy. She spent two days in clearing the patch until it was big enough, about four feet square; she kept the best bits of rubble to edge the garden, as she had edged the seaside gardens she had made on the sand in Bournemouth or Torquay or Margate in the halcyon days when she was sweet. I can put the bits close together and they'll look like pebbles or shells, she thought.

The ground smelled of stale rubbish and soot and—the loo, thought Lovejoy, wrinkling up her nose. Each piece of rubble had to be cleared and put down with a gentle hand; she did not dare throw it on a pile or make any noise; it was neat work but slow, and very grimy; she grew blacker and blacker; her hands were like a sweep's and her knees looked as if they had black caps on them.

She spent every moment she could in the garden. Nobody came—no boys, only cats; once Istanbul stalked through the rubble and, after springing up on the gap that led to Catford Street, disappeared into Mrs. Cleary's and Miss Arnot's house —or was it his house? thought Lovejoy. He made her wonder again why Sparkey was not on his step; she had kept a weather eye open for Sparkey, but all these days his step had been empty. He's probably ill, thought Lovejoy, who knew the ways of Sparkey.

The busy feet passed and repassed in the High with the blur of traffic noise behind them; nobody looked over the wall and it would not have mattered if they had; Lovejoy kept well down. Before going into the site at all she looked carefully up and down the street and seized an empty moment to sidle through the gap in the wall, jump down the bank, where she waited; if no heads came over, no footsteps sounded above her, she dodged across from one old wall to another, keeping behind the pyramids of earth and brick; sometimes even she could not tell which walls were hers. "Nobody will find it," said Lovejoy.

It took a whole week to clear the rubble and make the edges; the middle was hard black earth with a few blades of grass and weeds in it. I must dig it, thought Lovejoy, but with what?

She asked Mr. Isbister. She appeared suddenly in front of him as a robin appears on the handle of a spade, only she was not as attractive as a robin. "What do you dig the earth up with?" she asked.

"Small? Little bit?" Lovejoy nodded. "Fork," said Mr. Isbister and went back to his work.

"Mrs. Combie, will you lend me a fork?"

"What do you want it for?" asked Mrs. Combie.

"For something."

"Yes, but what?"

"It's a secret. Please let me have a fork."

"You'll spoil it," said Mrs. Combie.

"Ettie, no one can spoil a kitchen fork," said Vincent.

Reluctantly Mrs. Combie opened the kitchen drawer and took one out.

It was not much later that Lovejoy appeared in front of Mr. Isbister again. "Now look what you've done," she said and showed the fork with its prongs bent up and one broken. "You told me to use a fork," she said, glaring at him. "It's Mrs. Combie's"—and she wailed, "I have to take it back."

"*Garden* fork!" said Mr. Isbister. "Look"—and he showed her a small stout garden fork and a trowel. "Real garden needs spade," he said, "but you could manage with these."

Lovejoy looked at the tools and then at Mrs. Combie's broken fork. "You wouldn't lend me them?" she asked.

"No," said Mr. Isbister and put them away. He had a cupboard made out of a box in among his barrels, and now

Lovejoy saw in it a horde of garden things; there were a spade, a watering can, some flowerpots and wooden labels, packets of seeds, and a bundle of raffia. Her quick eyes saw all these before he shut the cupboard door and, You need all that for gardening, she thought. Perhaps I could pinch— But garden things, it seemed, were precious and well guarded. Mr. Isbister, for instance, was taking no chances; he had a padlock on the door, which he locked, and put the key in his pocket. "You go and get your own things," he told Lovejoy. She went silently away to face Mrs. Combie with the broken kitchen fork.

A fork. A trowel, a fork. How can I get a fork? At last Lovejoy came to the Square Gardens, and there Lucas—though she did not know his name was Lucas—had left his wheelbarrow on the path while, as Angela was out of the way, he had gone to have a smoke and some tea from his flask. Lovejoy saw tools in the barrow; she could see a twig broom and a spade, and a big fork; Who knows? thought Lovejoy, he might have left a little fork as well. She pressed her nose against the chestnut palings which had taken the place of the railings that had been there before the war.

In the war the railings had been taken away. "Every bit of iron was needed," said Angela when she told this story. "Railings were taken from all over London. When they took ours we didn't mind at first. We thought we should like the people from the Street to share our garden; we truthfully welcomed them," said Angela, "but very soon we found out our mistake. They scuffed up the grass, the boys played cricket on it, they threw paper about, they even picked the flowers and broke off the trees. Lucas said—"

"I don't like Lucas," Olivia had interrupted once. "He's a toady. He treats the children like the cat."

"The cat?"

"The cat did this, the cat did that," said Olivia.

"Nonsense, they are little hooligans, you know they are," said Angela. "They nearly broke Lucas's heart. They simply don't understand about gardens."

"How can they?" asked Olivia hotly. "I mean what chance? In the whole Street there isn't a tree, not a blade, for any of them. Each child should have a blade, at least," said Olivia.

"Well, we shouldn't have one if they all came in," said Angela, and she ordered the new palings. They seemed very tall to Lovejoy and they had sharp pointed tops. Still, I might get over them, she thought.

The Gardens looked an oasis of green and deep-down freshness after the Street; they smelled fresh, of grass and leaves and freshly turned earth; a few daffodils were out along the paths, and hundreds of crocuses in the grass. "You *have* been successful!" the residents said to Angela. "The Gardens have never looked better." To Lovejoy they were a revelation and she forgot the fork as, holding two of the palings, she pressed her face in between them to look.

"What are you doing here?"

Angela had a new spring hat; it was blue, trimmed with blue feather wings, which gave her a look of extraordinary swiftness. When she pounced on Lovejoy she might have been an avenging angel.

"What are you doing here?"

Lovejoy, her back against the paling, stood mute.

"Answer me," said Angela. "What are you doing?"

"Lookin'." Lovejoy let the word out and shut her lips.

Angela did not know it, but one of the Catford Street children was doing what she had always hoped they would do, appreciate the Gardens. If Lovejoy had asked her question, "Is that good garden earth?" or been able to say what she felt about the crocuses, the whole history would have been different, but she was silent and sullen and dropped her eyelids in the way Angela knew meant that a purpose was being concealed.

"You were going to climb the palings," said Angela.

Lovejoy was suddenly filled with a terrible feeling of the power of grown-ups, the power and the knowledge. No one knew better than she how to behave, pretty manners had been drilled into her when she was a very little girl, but now her helplessness enraged her; she had thrown the potato knife at Cassie, and what she did now imprinted her forever on Angela's mind. She spat. The spit landed hard on the pavement by Angela's shoe. Both of them looked a little frightened at that dark spot of venom on the pavement, then, skipping as if nothing had happened, skip-hop-jump, Lovejoy turned her back and disappeared towards the Street, while Angela, with a heightened colour, went home.

Lovejoy gave up trying to get a fork for nothing. "Where would I buy garden things?" she asked Vincent.

Vincent, as usual, ignored Woolworth's or any shop in the High. "There's a garden shop in Mortimer Street by Driscoll's," he said.

"It's expensive over there," said Mrs. Combie.

"That's where you get good things," said Vincent in rebuke.

When Lovejoy found the garden shop it was like Mr. Isbister's cupboard multiplied a hundred times. She blinked at the riches; there were shining green- and red-painted garden tools, trowels and forks, spades, big forks, big and little rakes; Lovejoy longed to handle a rake. There were twig brooms, and watering cans with bright copper nozzles and tiny green watering cans with long spouts. It was a delectable shop; there was a smell of fresh wood from lengths of trellis; there were clean, inviting-looking flowerpots stacked in different sizes. There were wheelbarrows. If I had a wheelbarrow how I could move those stones, she thought, and stopped to read its label. "The Super-Nimble Wheelbarrow," she spelled out,

"£4.10.0." Four pounds ten! She dropped the label as if it were red-hot.

A showcase, the whole of it used for seeds, was so brilliant with the colours of the flowers on the packets that Lovejoy was dazzled. Before she could touch them or read the names a shopgirl was beside her; shop people were always vigilant if a sparrow-child came in. "What do you want, dear?" said the girl briskly.

Lovejoy had seen a trowel and fork with red handles; they were tied together with string and laid in a wooden basket. "How much are those?" she asked.

"Eight-and-a-penny," said the girl more briskly. "You haven't got that, have you? Run along home."

"Don't you have cheaper ones?" asked Lovejoy. "What are those plain ones?"—and she showed a pair without any red paint.

"Those are stainless steel," said the girl without pity. "Thirty-three shillings the pair."

Lovejoy went out. She walked slowly back across the Square into Motcombe Terrace; there she paused, and suddenly her face cleared. Of course, I'll go to Dwight's, she thought.

DWIGHT'S REPOSITORY AND SALE ROOMS, *Established 1889* was a few doors down the Terrace from the Street. People said it was the same Mr. Dwight who kept it now. Sooner or later everybody in the Street bought or sold something at Mr. Dwight's; he seemed to have the flotsam and jetsam of all the streets round; in the window and inside the shop, from the floor to the ceiling, was junk: furniture and clothes and china, toys and bits of bicycles and perambulators, birdcages, parts of wash-hand-stands, and nearly new washing machines, shoes and books and radios; things were thick along the pavement and nobody knew how Mr. Dwight managed to get them back into the shop at night.

As Lovejoy came up, Mr. Dwight was there as he always was, with his boy, putting out more things on the pavement: a bookcase of books, a sofa, a jug and basin patterned with ivy on a Japanese table, another basin full of old stirrups under the table, a sewing machine, some dinner plates on two card tables, and a tin bath. Lovejoy waited until Mr. Dwight looked up, then said, "Mrs. Combie sent me to ask, have you a small garden fork and a trowel."

There was a pause while he put some bundles of spoons on the stirrups; Lovejoy looked at the back of his neck where the grey hairs were stiff; the band of his striped shirt was not very clean, he wore no collar, and the green sweater under his apron was baggy and stained. After the overwhelming beauty of the hardware shop it was a relief to get back into her familiar shabby world. She said, "A fork alone would do."

"Is *she* starting window boxes?" asked Mr. Dwight.

When he had finished arranging the spoons he went back into the shop and began turning things over. Lovejoy followed and watched. "I did have one, somewhere," he said under his breath and moved a pile of cookery books. "Somewhere," breathed Mr. Dwight and lifted a folded tablecloth, some old tennis balls in a net, a hat, and at last, from under a long-clothes baby doll, he brought out a small dusty fork; the varnish had come off its handle, its prongs were crusted with dirt, but it was a fork. "There's a trowel to it somewhere," said Mr. Dwight. "Maybe not its, but it'd do. I'll look for it. Tell Mrs. Combie I'll let her have it this evening."

"How—much?" asked Lovejoy.

Mr. Dwight looked earnestly at the fork. "It's a nice little fork," he said slowly. "It's handy."

"It's dirty," said Lovejoy.

"It's strong," said Mr. Dwight.

"One prong is bent," said Lovejoy.

"Well, she can have it for one-and-six," said Mr. Dwight.

"The same for the trowel. Two-and-nine the pair. Take it or leave it."

Lovejoy did not know why she bargained; no more than thirty-three shillings had she two-and-ninepence, and April was begun, and the seeds were still in her pocket. She looked at the fork, where he had thrown it on top of the tablecloth in all its usefulness and dirt. "You wouldn't hire it?" she said.

"No, I wouldn't," said Mr. Dwight. "One-and-threepence. Two-and-six, the two."

*　　*　　*

"Mr. Vincent, can you lend me half a crown?"

It was a bad moment to choose; Lovejoy saw that too late. She was finding out how difficult it is to notice other people when one is busy. Vincent was at his desk in the restaurant, doing his eternal accounts, and his face when he looked up was even whiter, more knotted with worry, than usual. "Half a crown?" he said. "I'll soon need half a crown myself."

He and Lovejoy gazed down at the figures, meticulously written, in the long, thin account book. "There are nine million people in London," Lovejoy had once told him, but Vincent had shaken his head. "There are about three thousand," he said solemnly, "three thousand real people, if that." Still, three thousand was a large number. "You'd think some of them would come," he said.

"Some do," said Lovejoy.

"Not enough to do any good, not real people." He shook his head as if he could not understand, and Lovejoy tiptoed away.

*　　*　　*

"Do you know what that child has been doing?" asked Cassie, outraged. "Singing in the Square."

It was lunchtime; Cassie had been in that morning; she

dropped into the restaurant every day—"or twice or three times a day," said Vincent bitterly—and on her way home had gone across the Square to Mortimer Street, meaning to go into Driscoll's and see if she could discover what extravagance Vincent had bought that day; she had caught Lovejoy in the act and brought her back. Now Mrs. Combie, who was serving vegetables for Vincent—there were three people in the restaurant—let the pots stand on the table and, leaning her weight on it, as she did when she was tired, looked at Lovejoy across the potatoes. Lovejoy defiantly looked back.

"Like her mother!" said Cassie.

"Don't be silly, Cassie. Mrs. Mason is a concert artist," said Mrs. Combie, and Lovejoy could have put her arms round the flowered overall and kissed her.

"Singing. Begging!" said Cassie.

"Did you, Lovejoy?" asked Mrs. Combie. Her voice sounded damped and sad and Lovejoy hung her head.

"It wasn't any use," she said. Standing on the edge of the pavement, she had sung some of her mother's songs. One lady had opened a window and thrown her threepence—a queer dark lady who stayed at the window to listen. "I couldn't help myself," said Olivia when Angela said she had encouraged the children to beg. "It sounded such a cheep in the Square." A maid came out from another house and told Lovejoy to go away, and a lady came from the gardens and said the noise was waking her baby. Lovejoy moved to another house and was told to go away from there, and then Cassie came. "I want two-and-six," said Lovejoy hopelessly, "—two-and-threepence, I've got threepence from the lady. Could—could I write to my mother? If you would lend me a stamp?" she asked Mrs. Combie.

Mrs. Combie looked more tired and said, "Dearie, I don't know her address."

"You don't *know*—" began Cassie.

"She'll write presently," said Mrs. Combie with dignity and put some buttered carrots in a dish and carried them to Vincent.

"If you ask me you'll be landed, Ettie," said Cassie when she came back.

"Mrs. Combie," asked Lovejoy when Cassie had gone, "couldn't you lend me half a crown and put it on the bill?"

Mrs. Combie looked over Lovejoy's head without answering for a moment; she was looking through the glass door into the restaurant, where Vincent for once was busy—"But chops and liver and bacon, and an omelette, there's nothing in that," she said to Lovejoy. Her eyes stayed troubled, on Vincent as he moved about, and Lovejoy knew again that for all Mrs. Combie's kindness and the way she understood, Lovejoy and Mrs. Mason and everyone else could be drowned or lost or starved for Vincent. "Half a crown?" said Mrs. Combie. "I couldn't do that. I daren't. You see, your mother hasn't paid, not for two months."

Lovejoy went back to the bomb-ruin, slipped through the gap and down the bank, bent and ran, doubling in and out of the walls, to the garden. She crouched in the middle of it, trying to dig a hole with her finger, but the earth was too hard; all she did was to stub her finger so that it swelled and sent pain up her arm. Then she sat, nursing the throbbing finger in her armpit, her head on her knees.

* * *

The places where money was kept were these: telephone boxes, the coppers put down for the newspapers while Sparkey's mother was at lunch or tea, gas-meters, and the boxes on the doors in the Ladies'. Lovejoy had inspected these; she had been the round of the kiosks, pressing button B, and collected nothing at all; the people round Catford Street were too poor to forget their threepences. The kiosk boxes, like the gas-meters and the lavatory boxes, were impregnable to her; her hands were small and she had no tools. There were tills in the shops, but shop people in the High and down the Street took no risks; the tills were behind the counters or enclosed in wire cages with cashiers in charge of them. There was a till on Vincent's desk but from the beginning Lovejoy ruled out Vincent and reluctantly she ruled out taking the money from the newspapers; there was something too trusting in the way it was left there; the very innocence and stupidity of it protected it; even the boys, who had been known to break open a telephone box, did not touch those coppers.

There was one more place Lovejoy knew where money was kept: in churches.

Like every other child in Catford Street, Lovejoy had looked into St. Botolph's and Our Lady of Sion. At St. Botolph's, just inside the door, were two collecting boxes, one labelled in Mr. Wix's colloquial way "People are still poor," the other "Our Organ Fund," but it was no use trying St. Botolph's because, keeping guard in it, were church ladies; Lovejoy had been chased out of it before now. The Catholic church was different; nobody watched there. "There's nothing worth stealing," Angela would have said. That was true; St. Botolph's was beautiful, Our Lady of Sion was makeshift and gimcrack; the statues were of the cheapest plaster and the Stations of the Cross that hung along the walls were coloured prints in cheap wood frames; the altar cloth was plain linen, the screen behind, plain blue; Father Lambert had no ladies to embroider for him, the hands that helped him were too rough for silk and gold thread, and yet there was far more money in the Catholic church—boxes and boxes, thought Lovejoy. There were four boxes at the entrance, two for guilds, one for payments for the small paper books that were for sale in the rack above it—but anyone could take one for nothing, thought Lovejoy, and no one would know—one for the poor, and one

"To Build Our Church and Schools," like the aeroplane outside. "Yes, we're fearful beggars," Father Lambert would say
often. That was not all; inside the church were more: a box
called "Sisters of Nazareth" and a box for candle money.
There were always candles burning on the small candle rails,
though here again anyone could take a candle and light it
without paying; sometimes people lit three or four but they
always put in their twopences; probably the boxes were full
of money, thought Lovejoy longingly.

It was not easy to steal in the Catholic church because it
was never empty; it was busy, not with church ladies but with
people. At St. Botolph's the people came to the services but
here they came in and out all day long; they knelt for a
moment, to say a special prayer, or prayed a long time, or they
lit candles. This traffic was a disadvantage from Lovejoy's
point of view, but it was balanced by the fact that no one took
any notice of anyone else; anyone could pray at the candle
rail for an hour and no one would think it queer. You can
do just as you like, thought Lovejoy, but you have to kneel
down, or bend your knee, as you come in and go out. Well,
I can do that, said Lovejoy.

She prospected and pondered till the second day, when,
after she had helped Mrs. Combie wash up, she quietly stayed
away from school and went to the church. She had thought
it might be empty after lunch when the shop and factory
workers had gone back to work and the children were at
school. At this time people were in their houses, either washing up or feeding babies or sitting a moment to read the paper,
listen to the radio, or snatch a few minutes' peace, like Vincent. It should be empty, she thought and skipped up the
flight of broken steps that led from the Street to a landing
that had been the old church porch and where the bell hung
now on a makeshift crossbar; from the landing more steps
had once led into the crypt; now they were the church

entrance. Lovejoy went stealthily down them; she had Vincent's screwdriver in her pocket and she felt like a burglar.

But the church was not empty. "Damn!" said Lovejoy. Two
girls with scarves over their heads knelt at the back, but it
was not hopeless; Lovejoy knew, by the white overalls lettered
with blue that they wore under their open coats, that they
worked at the laundry in Garden Row and would have to be
back there at two o'clock. She went past them into the church,
almost up to the front, slipped into one of the flimsy pews,
and knelt down; she looked through her fingers at the candle
box.

The candles were lit on a rail that stood by the altar; the
box was fixed to the wall; the label on the top read: *Candles
2d.*; twopences and twopences, thought Lovejoy; there were
nine candles on the rail. One-and-sixpence! thought Lovejoy.
She might be slow at reading but she was quick at adding up,
especially money. She meant to go closer in a moment, but as
she knelt she saw a subdued shine from the opposite corner
of the church and she noticed what, in her brief runnings in
and out, she had not seen before.

The long hut that now made the church had been put up
over the ruins and, rising through the temporary concrete
floor were three of the old church pillars; probably they had
been too heavy, too expensive to move until the remains were
razed altogether to build the new church; the pillars had been
left as they were, broken off short, and they made a side aisle
to the church; bookshelves and cupboards had been put along
it, but at the far end, up by the altar, screened from the
main church by the top pillar and a blue curtain, a chapel
had been made; as Lovejoy looked, a man came out from it,
pausing by the pillar to genuflect and cross himself before
he left the church. After a moment Lovejoy stood up and tiptoed across to look.

It was like another tiny church; there were rows of chairs,

a small altar with another blue screen behind it, a vase of
paper roses, and above it, on a pedestal, a plaster Mother and
Child.

Below the statue was another rail of candles and another
candle box.

A girl was kneeling on one of the prie-dieux—nothing but
girls, thought Lovejoy crossly, girls going gabble, gabble, gabble. This one had a string of beads in her hands and as she
prayed she played with it. A necklace in church! thought
Lovejoy primly. Even she knew better than that.

It was quiet, remote, almost secret in here. Lovejoy knelt
down, watching the girl, willing her to go away, and in a
moment the sliding beads grew still, the girl put the necklace
in her pocket, stood up, and went to the candle stand. She
took a candle out of the holder, lit it from another candle,
looked up at the statue, and, letting the wax run down to
make a warm bed in the socket, fixed the candle upright.
Then she took out a purse, found two pennies, and put them
in the candle box; Lovejoy heard them clink as they fell, and
the box top moved as if it were loose. Lovejoy could not look
properly, only through her fingers, but her heart began to
beat quickly. As the girl moved aside to kneel again before
she went, Lovejoy saw that the padlock on the box was open.

For a moment she could not believe her luck; she looked
so hard that her eyes blurred and she had to rub them and
look again. There was no doubt about it, the box was open, the
small strong padlock dangled from the hasp undone; the girl
walked away down the church, and Lovejoy was alone with
the open box.

"I must have left it open," Father Lambert was to say afterwards. "Now I wonder how the devil I came to do that." He
thought for a moment and said, "Perhaps it wasn't the devil."

Lovejoy was alone in the church too, as far as she could
hear. Getting carefully up, and being careful not to knock

over a chair, she looked; one girl, the girl who had been in the chapel, was still there but she was by the wall—praying to the pictures, thought Lovejoy. It seemed odd but it suited Lovejoy well; the girl had her back to Lovejoy; she stood up, passed to another picture, and again knelt down. Lovejoy did not in least know what she was doing, but as the pictures went right round the walls it seemed likely that she would be some time.

Lovejoy came back into the chapel and stood by the candles, looking at the box. The whole church seemed hushed, waiting. Do it. Do it, said Lovejoy, and the church seemed to say it too; the open box was like an invitation, like—a little too like— the newspaper coppers. In spite of all the boxes, she knew by the aeroplane outside that the church had no money to spare. She hesitated; then she remembered Cassie and her mother, and her face hardened.

Delicately, with her finger, she slid the padlock off, caught it and laid it quietly down, lifted the hasp, and opened the box; there was not much money inside but she put in her quick little claw and scooped some of it out. It did not chink much; not more than twopences being put in, thought Lovejoy. Experienced in hiding things, she did not put all the money into her pockets but some into her thick woollen socks and some into the handkerchief pocket of her knickers. There was a sixpence; her fingers, feeling for pennies, nearly dropped it; but all the rest was in coppers and it was heavy; I hope my socks don't come down, thought Lovejoy. Three times she dipped, then pulled the socks up, gave a hitch to her knickers, shut the box, closed the hasp, slid the padlock into place and locked it. The whole thing had not taken two minutes; she peeped into the church; the girl had moved one picture down.

Lovejoy unmistakably chinked as she moved. I'd better go, fast's I can, she thought and had begun to move heavily away when the statue on its tall pedestal caught her eye.

Angela said the statues in the Catholic church were cheap and vulgar, but to Lovejoy they seemed beautiful, especially this one of Mary. "Her robe's a beautiful sky blue," she told Vincent afterwards.

"Plaster blue!" said Vincent with scorn.

"Yes," said Lovejoy happily, "and she has a white plaster veil and plaster lilies."

"Ough!" said Vincent as if that hurt him.

"It isn't ough," said Lovejoy, offended, and did not tell him any more. Mary's pink hands and face were a little bright, perhaps, but she had pretty, shiny painted nut-brown hair and on the back of her head was the usual gold plate. Lovejoy did not know the purpose of that but she thought it decorative; like a dear little new kind of hat, she thought. The Baby had one too.

To Lovejoy the statue was exquisite, but now, as it caught her eye, its eyes were looking down at her—down *into* me, thought Lovejoy uneasily; she had the uneasy feeling that the statue was real and had seen what she had done, had seen but was not angry; the eyes had been sad and gentle before, they still looked gentle and sad—not even cross, thought Lovejoy; that mysteriously offended her.

It was against the code she had been brought up in all her life, the code of all the children in Catford Street: an eye for an eye, a tooth for a tooth, or two eyes, two teeth, if you could get them. This steadfastness—and yet what could a statue do but be steadfast?—its unchangingness seemed to put her guilt squarely upon Lovejoy and she did not like it. "Yah! Boo!" said Lovejoy rudely, but the statue stayed the same.

She began to panic. It had all been too easy, as if it were a trap; but it was not a trap; there was the church door open, the girl still murmuring her prayers. Lovejoy had only to walk out, carefully, so that she did not chink, and the money was hers.

Instead she had a strong feeling that she could not walk out, that she should put the pennies back. Almost she did. She had been perfectly collected and calm when she opened the box, but now her skin prickled, and her hands and her forehead, under her fringe, were wet. Why doesn't she look *away*? thought Lovejoy. Turn your head, she wanted to say sharply, but of course the statue could not, it was only plaster. "Silly little fool!" said Lovejoy scornfully at herself and with a mighty effort she walked down the side aisle. At the bottom she turned. The eyes were still looking.

CHAPTER IX

WHAT happens when a sin is committed? Usually the sinner flourishes.

Lovejoy bought the fork and trowel from Mr. Dwight and dug up the ground, doing her best, with the small fork, to make the earth smooth and fine, like the beds in the Square gardens. She sowed the cornflowers at either end of the garden, trying to put the seeds in rows like cabbages in an allotment, but they got lost in the furrows; she sowed them as evenly as she could and scattered earth over them. There had been three-and-eightpence in the candle box and from the one-and-fivepence she had over she bought grass seed to grow in the centre. "How much would I need," she asked Mr. Isbister, "to make that much grass?" She showed him the length and width with her arms.

Mr. Isbister paused and then grunted, "Half an ounce."

Lovejoy knew how to sow grass. She had watched the men doing it when the new council flats were made; they had lawns, not asphalt, and she had seen the men sow the seed and then stretch nets over the places to keep off the sparrows and children. Lovejoy, of course, had no net but that was soon solved. She had stolen the money, so it seemed to make no difference now if she stole a net, and she took the cat net off a perambulator when the baby was put outside to sleep. First she unfastened the net—if anybody comes I can pretend I'm looking at the baby, she thought; they'll scold me but that's all they can do—then she waited, looking up and down the Street and into the baby's house through the windows; the moment came; she dexterously peeled the net off, slid it under her coat, and sauntered away.

That gave her a bad few minutes in bed that night. People put nets over perambulators in case cats—Mrs. Cleary's or Miss Arnot's, perhaps—sat down on the babies' faces and smothered them. "Old women's tales," said Vincent, but Lovejoy could see how a cat could sit on a baby who had no net; the warmth, the soft pillow, would tempt it. The thought of the weight—of Istanbul, for instance, on a baby's face— filled the night with horror; she saw the baby choking in the tabby fur, beating with helpless fists, writhing, and no one would hear. In the night she decided to take the net back; I should be a murderer, thought Lovejoy, but in the light of morning she went firmly to the garden shop and spent two- pence on a dozen small wooden name-pegs, took them to the garden, and, after sticking them where the grass was sown, stretched the cat net over them; when it was done it looked so professional that she was charmed.

"If it was stolen, it couldn't have been a good garden," Tip was to say.

"It was a good garden," said Lovejoy, which was true. It all seemed to come together under her hand—"And why not?" asked Lovejoy defensively. It was not her fault, she argued, if she stole. The comics were unguarded on the stand, the little boys looked away from their ice-cream cornets, Sparkey had stood right out on the pavement to look at the flowers on the packet, the baby was left out with the net, the candle box was open. "What do you *expect*?" asked Lovejoy furiously.

Now the garden was ready to grow. In the earth the seeds were changing into plants—"or presently they'll change," said Lovejoy when she dug one up with her finger and found it was still the same.

"Hey! give them time," said Mr. Isbister.

"But how much time?" asked the impatient Lovejoy.

At night now, when she went to bed, she did not lie awake feeling the emptiness; she thought about the garden, the seeds, their promised colours. She had never before thought of colours—except in clothes, thought Lovejoy; now she saw colours everywhere, the strong yellow of daffodils, the blue and clear pink—or hideous pink—of hyacinths, the deep colours of anemones; she was learning all their names; she saw how white flowers shone and showed their shape against the London drab and grey. She was filled with her own business. She had never had her own business before; directly after breakfast, on her way to school, she went to the garden and was thinking about it all day long.

Each day she discovered something new. In Woolworth's she haunted the garden counter. It was piled high with packets of seeds and she needed seed; she had ambitions beyond cornflowers now. It's no use trying to swipe a whole packet, thought Lovejoy longingly but she found that if she handled them as if she were turning them over, she could, by pinching sharply and quickly, make a little hole in the paper and sometimes a seed, or a few seeds, trickled out. It took time. She did not dare to go often in case the girls grew suspicious;

though there was always a crowd round the counter, they might notice her; there was danger too from the people on each side, but with cunning and caution Lovejoy managed it. The packets looked as though a mouse had nibbled them, or a bird had pecked them. "But no birds come in here," said the manager. By the time she got them home Lovejoy did not know what the seeds were; she kept them in an old pillbox of Mrs. Combie's and slept with it under her pillow at night. When she had a dozen she sowed them an inch apart. She had no idea how close to put them or how big they would be but—"Love-in-a-mist, mignonette, alyssum," as if they were a charm she said them when anything unpleasant came into her mind; there were several sharp-edged things that came: "If I had a little girl I'd come from John o'Groat's . . ." "You'll be landed, Ettie . . ."

Sometimes Lovejoy was back in the church with the candles shining and the statue looking into her; it never looked at her, always into her, and she wriggled uncomfortably because, unaccountably, it seemed to find something in Lovejoy that matched it. How did it know that inside the hard, tough Lovejoy was something as gentle as those eyes? The something that worried about the baby not having a net, for instance? Lovejoy resented it; she felt as if she were being poked by a sharp pointed stick.

A murderer, they say, always goes back to the scene of his crime; Lovejoy went back to the church; she slipped in up the side aisle and stopped, quivering with shock. "Coo!" whispered Lovejoy. "*Coo!*" The hairs seemed to rise on the back of her neck and her legs felt cold. The statue was covered up.

Standing there, Lovejoy looked slowly round; all the statues were covered up; the altar candles, the vases of flowers were gone, everything was swathed in purple, and the hooded figures were frightening. Lovejoy had never heard of Holy Week but she felt as if a cataclysm had happened, and a tumult of grief and fear lifted up in her. "Coo!" she said again. "Cripes!"—and turned and ran.

When she came out she did not go to the garden; she had a sudden odd distaste for it and she walked down the Street, kicking her shoes crossly on the pavement.

The distaste did not last; she went to Woolworth's and from a packet she stole a big round seed; "And I know what it is," she told Mr. Isbister triumphantly. "It's a nasturtium, Golden Gleam." The nasturtium took the feeling of sadness and wrong away. With all the troubles that rose up in Lovejoy's mind at night, she had only to put out her finger and touch the pillbox and begin to intone, "Nasturtium, love-in-a-mist, mignonette, alyssum," and she was asleep.

"What have you been doing with yourself?" asked Vincent. "You look"—and he considered her—"fatter," said Vincent, but that was not quite the right word. "And younger," he said suddenly.

"I don't know what's happened to that child," said Mrs. Combie. "She's dirty."

That was a nuisance Mrs. Combie had never had with Lovejoy but, oddly, she was glad. "Perhaps she is a child after all," she said. Then, in the midst of this happiness, the postcard came.

*   *   *

It came at breakfast time and was addressed to Mrs. Combie. *Expect me Thursday. Love to my baby. Bertha.*

The postmark was Harrogate. "*That's* where she has been," said Mrs. Combie. "Harrogate's a good-class place." She turned the postcard over to look at the picture, which showed a panorama of good-class hotels in the distance, green lawns and red and yellow flower beds near to. *The Valley Gardens,* read Mrs. Combie with admiration. "So much for Cassie," she said.

Her whole face looked smoothed as she poured herself out another cup of tea; her hand was steady and her eyes looked happy. Then she *was* afraid, thought Lovejoy.

She, Lovejoy, felt as if a thunderbolt had gone through her she was so surprised—surprised at herself, not at the postcard. When Mrs. Combie had read it out, it felt like—an interruption, thought Lovejoy. I shan't be able to garden, she had thought at once, and into her mind had flashed the undeniable thought that when her mother was there she, Lovejoy, spent most of her time waiting—waiting still as a mummy, hushed as a mouse, for her mother to wake in the mornings; waiting to go out while her mother talked to Mrs. Combie or Vincent or anyone—anyone! thought Lovejoy, annoyed—waiting in the shops while her mother tried on clothes; waiting in Mr. Montague, the agent's, waiting room, or outside dressing-room doors, outside pubs, or in restaurants; waiting at home, sitting on the stairs. Why did people take it for granted that children had all that time to waste? I want to garden not wait, she thought rebelliously.

It was only for a moment; as if a spell had lifted and come down again, a moment later she was shocked. Garden! when *Mother* . . . she thought and she began to quiver.

"When is she coming? When?"

"Thursday," said Vincent.

"This Thursday? That's tomorrow."

"Yes, Maundy Thursday," said Mrs. Combie.

"Why do we shut on Good Friday, Ettie?" said Vincent. "On a holiday somebody might come. Do you think your mother'll bring you an Easter egg?" he said teasingly to Lovejoy, but Lovejoy had wrinkled her forehead and the old peaked look had come back.

"Coming at Easter," she said, and she looked from Vincent to Mrs. Combie. "That's queer. We never could get away at Easter time."

CHAPTER X

MRS. MASON had been home for three weeks—"Three years," said Cassie, and Lovejoy did not contradict her—when Vincent announced he was taking Lovejoy for a walk.

Now and again, on a Sunday, Vincent went for a walk; it was almost an expedition as far away as he could get in spirit from the Street; "I need—I need to breathe a different air," said Vincent. "Somewhere—elegant," he said, breathing through his nostrils as he did when he was offended. It was no use taking Mrs. Combie; loyal as she was, elegance was wasted on her; the perfect companion for these walks was Lovejoy. "She doesn't *know* anything," said Vincent, "but she has feeling," and together they visited St. James' or Berkeley Square or Bond Street and looked, not enviously but most fastidiously, into the windows of the little shops; Lovejoy

84

would instruct Vincent about the clothes and he would instruct her about the furniture, the china and glass, and the pictures. Sometimes they walked in streets of private houses, catching glimpses of expensive rooms, of a moulded panel, a curtain, a lampshade made of silk or lace, a vase of flowers.

As Lovejoy walked along, her head just touching Vincent's sleeve, the only thing she wished was that she and Vincent were more fitted to be where they were. Vincent, in his outdoor clothes, looked small and shabby and dusty; his overcoat was worn to threadbare places, its tweed had lost its shape and sagged, his hat and scarf were stained, and he had not any gloves. Lovejoy knew that her own coat, the dog-tooth check, was too short; her socks were short too and left too long an expanse of leg between; if she moved her elbows at all the coat split, and the red shoes hurt her so much that she had to go along like a crab, but while she had any clothes left at all Lovejoy would not have forgone those Sunday walks.

"It's not Sunday," she said now in surprise when Vincent asked her. Mrs. Combie was surprised too, but, "Come along," said Vincent firmly. He and Lovejoy went on a bus all the way to Hyde Park Corner and walked down Knightsbridge to Sloane Square; when they came back Mrs. Mason had gone.

"She had a telegram from the Blue Moons," said Mrs. Combie. Vincent opened his lips but shut them again; Mrs. Combie and Lovejoy were looking at each other with radiant faces. "She went at once," said Mrs. Combie.

"Of course," said Lovejoy.

The Blue Moons! Lovejoy had forgotten how the Blue Moons governed their life—mine and Mother's, she thought, lifting her chin proudly. She had often resented them but now they were dear, familiar, the dear Blue Moons. The stiffness went out of her bones, the pain and jealousy out of her heart. "Where? Where are they?" she asked.

"Brighton. She said it was a wonderful booking; they hadn't

one for Easter, that's why she was so worried." Mrs. Combie's face looked easy and clear; she seemed to feel the same as Lovejoy. "Tell you what," said Mrs. Combie, "you and me'll go down and see her one weekend. She gave me fifteen pounds. Now go and tidy the bedroom, dearie; I must help Mr. Vincent with the lunches." Neither of them had noticed that Vincent had gone into the kitchen without saying a word.

The bedroom needed tidying; it looked as if a whirlwind had been through it and had swept it almost bare; Lovejoy's clothes were thrown down in a corner of the cupboard, but her handkerchiefs were gone. "She even took my toothpaste," she said afterwards, "and my shoe cream and my soap." The cupboard doors were open, the drawers wide, bits of paper and old tickets and labels lay on the floor; the wastepaper basket was full of bottles and there were wisps of hair and cotton wool, red with lipstick, on the dressing-table; Lovejoy thought of how it had all been carefully made ready, and tears pricked her eyes.

The room still smelled of her mother; when Lovejoy burrowed her face against that spot on the armchair, instead of hard plush she seemed to be burrowing against the warm, soft flesh she knew so well, which smelled of scent—gone a little stale, thought Lovejoy—of scent and powder and perspiration—Cassie had taught Lovejoy never to say sweat—of clothes and the warm elastic of stays, of cigarette smoke and drink; it was not altogether a pleasant smell, but it was the smell of Lovejoy's babyhood, of her kitten-dance time, when she had been sweet and the world was safe.

"And when's your mother going to buy you all those new clothes?" Cassie had asked.

Lovejoy could still hear Cassie asking it and she bit her lip as she stared at the wall.

"Your clothes are perfectly good," Mrs. Mason had said.

"Yes, but Mother, I've grown," said Lovejoy and she had

shown how the pleated skirt and the check coat were far, far too short.

"They must be let down," said Mrs. Mason sharply.

"It's here, as well," said Lovejoy, showing how tight and stretched the coat and suit-jacket were under her arms.

"You must manage."

"But I can't breathe," said Lovejoy.

Mrs. Mason had not even objected to the plimsolls; she had not seemed to notice them. "It doesn't matter what you look like," she had said.

"Doesn't *matter*!" That was blasphemy to Lovejoy. She had had to persist, but when she showed how the red shoes had given her corns Mrs. Mason was angry. "You seem to think I'm made of money," she said.

"I don't," said Lovejoy, "but what can I do?"

"And what can I do?" asked Mrs. Mason.

Everything had been—queer, thought Lovejoy. At the Agency, Montague and Blewitt's, Mrs. Mason and Lovejoy had always gone straight in. "Mr. Montague's expecting you," the secretary would say and smile. Mr. Montague had a photograph of Lovejoy in her kitten dress on his office wall—or used to have, thought Lovejoy; she was not sure because everything seemed changed; they had gone to see Mr. Montague four times in these three weeks and had not seen him once. The last time Mrs. Mason would not let Lovejoy go in with her but told her to wait in the street—because of my clothes, thought Lovejoy, and her lips shook; but there had been something even worse than the clothes.

When Lovejoy took her nose away from the armchair she smelled another smell; on the table was a tumbler with a little whisky in it and an ashtray that held the butt of a dead cigar; the smell of them was stronger than the smell of her mother. Lovejoy took the tumbler and ashtray and put them outside the door; then she opened the window wide.

"Who is this gentleman that comes to see your mother?" Cassie had asked.

"Colonel Baldcock," said Lovejoy stiffly.

"As much Colonel as that cup!" said Cassie, and for once Lovejoy had agreed with her.

The other gentlemen had gone away; the colonel did not go away, and Mrs. Mason told Lovejoy to call him Uncle Francis.

"I won't," said Lovejoy.

Children are shocked when they first see grown people lovemaking but Lovejoy's ideas were, in some ways, the reverse of most children's. "But it's grown-ups who kiss," she was to say to Tip in surprise. To her it was an entirely grown-up occupation, like being cuddled and held on knees. "That's not for children!" she was to say, shocked in her turn. It was for ladies and gentlemen, she knew that; then why did it seem so terrible when the lady was her mother and the gentleman was Uncle Francis? And the strange part, she said to herself now, as she began to make the bed, the strange part is that she didn't like him either. Who could like him? thought Lovejoy, seeing again his red wet forehead and thick fat hands. He was thick all over, she thought, wrinkling her nose in disgust, and his clothes were horrid and he smelled, like the old ashtray and the dirty glass. Then why, she thought in anguish, did she let him stay and put me out?

Lovejoy had fought; she had brought out all her reserves. "I've got a secret," she had said.

"Have you, lovey?" asked Mrs. Mason idly.

"It's a garden." Lovejoy had said it with a rush because she had not really wanted to tell about it, even to her mother. Suppose she wants to see it? she had thought. She need not have worried.

"Think of that!" said Mrs. Mason and put up a hand to hide a yawn.

"You go to the pictures," the colonel said and gave Lovejoy ninepence. It was hard to refuse that, but Lovejoy put it coldly on the table.

He tried to wheedle her. "Go and buy yourself a nice ice cream."

"I don't like ice creams," said Lovejoy, which was a lie.

Well, he's gone now, she thought. She had finished the room and she picked up the tumbler and ashtray and took them downstairs.

"Wash them and put them away," said Vincent. He did not meet Lovejoy's eyes, nor did she look at him.

Once or twice the colonel and Mrs. Mason had had dinner in the restaurant and Vincent had served them silently, going back to his desk between each course and leaving them alone.

"It brings you business," said Mrs. Combie helplessly.

She was trying to find a bright side, but, "I don't want that business, thank you," said Vincent.

After dinner they would go out, as they went out every evening. Later Vincent heard them come in but he did not hear the colonel go home, and the child is there, thought Vincent. Once or twice he got up and stood hesitating, then he shrugged and sat down again.

One night it had been even later than usual when Vincent switched off the restaurant light to go to bed. Mrs. Combie always left a gas jet burning for him on the second floor, and by its faint glimmer, as he came up, he had seen something white. It was Lovejoy as he had first seen her, sitting on the stairs. But it's one o'clock! thought Vincent. She was in her ragged pyjamas, a blanket had been put round her, but when he touched her bare feet they were as cold as stones; her head leaned against the banister, and her cheek, when he brushed it with his finger, was wet.

Vincent stood up, his mouth in a small straight line. He had stayed for a moment, looking at the closed door; then he picked Lovejoy up, carried her downstairs, put her on the old sofa in the kitchen, tucked the blanket round her, and went back. After a moment he had quietly and firmly knocked.

Now Lovejoy, washing the ashtray and emptying the dregs of the whisky down the sink, began to sing one of her mother's songs. Vincent heard her little pipe and sat still listening. Thoughtfully he drew circles on his pad, but Lovejoy was not thinking of Vincent. Tonight, or tomorrow night, thought Lovejoy, her mother would be back in her place, Bertha Serita, in the blue dress, the silver ruff, the little saucy hat, the glittering sequins, her big throaty voice floating out across the audience in the Pier Theatre? The Pavilion Rooms? The Winter Garden? One of them; it did not matter which. Presently the song ceased; Lovejoy had gone back upstairs.

Though the bedroom was perfectly tidy she began to dust it again, wiping down the window with her duster. The glass was dirty with steam and smoke, and slowly, with her finger, she began to write on it. *Mother*, wrote Lovejoy. *Mother*. She got as far as the second M when the letters all ran together in a blur. She rubbed them out with the duster and then knelt down, her head on the window sill.

She had meant to cry, but before any tears could come she saw on the sill, level with her eyes but hidden under the curtain where it had been forgotten all these days, the pillbox of seeds.

CHAPTER XI

BEFORE going down into the bomb-ruin, Lovejoy cast her usual wary look up and down the Street, and there was Sparkey, in an overcoat and muffler, being led away by his mother from the newspaper stand for his tea. She crossed over to speak to them.

"Where's Sparkey been?" she asked.

"Having his spring bronchitis," said Sparkey's mother. Lovejoy nodded; that was an annual fixture. Sparkey's mother looked gaunt and tired and had black marks under her eyes, while Sparkey was more than ever thin and transparent-looking, but they had not forgotten the packet. Sparkey put out his tongue, and, "You leave him alone," said his mother

"Of course," said Lovejoy distantly and walked away.

Sparkey's mother went on towards Garden Row, but presently Sparkey slipped his hand and came, dodging from one portico to another, back to his step. He watched Lovejoy go through the gap; then he stood up on tiptoe to see more.

I haven't been for three weeks, Lovejoy was thinking, and she realized what an interference her mother and Uncle Francis had been. Well, he has gone, she thought comfortably, and her mother was back with the Blue Moons where she belonged. Lovejoy felt as if dozens of tight threads that had been sewn tightly into her were being loosened one by one.

As she came across the rubble, she noticed that there were rather more nettles and weeds between the walls; it had been raining, there were puddles on the ground, but the sun was drying them up. There was the usual smell of rubbish and soot and cess. Lovejoy sniffed it as she looked round carefully; then she bent and scuttled between the walls, behind the pyramids, till she came round her own two walls to the garden.

There she stood still.

The packet had said that the seeds would come up; Mr. Isbister had said that too; when Lovejoy had planted them she supposed she had believed it, but it had been more hope than belief. Now, on the patch of earth under the net, had come a film of green; when she bent down and looked closely, she could see that it was made of countless little stalks as fine as hairs, some so fine that she could scarcely see their colour, others vividly showing their new green. They're *blades*, thought Lovejoy, blades of grass! In the borders were what she thought at first were tiny weeds, until she saw real weeds among them. The weeds were among the grass too; she could tell them because they were bigger, a different pattern, and when she looked again the borders were peopled with myriad heads, all alike, each head made of two flat leaves, no bigger than pinheads, on a stalk; they were so many and so all the

same that she knew they were meant; no weed seeded like
that. They must come from a sowing—my sowing, thought
Lovejoy suddenly, the seeds *I* planted.

She knelt down, carefully lifted the net away, and very
gently, with her palm, she brushed the hair blades; they
seemed to move as if they were not quite rooted, but rooted
they were; when she held one in her thumb and finger it did
not come away. "It's like—earth's fur," said Lovejoy. She said
it aloud in her astonishment, and the sound of her own voice
made her jump and look up. It was then she heard the whistle.

It was the kind of whistle that is made by blowing on
fingers in the corners of the mouth, a boy's whistle. Boys!
Lovejoy crouched down, tense and still.

*   *   *

Lovejoy thought the bomb-ruin was deserted, but there was
a camp there and it belonged to Tip Malone.

Sparkey knew why the gang had not been to the camp all
this time; just as the girls had suddenly taken to skipping—
three months ago not a skipping-rope was to be seen in the
Street—now the boys were playing baseball; Tony Zassi, the
little American, had taught them. Sparkey knew where they
played in the park across the river; they had been there every
day all the holidays. "Well, you can't go," said Sparkey's
mother. "It's too far and the ball's too hard." Sparkey trembled
in case any boy heard her.

But now school had begun and the boys were back, and as
Sparkey stood straining to see, while his mother called him,
he heard the familiar rabble sound of voices, of scuffling, and
the boys came into view, walking and twisting together in a
huddle of jeans, corduroy trousers, and shorts, old darned
sweaters and jackets, cropped heads, short-cut hair, and weap-
ons, knives and catapults; it was the gang, and in the middle
walked Tip. All the Malones were big, and Tip was a head

above the other boys; he was carrying a bat—it was not his but Tony's. Tip was swinging it and talking in his big Irish voice. Sparkey stood up on his step; his eyes glittered so that if his mother had seen them she would have thought he was feverish again and taken him in, but a neighbour had come up to talk to her. Sparkey was husky with emotion as he called, "Tip. Tip Malone. Tip."

One of the boys, Puggy, glanced across the pavement but when he saw it was only Sparkey he took no notice.

"Tip," croaked Sparkey. "Tip."

In a pause in his stream of talk, Tip heard; unlike Puggy, when he saw it was only Sparkey he stopped. The other boys, even Puggy, stopped too. "Well, young 'un?" said Tip.

Sparkey's bowels could have melted within him at Tip's kindness but he held firm. He had an end in view. "I know something you don't," he said.

"Blimey. What cheek!" said John.

"I do," said Sparkey.

"What do you know?" asked Tip, amused at this strange little creature with owl eyes and spindly legs.

" 'F I tell you kin I be in the gang?" Sparkey flushed as the boys guffawed. They all guffawed but Tip. Tip looked down at Sparkey and said, much as Sparkey's mother had done, "But you can only be six—or seven," said Tip as a compliment.

"Aw, c'mon," said Rory, and Puggy twitched Tip's sleeve, but Sparkey looked so miserable that Tip was moved to ask, "What do you know?"

" 'F I tell can I be in the gang?"

"He *can't* know anything," said Jimmy Howes.

"I do." Sparkey forgot to croak; his voice was so shrill that it carried right down the Street.

"Ssh," said Tip. "D'you want everyone to hear?"

There were murmurs from the gang because Tip was taking this seriously. "C'mon," "Le's-go," "*Aw, c'mon*," they said, but Tip was a dictator. "Shut your mouths," he said. "This may be important."

Sparkey swelled with joy and hope; he almost told there and then but he wanted to make his bargain. " 'F I tell—" he began when Tip interrupted.

"You can't be *in* the gang," he said reasonably. "You couldn't keep up; you're too small, you'd get knocked about, but I tell you what: we'll keep a place open for you and for now you can be our look-out, our spy."

"A—spy!" said Sparkey. His bronchitis had left him weak and he nearly fainted from joy. "I'll do anything for you, Tip," he said huskily.

"Well, tell us what you've got to tell us, if it *is* anything," said Puggy impatiently.

Sparkey drew himself up; he felt twice as big and as important as he had a minute ago.

"I'll tell Tip," he said, "not you," and he looked at Tip. "There's a girl," he said, "on your ruin."

There was silence while they all turned and looked at the bomb-ruin, where nothing, no life, stirred. "Don't be bloody silly," said Tip.

"There is. It's Lovejoy Mason." As he told that Sparkey felt an immense satisfaction. Now he was even with her for the packet. "She goes in and out," he said.

"What for?" asked Rory.

A garden had not crossed Sparkey's mind, and, "I think she's building herself a camp," he said.

"A *camp*?" They were outraged.

"What d'you know about that!" said Ginger, flabbergasted.

"Blasted cheek," said John.

Tip's camp was the best-hidden for miles; screened by a bit of an old wall, it was like an igloo built of rubble; there was only a little hole, close to the ground, by which to go in and out; even the smallest of the boys had to lie down and wriggle. Outside it looked just another pile of bricks and stones; inside it had bunks made of orange boxes, an old meat safe for keeping things in, and an older cooking stove in which it was possible to light a fire or heat up a sausage or soup over a candle; drinks were kept in a hot-water bottle. "It's real drink, sometimes it's beer," whispered Sparkey—he always whispered when he spoke of the camp—and sometimes the boys had cigarettes.

"Do you have to smoke?" Mrs. Malone asked Tip when, for the tenth time, he was sick.

"Yes, I have to," said Tip desperately. "They wouldn't think anything of me, else."

The gang had thought the camp completely secret, but, "She's there now," said Sparkey breathlessly. "I just seen her go in."

For a moment they stood still, then Tip put his two little fingers in the corners of his mouth and whistled. The next moment they were through the gap, down the bank, and in the bomb-ruin. There was a violent noise of boots on stones, of hoots and cries, as they hunted among the walls; then they found, and Lovejoy was surrounded.

One minute the garden was there, its stones arranged, the cornflowers growing, the grass green; the next there were only boots. To Lovejoy they were boots, though most of the boys wore shoes, but boys' shoes with heavy steel tips to the soles and heels. She crouched where she was, while the boots smashed up the garden, trampled down the grass, and kicked away the stones; the cornflower earth was scattered, the seedlings torn out and pulled in bits. In a minute no garden was left, and Tip picked up the trowel and fork and threw them far away across the rubble. "Now get out," said Tip to Lovejoy.

Lovejoy stood up; she felt as if she were made of stone she was so cold and hard; then, in a boy's hand, she saw an infinitesimal bit of green; he was rolling a cornflower between his finger and thumb; suddenly her chin began to tremble.

"D'you know what we do to girls who come on our land?" said Puggy. "We take their pants off and send 'em home without them."

The boys guffawed again. "Shut up," said Tip. "I'm talking."

Tip had seen two things the other boys had not; being in front as they attacked, he had seen the garden whole; he had not had time to look properly but he had a vision of something laid out, green and alive, carefully edged with stones; the other thing he had seen, and saw now, only he did not want to look, was the trembling of Lovejoy's chin. She had not uttered a sound, not screamed or cried or protested; the Malones were vociferous, Tip connected females with screams and cries, and here was only this small trembling. It made him feel uncomfortable; he remembered how a puppy's legs, when he had seen it run over and killed, had trembled like that.

"Get out," he said to Lovejoy but less fiercely. As she still seemed dazed he put his hand on her shoulder to turn her, but he should have known better than to touch her; this was Lovejoy, who had thrown the potato knife, who had spat at Angela; she turned her head and bit Tip's hand.

She bit as hard as she could, and ran.

When she came through the gap, the boys after her, Sparkey looked down at his shoes and smiled.

CHAPTER XII

ONE of the things that has to be learned is that even sorrow cannot be had in peace, because other people have sorrows too; no boy could catch Lovejoy, and she had had only one thought as she ran, to get to Mrs. Combie, but when she got home Vincent and Mrs. Combie were quarrelling.

It had begun with Mrs. Mason's fifteen pounds.

"Fifteen pounds?" Cassie had said. "You can pay me back the three you owe me." But Mrs. Combie could not.

"Never, never borrow money from Cassie, *please*," Vincent had said, but once or twice lately Mrs. Combie had been forced to it. Now she was silent, flushed and embarrassed.

"You mean it's spent already!" said Cassie, her voice shrill. The spots on her face stood out as they did when she was angry. She looked at Mrs. Combie with the small blue eyes that seemed to bore holes—right down into you, thought Mrs. Combie, flinching—and, "You've given it to George," pronounced Cassie.

Mrs. Combie did not let Cassie call Vincent, "George." "Vincent had bills to pay," she said distantly.

That was true; the difficulty was to know which to pay first; the cash bills? thought Vincent, or pay the money into the bank? Money going in and out of the account makes it look alive, he thought; but no, better to pay the bills, but which? Bobby and Bax, the High Street grocers? Or Mr. Nichols, the butcher who had been so patient? Or the dairy, or the shoe shop for mending shoes, or Driscoll, the greengrocer?

"If he bought off the barrows and paid cash, which he's too mighty proud to do, there wouldn't *be* bills," said Cassie. Vincent had gone out to distribute the fifteen pounds as best he could but—though Mrs. Combie felt she would die rather than tell Cassie this—he had not paid anyone. He had come back, his face paper-white with excitement, and so exalted that he seemed to be walking on air although he was carrying a heavy parcel.

In it he had a set of dessert plates in different colours, deep green, royal blue, crimson—Mrs. Combie had never seen such colours—and in the middle of each plate was a painting of a lady's head, delicately done in ivory or pink with roses.

"Did you get them at Dwight's?" asked Mrs. Combie uncertainly.

"Dwight's! They're Angelica Kauffman. At least, they might be Angelica Kauffman. I'm nearly sure they are, Ettie. I saw them in a shop off Hanover Square weeks ago. I got them for thirty pounds," said Vincent.

"Thir—" Mrs. Combie's voice went quite away; it was a long time before she got it back. "Fifteen pounds down," Vincent was saying. "The balance over twelve months. I was lucky they let me have them." He stared at the plates with his soul in his eyes. "But George," said Mrs. Combie when she could speak, "what are they for?"

"We shall serve dessert on them," said Vincent, "for very special clients."

But George, we haven't any special clients. We haven't any proper clients at all, except Mr. Manley, and we haven't— George, it's fifteen pounds *still* to pay! Mrs. Combie did not say any of that but it was said in her silence.

"We can get the bank to give us an overdraft," said Vincent uneasily.

"We have an overdraft, George. Mr. Edwards said he can't do any more."

"Well, I've always said we should mortgage the house."

"It is mortgaged, George."

"Ettie, you're like a raven, a raven!" said Vincent.

He walked up and down the kitchen, still in his shabby overcoat. "Very well, take them. Sell them," he burst out at last. "Sell them. Or smash them."

"Smash them?" said Mrs. Combie, shrinking.

"You have smashed them." Vincent was shouting again. "Don't you see that for me they're smashed?"

Lovejoy heard Mrs. Combie weeping and took herself out of the way upstairs.

*　　*　　*

It was an hour or two later that Cassie burst into the Masons' room. She never knocked. One does not knock for children.

"There's a boy wants to see you," she told Lovejoy.

"I don't want to see a boy," said Lovejoy.

"Hoity-toity!" said Cassie. "Well, I'm making poor Mrs. Combie a cup of tea. You'd better come down and have yours now."

"I don't want any tea."

"Don't you feel well?" asked curious Cassie.

"Quite well," said Lovejoy but she felt neither well nor ill; she felt nothing, nothing at all; she might have been dead. "You can come down or go to bed," said Cassie.

Lovejoy came down, but in the kitchen they had started again. "The whole of Dad's money gone!" said Cassie.

"We'll get it back," Vincent shouted at her.

"There's a place called Queer Street," said Cassie.

Lovejoy left the kitchen so that she would not have to hear any more. Her fingers, gripped in her pocket, found the pill-box. Thoughtfully she took it outside and emptied it down the gutter.

The seeds fell down like rain; she wondered if they would stick in the gutter and grow, and she thought of nasturtiums flowering on the pavement edges and at once the familiar feeling stirred in her, the garden feeling. But what's the use of that now? Lovejoy was thinking wearily when a boy came up from the shadow by the side door. It was Tip.

Lovejoy stiffened. "What do you want?" she said, backing against the house wall.

Tip did not see why she should flinch and back away like that. He had not hurt her, while she had left a half-circle of bleeding little purple marks on his hand; "The first thing she ever did for me she bit me," he was to say afterwards. The bite ached still. Nor did he at all understand why he was doing what he did now. "I came to bring you this," he said and held out the garden fork. "I couldn't find the trowel," said Tip, "but we've got a little old shovel you could use."

Lovejoy made no attempt to hold the fork; as she walked away to the edge of the pavement she let it drop from her hand into the gutter; then she sat down on the curb and began to cry.

Tip was one of those boys who are so big and strong that

people do not really look at them; they look at their boots, their big young knees and shoulders, their jaws, perhaps, but not at them. "What a young tough," people said of Tip, but Mrs. Malone, who knew him better than anyone else, said, "He's not tough. He's gentle." Few people divined this. Yet Lovejoy divined it, at once.

To Lovejoy, Tip was a bitter-enemy boy, the biggest and worst of the ones who had smashed her garden, and yet she, who never cried in front of anyone, who had not cried then, was moved to cry now, in front of him. He did not jeer at her, nor did he go away embarrassed; he picked up the fork and sat down on the curb beside her.

The curb of a busy street may seem a poor place to talk but on an early May evening, almost warm enough for summer, when people are taking their ease outside, there is something relaxed about it; if the street is familiar it can even be peaceful. The stone Tip and Lovejoy were sitting on was warm, it was the right height from the gutter to be comfortable. Scraps of conversation fell into their talk as people passed, but that only made it seem more private; a Sister of Charity came by with her quiet skirt and noisy beads and she smiled down on them; the man with the two dogs passed on the opposite side of the road; a gang of big boys stayed, shouting and laughing on the corner at a group of girls. A little farther up the Street, Yvette and Susie Romney were practising handstands against a wall. Pooh! I could show them, thought Lovejoy. The pink and white of their thighs flashed each time their legs went up and their skirts fell back. One of Mrs. Cleary's and Miss Arnot's cats—not Istanbul but a white blear-eyed cat—came down the Street, arching its back against every pillar, and mewing as it stalked the smell of the fried fish and chips that two big girls were eating out of a newspaper as they walked. A few smaller children, up late, were playing hopscotch. Lovejoy heard all this and saw it as if she were in a dream; she was too tired, too dead to think or feel or care for herself or Vincent or Mrs. Combie, but she felt Tip beside her and she noticed him acutely.

She saw the shabby blue jeans, the way his wrists came far out of his grey-coloured sweater—it was halfway up his arms—the way his shoes were rubbed and the heels worn down. He did not seem to mind any of these things; she thought that her plimsolls, the threadbare plaid of her coat might seem to him entirely natural and that gave her a feeling of ease. She noticed other things: how hard and bony Tip's arms were, where hers showed round and soft; the funny look of his cheek that was bony too and freckled, freckles all over it, thought Lovejoy; his hair was rough; Lovejoy's head only came up to his shoulder, and when he turned to look at her his eyes were dark blue. A boy with blue eyes? thought Lovejoy, surprised. She had never thought of a boy's eyes as having a particular colour before; for Lovejoy that made him seem suddenly human.

As for Tip, he only stole glances at her but she seemed to him small and curiously clean, and he noticed that her hair was beautifully brushed.

They sat together and the tears dried on Lovejoy's cheeks; fixing her eyes on the hopscotch, watching it without seeing it, she told Tip about the garden, beginning with the packet of cornflower seeds and going on to the buying of the fork and trowel—she left out the candle box—but Tip did not seem to be listening.

"Who brushes your hair?" asked Tip.

"I brush it." Tip, thinking of the screams and protests of his young sisters Josephine and Bridget when his mother brought out the family hairbrush, marvelled, but Lovejoy was telling him about Mr. Isbister and the grass seed, and the net—leaving out how she took it; she told about the seeds—leaving out how she stole them from Woolworth's—and of how the grass and the cornflowers had come up. There she stopped.

Tip listened, hitting his leg thoughtfully with the fork. Boys have to hit something, thought Lovejoy irritably. "That's how I made the garden," she said, staring across the road. "My garden," and she gave a little hiccup of misery.

"Make another."

It sounded so unsympathetic that Lovejoy sat up indignantly until she saw Tip was better than sympathetic, he was interested. "You were silly to make it there," he said. "Make another somewhere else."

That was what Mr. Isbister was to say. He was quite angry. "Catford Street?" he said. "What d'you expect? Cats—boys, frost, drought—or a dang—great thunderstorm. Make a garden, you're in for it. Then don't come mewling here," said Mr. Isbister.

"But is it any good? Do things ever grow?" asked Lovejoy.

Mr. Isbister grunted and said, "Look." He had been putting in cuttings of geraniums, plain little pieces of plants with three or four leaves.

"They haven't got a root," said Lovejoy.

"They make one," said Mr. Isbister. "Stick 'em in the ground, they grow."

"Just bits of plant?" asked Lovejoy incredulously.

"Bits of plant," said Mr. Isbister, poking at them with his finger. "That's earth," he said, "and not boys, cats—hailstones —can—beat that, all the time." And he said what Tip said now. "Make another."

"You were silly to make it there," said Tip.

"But *where* else can I make it?" Lovejoy's voice was as sharp and irritated as Cassie's. "There isn't anywhere," she said scornfully. "Nowhere that boys don't spoil. It wasn't a very good garden," she said, "not what I wanted but—" Her voice trembled as if she were going to cry again.

"What kind of garden do you want?" asked Tip hastily. He only asked to divert her but it brought an answer from Lovejoy, an answer she had not dreamed of before.

"I want an Italian garden," said Lovejoy.

There was one walk she had been with Vincent—long ago, while I was still looking for a garden, thought Lovejoy now. It was a street along the river, with gardens, embankment gardens, thought Lovejoy, in front. Its houses were dark red. "What is it called?" she had asked Vincent.

"Cheyne Walk," said Vincent.

Most of the houses had small private gardens. "That's what I want," Lovejoy had said, looking into them, "a small private garden."

Those in Cheyne Walk were not very private; they could be looked into easily; Lovejoy had thought, I'd want mine to be more private than that. They were all different; some had small lawns, edged with coloured cobbles; some had clipped bushes, in some there were beds of daffodils and wallflowers; one had a rock garden built of rough stone; one or two had round beds with rosebushes cut back; some had empty beds, ready for planting or sowing—in April, thought Lovejoy. She had stopped to study one of these carefully; the soil was finely raked and black-looking. "Is that good garden earth?" she asked.

"I suppose it is," said Vincent. "Come along."

Then they had found a garden they both liked.

It was different from the others. It was worked out in stone and it was shapely; in the middle was a small stone urn filled with earth and standing on a pedestal; round the pedestal was a square of grass, clipped smooth and green, and this was bordered with narrow flowerbeds that were edged with fluted stone.

"The flowerbeds in the Square Gardens don't have stone edges," said Lovejoy.

"The Square Gardens are ordinary gardens," said Vincent with scorn. "*This* is Italian."

Vincent had schooled Lovejoy into thinking that everything superbly good was Italian, that everything Italian was superbly good, and she looked at the garden with awe.

"Italian gardens," said Vincent, who had never seen one, "are stone and green, with fountains and vases and walks, not just flowers."

This instant, as she sat beside Tip on the curb, that came into Lovejoy's mind.

"I want a garden with stone," she said. "With a vase in the middle and walks—"

When she said "stone" Tip looked up. He stopped beating his leg with the fork. "I know where," he said.

*   *   *

"But we're going into the church," said Lovejoy and stopped. She was wary of going into Our Lady of Sion now.

"That's all right, it's my church," said Tip serenely.

"Yours?" Lovejoy was astounded.

"Yes," said Tip firmly, "where I go."

"Go to *church?*"

"Yes. Don't you?"

"I've never been," said Lovejoy, and she looked at him as if he were a phenomenon. "I've never known anyone who went to church," she said.

Tip was suddenly moved to take her hand. "C'mon," he said.

Lovejoy followed him up the church steps to the landing where the rusty bell was; Father Lambert had put it into a cage because the boys slipped in and rang it.

"Look," said Tip, and, going to the top of the opposite flight that led down into the church, he hoisted himself up, in the footholds made by the broken bricks, till he was sitting on the wall above. "Can you do that?" he asked.

"Of course," said Lovejoy and came up after him, more nimble than he.

"Turn yourself round," said Tip, "and come down." He disappeared behind the wall. "Slide down," he said. "Feel with your toes." There were some broken bits like ledges in the wall. "You kin put your feet on them," whispered Tip. "Gimme your foot and I'll show you. No, the other one. Now down. Hold on tight." It was hard to hold to a ledge, hanging by a hand while the other groped for the next ledge; below was a heap of sharp rubble and stone that would hurt if one fell on them, but Lovejoy came on down. "Steady! Let yourself down now. You're there!" whispered Tip and she dropped lightly beside him. "Good girl," he said. "Bridget wouldn't have done that, but that's what you have to do, see? Look carefully, and when no one's there, get over the wall. It's difficult going back; you have to climb up by the bricks."

"I can do it," said Lovejoy.

She looked round. They were in a space behind the church that once, long ago, had been a graveyard. At one side was the Priest's House, but the two windows that looked on it were blank and curtained. "It's Father Lambert's bedroom," whispered Tip. "He's only in it at night, and the room above's a storeroom; I know. I've carried books up there." At the back a long blank wall ran the length of the graveyard. "That's Potter's garage," whispered Tip, "and that's the dairy." He nodded towards a wall on the third side with high gratings. "Nobody can get up there to look," he said, "and nobody comes here. Most people don't even know it's here. They don't look over the wall. They don't think of it because it's the church, see, but you could make a garden here, if you kin find a place," he added—the space was piled with rubble and debris. "There's a lot of stone," said Tip, looking at it.

There was more stone than Lovejoy had ever seen, bits of broken pillars, cornices; a great tombstone with cherubs on it—"Supernatural babies," whispered Lovejoy—had been laid against the wall. There were flutings and chippings and pieces, bits of faces, and hands and wings, and flowers. "They're from the old church," whispered Tip—instinctively they whispered here. "One day they're going to build it new."

"The aeroplane isn't nearly up," said Lovejoy comfortably. She was quite alive again. She could see already that this was a much better place for a garden. Protected by the church, it would be safe. Lovejoy had never heard the word "sanctuary" but she knew she had found a safe place. She felt like Christopher Columbus when he had landed on the shores of the Bahamas, and perhaps to have discovered in Catford Street a quiet, empty place for a garden was a feat almost as unlikely.

She took two steps over the rubble, and then stood still. The last sun was slanting exactly where she needed to look; at the back of the church hut, between stumps where a second row of the old pillars had been, was a space, empty and sunny; it was strewn with chips of glass and stone but it was earth; she could see its darkness. It was perhaps seven feet by four, the size of a hearthrug, but big enough, and at one end, as if it had been placed in readiness, was, not a vase but a bit of a small broken-off column, whiter than the stumps of the big pillars—"Pure marble," whispered Tip, who had come up; marble and fluted, "Like a piece of Edinburgh Rock," whispered Lovejoy, and, as if to prove the ground was fertile, up the little column grew a stem with green leaves, broad and shining, in the shape of hearts. "What is it?" Lovejoy was to ask Mr. Isbister when she took him a leaf.

"You never seen ivy?" asked Mr. Isbister incredulously. Lovejoy could not remember that she had.

But now it did not matter to her what the stem was; she simply gazed.

CHAPTER XIII

WHEN Lovejoy looked at the plot, measuring it with her eye, considering what to do with it, she found out a surprising thing; where before she had groped uncertainly, now she knew something about gardens; she began searching among the stone until at last she picked up a piece of fluted carving. "We must edge the beds with stone like this," she said.

"That's a bit of grave," objected Tip.

"The grave's all smashed," said Lovejoy, unconcerned, "and look." She had found another broken grave spread with fine marble chips. "We can make paths with this," she said.

She had said "we." Tip began to feel uneasy. He had shown her where she could make a garden, that was enough. "You do what you like," said Tip. " 'S your garden, not mine."

"We'll make a lawn here," said Lovejoy as if he had not

spoken, "and flowerbeds here, between the stone edges and the grass. Let's clear some of the bits." She squatted down and began picking up the stones. "We mustn't make a noise so don't throw anything, put it down gently," she commanded. Tip did not move. "Help me," said Lovejoy.

"Who d'you think I am?" said Tip. Lovejoy did not answer.

"I'm not going to make no sissy garden," said Tip. "I showed you where it was, what else do you want?" And he turned to go back to the wall.

He expected an outcry; when anyone crossed Bridget or Josephine Malone—or Clara or Margaret or Mary, any of his five sisters—there was always an outcry; that was a good name for it, a howling, it might almost have been called a bawling, that could be heard right down the Street; but Lovejoy said nothing. She stayed where she was, picking up the stones, only her head sank lower and the two sides of her hair swung forward, hiding her face and showing her neck; with her finger she poked in the earth.

The effect was curiously powerful. Tip went a few steps and looked back; the silence tugged at him; she seemed so small and solitary among the stones that he could not bear it; he tried to go, he went a step more, then he came back. "All right, then, I'll help you," said Tip angrily.

She kept him till it grew cold and eerie in the graveyard. "My mum'll lam me," he said.

"Does she lam you?" asked Lovejoy wistfully.

"Don't they care how late you are?" he asked.

"No," said Lovejoy briefly and worked on. Tip began to think there were advantages in being Lovejoy; she could stay out as late as she liked, she was free of church; he began to look at her with a mixture of disapproval and respect.

They worked on; he had to admire the way she did it, soundlessly moving and clearing the stone and glass. "Keep any little bits that will do for edging," she said, but to almost every bit Tip found she said, "No, that won't do." It was hard work. Tip's back had begun to ache when at last she stopped. "You've got spunk, I'll say that for you," said Tip, when she stood stiffly up.

"It isn't nearly done," was all she said. "You'll come to-morrow?"

"Me? No fear," said Tip.

She looked at him.

"I've things to do," said Tip loftily.

Lovejoy bent her head again in that quivering silence.

"I promised the others," said Tip not quite as loftily.

"I was going to move that big stone there an' I can't by myself," said Lovejoy sorrowfully. "An' that iron bar, I can't get that up." It was a lament. "*You* told me to make another garden," said Lovejoy. "How can I all alone? It was going to be so lo-ve-ly." In the darkness her whisper seemed to go on and on like a sad little ghost. Tip tried to shut it out but he could not.

"Oh, all right," he said crossly, "I'll come for a little while." He was soon to learn his mistake. Lovejoy was a tyrant.

"I only came to tell you I can't come," he would begin. "We're meeting down by the river." But mysteriously he stayed, and missed the meeting. "Come straight after school," begged Lovejoy. Her begging was almost as compelling as her silence.

On the second day the patch was cleared, and now began the work of finding the stone. Schooled by Vincent, Lovejoy was meticulous. "That doesn't match," she said to most of Tip's efforts.

"Why does it have to have a stone edging?" asked Tip rebelliously. "Other gardens don't."

"This is an *Italian* garden," said Lovejoy, "a real Italian garden." Words could not describe how she loved the smooth pale stone and the little broken column.

Tip began to be infected. It was oddly exciting. There was the excitement of stealing up the Street and into the church, of listening, clinging like limpets to the wall to hear if the way were clear before they came out. "*Never* come out without listening," Tip impressed on Lovejoy. "You can always hear; the stone makes footsteps sound loud if anybody comes." Lovejoy knew that, from when she herself had listened as she stole from the candle box. They worked, speaking in whispers, careful to keep their heads down in case they were seen from the church-hut windows. If either of them was there alone and heard someone coming, even though he was sure it was the other, they arranged that they should immediately freeze into stillness behind a big tombstone that was laid against the hut wall; they could glide there in an instant from the garden, and it was big enough to hide them. If either of them was trailed or saw the other in danger, he was to give three deep hoots that they thought were like an owl's. "Sparkey can do that too," said Tip.

"He won't be able to," said Lovejoy with scorn.

"I will," said Sparkey at once when Tip told him, but his hoots sounded more like a bat's squeak than an owl's.

Tip had had to tell Sparkey, though Lovejoy objected. "He'll tell if you tell him," she said.

"He'll tell if I don't," said Tip. "He's seen us. He sees everything in the Street. He doesn't stay on his step. Now he's our spy, he patrols."

A friendship had grown up between Tip and Sparkey, made of worship on Sparkey's side, kindness on Tip's; Tip had taken him one Saturday to the park across the river and let him watch a game of baseball, and Sparkey's mother had even let him go to the Malones' to spend the night; now Sparkey was in a quandary. He would have loved to expose Lovejoy—to torture her, he thought, his eyes glittering—but he would have cut his throat sooner than disobey Tip. "It's top secret," said Tip.

"Kin I see it?" asked Sparkey.

"Nope," said Tip, which was hard on a little boy. "You couldn't get down the wall, but we've let you into it. None of the other boys know," he said to take out the sting.

Lovejoy had been fearful of Father Lambert. "He lives next door in the Priest's House. He'll catch us," she said.

"Not he," said Tip. "He never knows anything. He's half asleep."

They did not see Father Lambert, up above them, carefully draw back his head from the wall and go on down the steps into the church. Every now and then he stepped up to the windows and glanced down at them as, absorbed, they carefully fitted in their pieces of stone to make the garden edges. They were well hidden. On the church side the windows were high up, only someone as tall as the Father could have looked through them. "*He* won't know," said Tip. "Besides, I can always pretend I'm going into the church to pray."

"But I can't," said Lovejoy.

Perhaps it was this conversation that made her think of the church; before she had not raised her head to look at it at all. The windows ran all along the back, and from the graveyard the ceiling, the lamps, the top of the altar, and the statues' heads could be seen. Lovejoy had been happily setting two bits of stone into the edging, which was now almost finished; as she looked up and into the church Tip saw her face change; for a moment she was still, then, forgetting, she stood upright. "Get down," hissed Tip, but Lovejoy said, in a strange polite voice, "Thank you very much, Tip, but I don't think I'll make the garden here."

Tip followed her eyes. He could see the ceiling, two hanging lights, and the top of a blue screen; that's the top of the

altar, thought Tip, the altar in the Lady Chapel. He could see
the statue of Our Lady, she stood on a high pedestal that
made her higher than the other statues; Tip could see her
head and white veil, the breast of her blue robe, her hand, and
the Holy Child's gilt halo. Through the glass she looked quite
close, as if she were watching them, but what was there
startling in that? But Lovejoy was still standing up, her eyes
wide open, not concealed as they usually were, and, as Tip
watched, tears of consternation ran out of them.

In the church Father Lambert dropped a pile of books; Tip
seized Lovejoy, dragged her down, and pulled her behind the
tombstone. She crouched, weeping, beside him. Do girls do
nothing but cry? thought Tip. "What's the matter?" he said
impatiently, then more patiently, "What's the matter? Go on,
tell," he said, resigned. After a moment he put his arm
round her.

"Well, no wonder," said Tip when Lovejoy had finished
telling. "No wonder!"

That was not very comforting and Lovejoy's hairs lifted
again. "You mean, no wonder the garden was smashed?"

Tip had not meant anything of the kind; he meant it was
no wonder Lovejoy was frightened, but he was suddenly filled
with an irresistible desire to torment this tormenting little
creature. He nodded solemnly and Lovejoy quailed.

"Will she smash this one?"

"You couldn't be surprised," said Tip solemnly, and was
gratified when the last of Lovejoy's control broke to smither-
eens. "But what am I to do?" she wailed. "What can I do?"

They had come out from the tombstone, and she knelt
down beside the garden while the tears ran down her face.
Tip began to feel uncomfortable. He did not know what she
could do.

"You could tell Father Lambert," he said at last.

"Tell *Father Lambert?*" That seemed to Lovejoy a really idiotic thing to do.

"He'd forgive you and give you a penance."

"What's a penance?"

"A penance is—a penance," said Tip. Then he tried to make it clearer. "It's a sort of punishment that makes things all right again. It would have to be a dreadful one for this. That was *holy* money!" said Tip, shocked.

Lovejoy thought deeply, her tears drying. Then she looked up at Tip. "You give me one," she said.

When Lovejoy looked at him in that trustful way, Tip felt a heady bigness. He said, "I don't know if it would work," but more in duty bound than anything else. The thought of punishing Lovejoy was so delicious that he had to look at his toes to keep from smiling.

"All right, I'll give you a penance," he said, and then pronounced, "You'll put all those twopences back."

There was a silence; then: "I don't like that punishment," said Lovejoy. "Give me another."

"The less you like it the better it is," said Tip glibly. That had often been said to him, but she did not take this view of it at all.

"I haven't any twopences," she said.

"You must get them," said the inexorable Tip. "Get them, not steal them," he said quickly.

Lovejoy's face fell. "How am I to get them, then?" she said, going back to tears. "Even with stealing, I took weeks to get the fork."

"You didn't—you took three days, you told me so," retorted Tip, but Lovejoy had already a woman's power of shrinking and expanding time. "Weeks!" she wailed, and in a way that was true. She was a child as well as a small woman. "They did it all so quickly," Angela was to say when she knew the whole story. "How could it happen like that? It was so quick!" But Olivia made one of her rare contradictions.

"It wasn't quick," said Olivia. "At least not to them. A month can go on forever to a child. To wait five minutes can be an agony. You've forgotten what it was like." And she said again, "It wasn't quick."

Now to get the three-and-eightpence seemed an impossible task. "I'll never get it. Never," sobbed Lovejoy, and soon, weakly, Tip found himself promising to help. "I'll help you earn it but you must put the money back yourself—in candles," said Tip, feeling his power. "And you'll pay twice as much for each candle, to make up," he said.

"Children are half-price," said Lovejoy, fighting, but Tip did not waver.

"You'll pay fourpence each and you'll light them one by one, each time we get a fourpence, and that'll be your penance. Three-and-eightpence is eleven candles. You'll go into the church eleven times. And," he added, seeing a respite for himself, "you're not to touch the garden till the penance is done."

Lovejoy looked at the garden and then up through the window at the statue. "I don't like her. I don't want to look at her," she said bitterly.

"That's because you're wicked," said Tip cheerfully; then he relented. "It'll get better with each candle. Each time you'll mind it less."

CHAPTER XIV

"Here's sixpence for you," said Tip to Lovejoy. It sounded lordly but that sixpence had taken a week to get. Even to Tip it had seemed an interminable time. "The Malones must be well off with all they earn," Angela had said when Clara Malone had got into the Dame Una Fanshawe secondary school—Angela was a governor—and Mrs. Malone had appealed for a grant towards the uniform. "There *must* be plenty of money." With Mr. Malone and the three eldest Malones in work, and Mrs. Malone doing night shift twice a week in the kitchens at the Corner House, it was indeed surprising the way money flowed into the house; the only thing more surprising was the way it flowed out! "Nine children, for food and clothes, and the price of food!" Mrs. Malone said. "Food and drink," she added, for she was an honest woman.

"Are they all at home?" Angela had asked.

"All at home," said Mrs. Malone with pride and pleasure.

Tip had only been able to get sixpence, and now Lovejoy looked at it with an absence of opinion that stung him.

"It's not much," said Tip defensively, and Lovejoy agreed, which stung him still more. "I'm going with Sid and Lucy on his round on Saturdays," he said, "soon's the boy he's got now goes to work proper. Summertime he sells ice. That'll be half a crown a Saturday," he boasted.

"Half a crown!" said Lovejoy. She was interested now. "We can buy lots of things with that!"

Tip could have pointed out that it would not be her half-crown, but as it was only in the future—Sid still had his boy— he did not think it was worth it. Meanwhile, he had decided the penance was too hard. I was too tough, he thought with the same kind of pleasure with which he had punished her, and he said gruffly, "You needn't do your penance. It's too difficult."

"But I've done it," said Lovejoy.

"You couldn't have."

"I have."

"Three-and-eightpence!" Tip could not believe it.

"I have."

He looked hard at Lovejoy. "You stole it."

Lovejoy was not offended; she knew it was only too likely, but, "I didn't. Honest," said Lovejoy, and it was honest.

"But how, then?" said Tip, bewildered. "How?"

"Ssh," said Lovejoy with a look at the statue. "Ssh, I'll tell you. I had sixpence to begin with," whispered Lovejoy, "left over from the first candle money—"

"You shouldn't have used that," said Tip.

"The penance was to put back the money," argued Lovejoy, "and that was the money." He supposed it was.

"Then I sold my shoes."

"You *what?*"

In the Malone family shoes were not owned by anyone; they were a child's for the brief period in which he, or she, could wear them, and then were handed down and down as valuable treasures.

"You sold *shoes?*" Tip could not believe it, but Lovejoy went on as if this were nothing strange. "My red shoes to Mr. Dwight for one-and-six." She had taken twopence from the telephone kiosks. I went round pressing Button Bs four times a day every bloomin' day; it should have been three-pence but it was two." She had let down the hem of one of Cassie's dresses. "She said she'd give me threepence, but then when I'd done it she said I had nicked the stuff and she only gave me two. Dirty cat!" said Lovejoy with venom. "Vincent gave me one for darning his socks—" She broke off there. She had a feeling she had not darned them very well, while for Cassie she had tried hard. How strange that one should be mean to the nice people, thought Lovejoy; her conscience was getting tender but only in places; she had not scrupled, for instance, to do an old trick of hers, getting on the bus and pretending she had lost her fare; some kind lady or gentleman would give the money to her, and, "Then I jump off and run away," she said.

"They're always doing that," Angela told Olivia, who had been fooled several times. Nor did Tip approve. "But it's hard work," said Lovejoy virtuously. "I had to try four times before I got anything." And she said, annoyed, "They *will* pay the conductor 'stead of giving the money to me. They have to give it to you before you can jump."

"I think that's stealing," said Tip. "It oughtn't to count."

"It's not stealin', it's actin'," said Lovejoy stoutly.

"And the other shilling?" asked Tip.

Lovejoy came closer to him and jerked her head towards the statue. "Tip," she said, "I'm frightened. She does things."

"Does things?"

"Twice," said Lovejoy, "and so quick." Her eyes were wide open, alarmed yet gratified. "Twice, like that," and she brought one palm down with a clap on the other to make a clap of thunder.

"But what did she do? What happened?" said Tip, asperated.

Lovejoy came even closer.

It had happened on the evening of the day when she had gained her eighth candle; if the time seemed short to Tip, to Lovejoy it had been endless. "Days and days and days," she said.

"Only a week," said Tip.

"Ages," said Lovejoy. "Ages—wasted." April was gone, May more than half through, and the garden hardly touched. "That—penance!" said Lovejoy through her teeth. She had been going into the church with the eighth fourpence—a penny from one of the bus victims, the twopence from Cassie, and the penny from Vincent—when she saw a big car coming down Catford Street.

The engine did not sound like any other car Lovejoy had heard; it was a low, powerful purring between the houses; that made Lovejoy think it was, among other cars, what Istanbul was among other cats, a kind of king. All the people in the Street turned their heads to look; they looked still more when the car drew to the curb and stopped. There were two people in it, and the gentleman got out; Lovejoy, rooted on the curb, noticed how he went round to the car's other door and helped the lady out; before he did it he threw his cigarette into the gutter. A whole cigarette! thought Lovejoy. She watched while they looked for a moment at the Street and the broken steps. They're Real People, thought Lovejoy. Somebodies.

"But what were they like?" Tip was to ask.

"He's dark and she's fair," said Lovejoy glibly, then paused. She, who photographed every detail about everybody she met, instantly and certainly, was uncertain about these two. "He's dark with dark eyes, and she's fair with blue." But was she, Lovejoy, just saying what she made up?

"They're both brown," said Tip disgustedly when at last he saw them. "Mousy brown, and he has brown eyes, she has grey."

Lovejoy was not even accurate about their clothes, which was extraordinary for her; she saw their clothes, of course, every detail of them, but oddly haloed. The gentleman had a dark grey suit—worsted, thought Lovejoy—a cream shirt—pure silk, thought Lovejoy—and a striped tie—his old school tie; this was, as a matter of fact, correct. He was hatless, his shoes shone, and in his breast pocket was a folded white handkerchief—fine Irish linen, thought Lovejoy; it would have a white embroidered monogram on it, like the ones she and Vincent had studied in the Piccadilly shops. On the little finger of his right hand he wore a ring, a signet ring—the family crest, thought Lovejoy, to whom Vincent had talked about crests. Perhaps he's a nearl, thought Lovejoy, to whom Vincent had talked about earls.

The lady was even better than the gentleman; she wore a plain grey suit—a soft suit, thought Lovejoy, what they call a dressmaker suit, she thought, which she knew was not at all the same thing as a suit made by a dressmaker. The blouse was shell-pink—and it's hand-made, thought Lovejoy—with it were slim, plain, high-heeled dark brown shoes—because it's a town suit, quite correct, thought Lovejoy—long, dark brown gloves wrinkled over the wrists, a brown bag, and a small brown hat, all to match her long bright brown fur stole. Mink! thought Lovejoy, transfixed; her very bones knew it was mink.

She followed at a respectful distance behind them as they

went up the steps to the landing beside the rusty bell. They were talking about the church. "I have to decide if they can have some money," said the gentleman, and he touched the broken netting where the cage had been torn round the bell. "They look as if they needed it."

"But *why* you?" asked the lady.

When the Catford Street children went to the pantomime— and almost the whole Street went each Christmas—none of them would have been pleased if Prince Charming and Cinderella, or Dick Whittington and Alice, or Jack and Jill, had declared themselves flesh and blood; Lovejoy, who was a stage child, knew drearily that pantomime people were people who blew their noses, washed their underclothes, ate sausages, drank beer, like anyone else. For the other children it was the Principal Boys and Girls who moved in a circle of glamour; now Lovejoy knew that for her it was Vincent's people, the earls, the Somebodies. When she heard the lady and gentleman talking, though she was fascinated, she did not want to hear. Their voices were too real. If she had been asked how she expected them to talk, she could not have said. But not like that, she thought; she would have approved of the old court languages.

"But Charles, why you?"

Charles? Lovejoy cocked an ear but it sounded right; there was, after all, Prince Charles.

"It's a trust," he was saying, "for rebuilding churches and making schools—Catholic, of course. My father did it, and my grandfather. It's called the 'Charles Whittacker Adams Trust.'"

"That's your name."

"Yes. That Charles was my great-uncle."

Charles Whittacker Adams—it was a rounded, satisfying name and Lovejoy repeated it over to herself as they went down the steps into the church. But what was her name?

wondered Lovejoy, and then Charles told her. "Careful, Liz," he said as they came to a broken bit of step.

Liz! could a Somebody be called Liz? "It's short for Elizabeth, goose," said Cassie. Nothing could be more royal than that, not even Charles, but it was a long time before Lovejoy was reconciled to Liz.

"What a funny little church!"

Liz stood in the doorway as Charles went in; he looked round him, then walked slowly along by the walls, looking at the floor, the ceiling, the old pillars. He stepped to the windows, craned up, and looked out; Lovejoy held her breath in case he saw the garden, but he obviously saw nothing interesting because he stepped away again.

There were people praying, and Lovejoy slipped past Liz to light her candle; I'll do it quickly and then I can see what they do, she thought.

She bent her knee to the altar as Tip had taught her, and went round to the chapel, where she bobbed again and knelt by one of the chairs.

"You mustn't just go in and take a candle," Tip had said. "First you must pray."

"Why?" asked Lovejoy, mystified.

"Because it's polite," said Tip.

"I don't know what to say," objected Lovejoy.

"Say Hail Mary," said Tip; as a cradle Catholic it had not occurred to him that any child could not know Hail Mary.

"Hail Mary," said Lovejoy as she would have said "How do you do," and got up to light her candle.

Out of the corner of her eye she saw that Liz had walked across at the back of the church. Is she watching me? thought Lovejoy. Oh, I hope she doesn't go before I've finished.

"You mustn't just walk out," Tip had said. "You must go back to your place and pray."

"*Again?*" asked Lovejoy; that seemed exaggerated.

"Yes. That's when you do your asking."

"Oh!" said Lovejoy, more reconciled.

"You can ask for anything you want," said Tip.

"Anything?"

"Yes."

"Let me get those flicking pennies quickly," prayed Lovejoy devoutly. She said that each time, but still it was hideously slow and as she rose from her knees she sighed. There were three more candles, twelve more pennies to get, a whole shilling, and she thought it prudent to add a word. "Quickly, mind," she said to the statue. "And do you know how quick it was?" she said to Tip now. As she had come down the side aisle Liz had smiled at her, beckoned, and given her a shilling.

"Blimey!" said Tip.

"It was blimey," said Lovejoy. "And that was not all."

She had taken the shilling, three fourpences, the ninth, tenth, eleventh candles, and, forgetting to thank Liz, she went straight back up the church, genuflected, and bought three more candles. Then she went and knelt down. She felt Charles and Liz come up behind her. "Did you see?" Liz asked him. "I gave her a shilling, and—"

"Ssh!" said Charles.

"Do you think she's a little saint?" Liz whispered.

"Little sinner, more likely," said Charles.

"Now we're quits," Lovejoy had said to the statue, but she was not quite quit; three candles meant three prayers, or she supposed they did. "You've got to do it properly," said Tip.

"Let me get those flicking—" But that, her routine prayer, was finished. There were no more candles to get. Well, what else? thought Lovejoy. "Let Mother come back"—that would have been the prayer a short while ago but, on the whole, she thought Mother was better with the Blue Moons. "Let Mother not come back"—that was safer, and, "Let my garden grow," that was sense, and it was suitable because now she could begin in the garden. There was one prayer left. "You can ask for anything you want, or anyone else wants," Tip had said; she could have asked for clothes but suddenly she thought of Vincent.

That morning Vincent had been in trouble again; he had come back from Driscoll's with two punnets of strawberries.

"Strawberries already?" Mrs. Combie had said.

"All good restaurants are serving them, Ettie."

"How much?" said Cassie, pouncing.

"Never you mind how much," said Vincent, but Cassie had found out. "She looked in my private market book," Vincent told Mrs. Combie.

The strawberries, with their green leaves, had looked pretty in their chip punnets, but there had been a scene about them. Mrs. Combie was fired to protest. "Can you *see* Mr. Manley, or *anybody*, paying for them?" she had asked. "And there's a chicken come in, and steaks. Oh, George!"

"We can eat them up," Lovejoy offered hopefully when the scene was over.

"At six shillings a basket! I should choke," said Mrs. Combie.

"Ettie, somebody will come. They must," Vincent had said desperately, and, "I used my prayer for that," said Lovejoy. "Send the lady and gentleman to Vincent," she had commanded.

"Well?" said Tip. "Well?"

"When I got up they had gone out of the church," said Lovejoy.

"I'll have to go in and see the priest," Charles had said. "We'll need to talk, but let's go now. I've seen all I need for the present."

"When I came out they were going down the steps," said Lovejoy. "They got in the car and drove—" She broke off dramatically.

"Well?" shouted Tip.

"Drove straight to the restaurant," said Lovejoy.

Tip looked squarely into Lovejoy's face. "Straight?" he asked.

"Well, nearly straight," said Lovejoy. The car had stopped when it was well past the restaurant, almost at the river, where it had waited a moment and then turned. "But they went to the restaurant," said Lovejoy obstinately.

It had been that rare thing, a perfect evening.

If Vincent had chosen a car to stand outside his restaurant, he could not have chosen a better than the big green one, and no two people could have been nearer his dreams than Charles and Liz. Like Lovejoy, Vincent gave them attributes at once. Charles was young, rich, handsome; Liz was charming. To Vincent they were that forever and ever.

When they walked in, the restaurant, he knew, had never looked better; driven by the quarrel, he had spent the whole day in polishing and cleaning. The flowers in the vases were extra good that day; infected by the strawberries, he had bought lilies-of-the-valley for every table.

"How did you know you should buy them?" asked Mrs. Combie, and Vincent answered solemnly, "I was inspired." He had lit the flame in the silver *réchaud* and put on the best napery.

"On your own head be it," Charles was saying to Liz as they came in at the door. Vincent smiled.

"Can you give us dinner?" asked Charles. He spoke half doubtfully.

"Of course," said Vincent as if to say, What else? "This table?" He led the way to the best table and pulled back a chair for Liz. As they sat down he saw them looking round in surprise and pleasure, and he smiled again. "We were just driving away when we saw the bay trees," said Liz.

"An apéritif?" asked Vincent as he brought his pad. That

was a dangerous thing to ask; he had only some sherry and Cinzano and bitter Campari—"And they would hardly ask for that." Don't let them ask for fancy cocktails, he prayed. They ordered sherry, "Medium dry," said Charles; Vincent thankfully poured his best dry sack into his best glasses, brought them to the table, and took up his pad again.

No one, Mrs. Combie often said, could ever tell what Vincent would do; now some inspiration told him to be modest; to Mrs. Combie's wonder—she had her eye to the glass panes—he did not produce his elaborately written menus but suggested something he could do easily, here and now, with what he had, and that fitted his little restaurant. "I shall make you an onion omelette," he announced. He did not mean to announce it but he was thinking aloud; eggs and onions of course I have got, he thought. "And then a nice rump steak Bercy?" That will be easy he thought and he quickly ran over all he would need—butter, parsley, chopped shallot, lemon juice. "Unless you would rather have fish?" he asked. That was dangerous too; there was no fish, but it was Vincent's lucky night. They ordered the steaks. "With sauté potatoes," said Vincent, his face intense, "and a salad?"

"What wine have you?" said Charles.

"I'll bring the list," said Vincent as glibly as if he had a real list, and then stopped. "A barbera would be good with the steak," he suggested, "or Chianti. I have a barbera 'forty-nine—"

Charles ordered the barbera. "The omelette will be about ten minutes," said Vincent, then he went through the glass door and called. "Ettie," he called. "Ettie. Ettie."

When Mrs. Combie came he took her in his arms, pressed a kiss on her forehead, and said, "They've come, Ettie. The people I've always wanted. They've come. Now help me. Help me."

"I'll help you, George," said Mrs. Combie.

If Vincent were pressed for time he became silent and swift, he took off his coat and hung it over a chair by the restaurant door, ready to slip on again, and gave rapid, low orders. Lovejoy was sent scurrying for fresh watercress for garnishing. "Knock and make Mrs. Driscoll open," said Vincent, "and run all the way."

He went back into the restaurant to clear the table Mr. Manley had just left. If they see me busy they won't get impatient, he thought. Thank God Mr. Manley has left, thought Vincent; to think of Charles and Liz in the same room as Mr. Manley seemed to Vincent sacrilege, but he was glad of Mr. Manley's used table. That evening he did not have to act, it was all genuine. He cleared the table and came to Charles and Liz. "Do you like your steaks rare or medium?" he asked.

Back in the kitchen he and Mrs. Combie worked with a quiet passion until, the omelette in the pan, the plates warming, Vincent cut bread, slipped on his coat, and took it in. "Put the steaks under," he commanded, "and pray God the potatoes brown in time."

A moment later he was back again, slipped off his coat, and went to the wine bin. "If we had a cellar," he said, "the barbera would have been too cold; it's an ill wind that blows nobody any good. Chop the parsley, Ettie," he said, "and the shallots finer than that; *fine*, I said," and he tweaked her ear as he passed.

To Mrs. Combie it was an onion-smelling evening. Now Vincent told her to arrange the salad, and she had to rub the bowl and the leaves lightly with garlic though her nose twitched with disgust.

When the steaks were done the savoury butter was piled on top; as Vincent put on his coat he said, "I'll bring the omelette plates out; come to the door and take them, then pass me the tray and the other things as I tell you. You, Lovejoy"—

Lovejoy had come panting back—"pass the things to Mrs. Combie from the stove."

In a chain they worked, Vincent's face absorbed, lumpy with worry as Lovejoy had seen it, but infinitely happy; Charles and Liz watched him, amused and pleased, as he slid the steaks onto their plates, garnished them with watercress—my watercress, thought Lovejoy, her eye at the glass door—served the crisp brown potatoes; then he rolled the trolley away and fetched the wine, which Mrs. Combie had kept in the hot kitchen to warm a little more after it had been shown in its cradle to Charles and carefully uncorked. "Let it breathe a few moments," Vincent had said, and Lovejoy had looked at it, not daring to touch it; she had not known wine was alive.

When Vincent had served the wine—and Lovejoy marked how he poured a little into Charles's glass and then waited until Charles sipped and nodded before he served Liz; Lovejoy took in all these mysteries and was never to forget any of them —he set the wine carefully down, then began to mix the dressing for the salad at the table. "In front of them? Is that polite?" asked Mrs. Combie.

"Very polite," said Vincent. Back in the kitchen he had asked her to bring him a clean cloth to mop his forehead. "I'm out of training," he said.

"Dearie, it's the strain."

"I used to serve eighteen," he said, his voice high with excitement. "Twenty—but then I had a waiter. We'll have a waiter, Ettie."

"And have you seen the car?" asked Lovejoy.

"We'll have rows of cars," said Vincent.

But—what was a car like that doing in Catford Street? thought Mrs. Combie. "It's probably just for once, George," she said. She had to caution him though it went to her heart to dash the hope in his eyes; it was not dashed. "They'll come back," said Vincent. "After this meal they'll come back."

"All right?" he asked as he went back into the restaurant.

"Superb," said Charles.

"He's Charles, she's Liz," Lovejoy whispered to Mrs. Combie as they peeped through the door.

A crack of reality broke through. "That's not mink," said Cassie—with her unerring nose for what was not her business, for what Vincent would rather she did not see, Cassie had seen Lovejoy running with the watercress and at once had arrived. "That's not mink. That's marmot," said Cassie, running her eye over Liz, but Lovejoy refused to hear.

"They're having strawberries," she said. Vincent brought out one of the baskets. He did not say, "I told you so," he said solemnly, "Bring me one of the Angelica Kauffman plates."

"You mean two, George?"

"No, one. For her."

"But—won't he mind?"

"You'll see. He'll be pleased," said Vincent.

When he took in the coffee cups, Liz was touching the deep red plate with her fingers; Lovejoy had chosen a red. "It's beautiful!" said Liz.

"I keep them for my most beautiful clients," said Vincent. His heart beat in case Charles thought he was impertinent, but, sure enough, Charles smiled.

"George," said Mrs. Combie when Vincent came out. "Do you think they're in love?"

"A good dinner helps love," said Vincent. "More coffee, Ettie." He had a delighted small grin on his face that made him look like a boy and he kissed Mrs. Combie as he passed. This is what Vincent is like, thought Lovejoy, happy and sure, not little and worried and small.

The bill came to three pounds, three shillings. "He'll create," said Cassie warningly as Vincent took it to Charles folded on a plate, but Charles paid it almost without looking. He put down four pound notes and when Vincent brought the change, "Congratulations to the kitchen," said Charles and left the silver.

"I didn't know there were people like that," said Cassie. For the first time there was awe in her voice.

Vincent gave Lovejoy sixpence. "From Charles," said Lovejoy reverently.

"If he gave you sixpence you won't want mine," was all Tip said to this story.

His voice was surly. What was the matter with him? Was he jealous? thought Lovejoy. She did not know that males do not care to be circumvented, however wonderfully, by their females.

"And you're a silly little girl," said Tip. "A statue, even if it's Our Lady, can't *do* things."

He was impressive but Lovejoy only said, "Huh!"

CHAPTER XV

"IT'S TOO late to plant seeds," said Mr. Isbister.

"Even grass?" asked Lovejoy.

Mr. Isbister grunted, which meant "Even grass."

"There, you see," said Lovejoy bitterly to Tip, "that's what you've done with your penance."

Lovejoy was tenacious in getting her way, even with her mother—though there she had not been very successful—even with the Virgin Mary, and there she had been singularly successful. She believed she could bend most things to her will. "You can't plant seeds now," said Mr. Isbister.

"What if I will?" asked Lovejoy.

Mr. Isbister spat on the area ground before he answered. "In England," he said, "there's—five months when grass—will grow. April to September." Lovejoy opened her lips. "But not in London," said Mr. Isbister. "Least, not in Catford Street. Hot spell, ground bakes—hard as a plate unless you can water, sprinkle—the whole blasted time."

"We can't," said Lovejoy. "How could we? There's no water where we are."

"Then leave grass alone," said Mr. Isbister, "and for flowers get—seedlings."

"Get seedlings." Lovejoy was beginning to learn that, as a gardener, she was one of a confraternity, moving in rhythm; as needs arose, things appeared to match them. She would once have said that not much gardening went on round Catford Street; then why, in every greengrocer's shop, on the counters at Woolworth's, had boxes and boxes of seedlings appeared? She tried the patience of the shopgirls asking what they were; some of the plants had flowers on them, so that she knew them, pansies—she had a particular affection for pansies, with their wise faces—geraniums, double daisies, but the others were just clumps of green.

"What are those?"

"Alyssum."

"What are those?"

"African marigolds."

"What are those?"

"Antirrhinums, snapdragons."

Lovejoy's eyes raked the stiff, queer plants, trying to imagine what kind of flowers they would be.

After a great deal of hovering with Tip's and the dinner sixpences, she bought two marigolds, two alyssums, a daisy, and a snapdragon.

"*One?*" said the shopgirl when Lovejoy bought the snapdragon. "We sell them by the dozen," and, "Don't ruin yourself," said the girl when Lovejoy bought the daisy.

The garden was not ready, she had no pots, and she had to plant the seedlings out in tins, a golden syrup tin, two cocoa tins, and a child's old seaside pail she found in a dustbin. "Just for now," said Lovejoy. "Till we're ready." She looked at the long roots of the snapdragon. "When we put them in the beds, we'll have to plant them deep," she said. She brooded over them, and went to tell Mr. Isbister.

"Must take care of them," said Mr. Isbister. "Young plants are the same—as babies; that's why they call—a seedling bed— a nursery. They need—food and—warmth and quiet and— loving," brought out Mr. Isbister.

"Loving?" asked Lovejoy, astounded. She had never thought of plants as being loved, but, "Yes," said Mr. Isbister curtly. He was giving a coat of green paint to an empty half-barrel in his barrel garden.

"Why is it empty?" asked Tip, looking at the way the other barrels were crowded. Nowadays Tip sometimes came with Lovejoy to see Mr. Isbister. "Why is that one empty?"

"That's my summer holiday," said Mr. Isbister. Tip and Lovejoy looked so blankly at the half-barrel that he chuckled. Lovejoy had never heard him do that before; it sounded as if he were excited. Then he straightened his back and told them. Every July since they were married—"Fifty-three years now," said Mr. Isbister—he and Mrs. Isbister had gone on an excursion to the sea, but this year Mrs. Isbister was going alone.

"Why is she?" asked Lovejoy dutifully as he paused dramatically.

That was the right question.

"Because I need m'ticket money," said Mr. Isbister in glee, "t'buy something special." He was going to the Chelsea Flower Show, he told them—"Well, every year I go," he said, "but I've never ordered anything. The prices is wicked, but this year, for once, just for once before I'm too old, I'm going to buy, up to twenty-nine-and-six, that's the price of the ticket and what we'd spend. You don't buy straight off, mind. You order. I'll order from one of those big slap-up nurseries," boasted Mr. Isbister.

"What will you order?" asked Lovejoy.

Mr. Isbister did not answer at once; then, "Might be a fuchsia," he said, "and a new chrysanth—but I'd have to wait till the autumn shows for that—or it might be a rose." When he said "rose" his voice took on a deeper, more respectful note. "Last year there was a new little rose, a polyanth," said Mr. Isbister; he was looking up at them through the railings but now his eyes looked over their heads. " 'Twasn't even on order then, but it will be now; I saw it in the catalogue, pink-orange, coppery, it was; they called it flame. Costs a guinea," said Mr. Isbister.

A guinea to Lovejoy was rich and exclusive; the things in the shops she looked into with Vincent, if they were marked at all, were marked in guineas. She had assessed Liz's suit in guineas. "Guineas used to be gold," Vincent had told her and she saw them as rare little round gold moons. "Can a plant cost a *guinea*?" she asked.

"It can," said Mr. Isbister proudly. "Look," and he searched among the catalogues he kept in a pile, took out a new-looking one, wet his thumb, and turned over the pages and then held one up for her to see; it was a coloured photograph of a copper-pink rose.

"I don't think it says 'rose,' " said Lovejoy, peering down as she tried with her usual difficulty to spell out what it did say. "Jim—Jim."

"Jiminy Cricket," said Tip, looking over her shoulder.

"That's its name," said Mr. Isbister complacently.

"Do roses have *names*?" To Lovejoy it made them come almost into the category of people.

"All special flowers have names," said Mr. Isbister. Not people, Somebodies, thought Lovejoy.

"Jiminy Cricket." She tried it over on her tongue. "Jiminy Cricket." For a moment she too was dazzled, then she sighed and came back to her own garden. It had too many problems to let her have guinea-visions just now.

The eight little plants looked naked and solitary against the pair of long stone-edged beds, each six feet long and nine inches wide. "I had dozens of cornflowers, but how can we buy dozens? How can we get them?" asked Lovejoy. "They're four shillings a box, that's twopence each, and the pansies are fivepence."

"I'll get you some," said Tip.

"It took ages to get the candle money." Lovejoy did not mean to be ungrateful but she was beginning to know how quick was time, how inexorable; even her stiff little neck had to bow to that. The earth in the beds was not even dug, she saw the whole garden doomed, and her voice was sharp as she said, "And all that time you only got sixpence!"

Tip did not answer. Soon the silence seemed so long that Lovejoy looked up. He was sitting on his usual bit of stone but he was not whittling anything with his old knife, not knocking anything with his shoe or a bit of stone; he was quite still; his head was bent and he was looking at a piece of skin on his fingers. "What's the matter?" said Lovejoy.

"Nothin'," said Tip. That was true; there was nothing the matter with his finger; it was Tip himself who was hurt.

A new feeling began to be in Lovejoy; it was the first time she had ever hurt anyone and minded. The unkind words seemed to go on and on in the air. Lovejoy suddenly found she could not bear Tip's stillness, his bent head and hidden face. She could not take the words back—words never will come back—and she looked round for something she could do. With the fork she began to dig up the earth in the beds; she was not really thinking of what she was doing but of Tip; she put in the fork, and there was a small hard sound as if it had hit something; she brought the fork up, put it in, and the sound came again. She looked down the hole she had dug, remembered the length of the snapdragon roots, and looked up with a horrified face. "Tip! Tip!" she cried.

No answer. Tip looked at his fingers.

"*Tip.*"

The unhappiness in her voice reached him. "What?" said Tip unwillingly.

And Lovejoy answered, as if the end of the world had come, "Tip, there isn't enough earth in these beds."

*   *   *

The little garden was laid out, enclosed in its stone; round the space that was to be the lawn they had made a path with the old grave's marble chippings; the broken pillar rose gracefully with its ivy trail at one end; the beds were outlined; at the entrance were two corner stones embossed with lions. The lions had wings, they were supernatural lions; Tip had found them on a shattered monument, and Lovejoy had identified them. There never would have been such a garden, but it seemed almost treacherous now. "We could have found a way to get the seedlings." Lovejoy lifted a stricken face. "We could have tried to sow the grass but we can't do anything, anything at all, without earth."

"Let me see," said Tip, but it was true; there was a depth of perhaps four inches of soil before the fork struck stone. Lovejoy threw the fork down in despair, but, "There's more earth underneath," said Tip.

"We can't get through to it."

"No," said Tip. He knelt, tapping the fork, which he had picked up. "Don't do that," said Lovejoy irritably.

"I'm thinkin'," said Tip with dignity. At last he said, "Flowers grow in window boxes and boxes have hard bottoms and are not very deep."

"Deeper'n that," said Lovejoy.

"We must build the beds up with earth," said Tip.

There was plenty of earth, of course, under the rubble, but there was no hope of moving the heavy pieces of stone; it had been as much as their hands could do to bring the bits they had used. Earth was there, as it was under everything, under the church, under the houses and the Street, the whole of London. "Why, the world's made of earth," said Tip.

"And we can't get through to it," said Lovejoy. She sat down on her chosen stone by the garden and began to cry.

It was a strange thing that Lovejoy, who before had scarcely ever cried, and certainly would have let no one see her, cried continually with Tip; as on the first day, he seemed to encourage her to cry and, when she did it, an equally strange thing happened to Tip; he became both weak and strong. The weakness seemed to come from somewhere above his stomach, where his counterpart, Adam, had lost a rib, perhaps, and it was sweet and powerful, a tug, as if the rib were attached and pulling; it made him do—"*Anything*," said Tip helplessly. Wrong things, silly things. Well, a man can't go against his own rib, he might have said. Tip—and probably Adam—had judgments of their own, good judgments, and knew they were running into trouble, but Eve, Lovejoy, made them feel strong, big and invulnerable, sometimes stronger than they could conveniently be, and now, "Stop crying," said Tip. "I'll get you some earth."

He meant, bring it from the old garden. After all, it's *my* bomb-ruin, he thought. I kin bring it when the boys won't be there; but Lovejoy's eyes, though they were still wet, were looking a long, long way beyond Tip. "Good garden earth?" asked Lovejoy tremulously.

That was something new to Tip. All dirt's the same, he would have said. "Wasn't your old garden good garden earth?" he asked.

"No," said Lovejoy firmly.

"What is good garden earth?"

"The—the Square."

Tip took a deep breath. "Oh well," he said magnificently, "I'll get it from the Square."

CHAPTER XVI

"Isn't it stealing?" Lovejoy asked when the plan was made. She asked because Tip was peculiar about stealing. "Love-joy!" he would say sharply when she as much as edged towards a box of seedlings.

"They won't miss one," she would say defiantly.

"Love-JOY!"

"Of course it's not stealing," said Tip now about the earth. "It's only dirt. If we took flowers, or broke off branches, it would be stealing, but dirt's dirt," said Tip reasonably.

"If it's not stealing why do we have to come at night?"

"Because we have to get over the railings," said Tip. "They wouldn't let us do that. They don't trust us," he said with animosity.

But that had its compensations; never, not even in the faraway days with Maxey, had he made such a perfect plot. Had he made it or had Lovejoy? He decided not to go into that, but he was beginning to feel that it was the time he spent away from her that was wasted. He did not, of course, let her know this. "You can't come tomorrow?" she would say as if the sky had fallen, and Tip would growl, "Can't I have one day off?"

It was not an easy plot; as Olivia was to say, they should have had a medal for persistence, "And full marks for carrying it all out," she said.

"Marks for stealing?" asked Angela coldly.

"They are not *big* children," said Olivia, "and to wake in the middle of the night, night after night, well, three nights running, shows—enterprise and daring," said Olivia. "I should have been frightened, at that age, to go out at night into the streets. Then think of the work, those heavy loads; two of them have small arms and legs. And look how beautifully they did up the buckets."

The buckets were deadened by being wrapped with two thicknesses of sack; the handles were wound round and round with rag. "They'll make first-rate thieves, no doubt of that," said Lucas.

The buckets had to be done up each night, undone again in the morning, because one was Vincent's and one the Malones'; the shovel and sacks were Tip's, and the rope with which the buckets were let down from the church steps into the garden was, in the daytime, Mrs. Combie's washing line. "Our line's too long," said Tip. "It's for eleven people's washing."

The most difficult part was the waking. Lovejoy had Mrs. Combie's alarm clock; she fetched it from the kitchen when Mrs. Combie had gone to bed and put it back as she crept out in the morning—"Only it isn't morning, it's still night," she said—but an alarm clock was no good to Tip; he slept on through it even if it were put close to his ear. For two nights Lovejoy waited and he did not come. "It's no good," he said. "I'll have to get Sparkey."

"Sparkey?" said Lovejoy with distaste.

"Yes. He'll stay awake if I tell him," said Tip. "He'll do anything for me."

"But—can he?" asked Lovejoy.

"He doesn't sleep very well, he's so delicate, you see; if there's a mouse he wakes up, and he'd be thrilled," said Tip.

"But would his mother let him?"

"She lets him go with me," said Tip easily. "She knows that I'll look after him. I will, you know. We'll make him put his gumboots on and a thick coat. It's only three nights," said Tip. "We ought to be able to take four loads a night."

"But he won't have to *come*," said Lovejoy. "You can leave him in bed."

"That wouldn't be fair," said Tip sternly.

Tip was woken by the dutiful Sparkey—"I thought you was dead," Sparkey said to Tip the second morning—but he had to dress Sparkey and then lift him out of the window— they slept in the basement flat—and grope up the area steps to the railings and the pavement. " 'F you hear a policeman or anyone, get into a porch and duck down," ordered Tip. It was light in the Street but a queer colourless light that made them feel as if they were not real; it was queerly cold, and their stomachs were empty, which made them feel more queer; after the first night Lovejoy brought some bread, but what they needed was something hot and their stomachs rumbled loudly. "What's the use of *us* being quiet?" said Tip.

"It was on the morning of May twenty-sixth," Father Lambert was to say when, later, he made his statement to Inspector Russell at the police station. "Priest's House," he explained, "adjoins the church steps, and I sleep in a room at the back, overlooking what was the old churchyard. It was a sliding sound, followed by a slithering."

"Is there a difference between sliding and slithering?" asked Inspector Russell.

"The one," said Father Lambert, "is an even sound, as of a rope being let down—which is what it was; the other is uneven, like legs."

"Was it legs?" asked the inspector.

"It was," said Father Lambert.

It was Tip who let the rope down with the buckets, one at a time; the legs were Lovejoy's, coming over the wall, groping their way down. She untied each bucket, staggered with it to the garden, emptied it on the beds, took it back, and tied it to the rope again, and Tip drew it up.

"Did you hear anything else?" asked Inspector Russell.

"Not a chink," said Father Lambert. He also admired the buckets. "They were cleverly muffled," he said.

He had heard the beginning of a lament from Sparkey, who wanted to see the garden, but that was instantly smothered.

"Did you recognize the children?" asked Inspector Russell.

"I knew Tip Malone, of course, and I recognized the little girl but I didn't know her name."

"Did you hear them again?"

"I didn't listen. I went back to bed."

"Didn't you *know* what they were doing?"

"Not exactly," said Father Lambert. "What I did know"—and he said this later to Angela—"is that children have to play."

CHAPTER XVII

To LOVEJOY it was very far from play. When the last
bucket was tipped out and she saw the two flowerbeds
filled with fine black earth, good garden earth, she had a
feeling of such triumph and satisfaction as she had never
known. "Who plants a garden plants happiness," says the
Chinese proverb. In that moment Lovejoy was absolutely
happy.

To Tip it was not play either. He had thought that, having
got the dirt, he would be allowed to rest on his laurels, or at
least to go back to the gang, but there was a story Olivia could
have told him, a story she and Angela used to ask for when
they were little girls, "The Old Woman Who Lived in a
Vinegar Bottle."

The old woman who lived in a vinegar bottle found sixpence one day when she was sweeping; she took it to the river

shore to buy a fish for dinner, but the fish was so small that she had pity on it and put it back in the water. "Bubble, bubble, bubble," went the water, and there was the little fish. "Call me, and whatever you ask I shall give you," it said. The old woman said there was nothing she wanted, but no sooner had she gone back to the vinegar bottle than she remembered the dinner she should have had; she went back to the river and called the little fish. The hot dinner was provided and then she thought she would change the inconvenient vinegar bottle for a house; but her furniture would not go with the new house and she asked for new furniture; her clothes looked shabby with the new furniture and she asked for new clothes; she could not do housework in her new clothes and she asked for a little maid; the maid sent her to the shops to buy chops for dinner and she asked for a pony-carriage. "Bubble, bubble, bubble," went the water all day long. If Tip—or Mrs. Combie —had heard that story they would have known just how tired the little fish became.

"Wanting is the beginning of getting." Vincent said that often.

"Then why don't people get things?" asked Lovejoy.

"Because they don't want hard enough." Certainly no one could have accused Vincent or Lovejoy of that.

"We can't put these poor little things in this beautiful earth," said Lovejoy, looking with disfavour at the snapdragon, the daisy, and the marigolds and alyssums. "We must have something special."

"What sort of special?" asked Tip warily. It was a word he was beginning to dread. Tip's face was beginning to look as no Malone face had ever looked before, careworn.

"Mum," said Tip, coming to sit on a box by his mother when she was washing up at the sink, "Mum, I do wish I had some money."

"How much money?" asked Mrs. Malone cautiously.

"I don't know," burst out Tip. "That's it. I don't know. I don't know where I am. There's never any end to it," said Tip and kicked the box.

Mrs. Malone looked at her son in astonishment. That was how Mr. Malone talked on a Friday night.

To give Lovejoy her due, some of her wants she achieved for herself; for instance, the lawn.

"In Catford Street you can't sow grass seed now." Lovejoy puzzled and puzzled how to get over that until one afternoon in school she was sent on a message to the infants' classroom. It was half-past three but the kindergarten teacher, Miss Challoner, was still there, cutting out paper figures for the next day's project. Lovejoy threaded her way among the small chairs and tables and, as she stood in front of the teacher delivering the message with parrot correctness, she looked round the room with its sandtray, its brown paper pictures thumbtacked on the wall, its shop, the tadpoles in a battery jar on the window sill, the pots of plants, the big cardboard clock, all the fascinating things the infants had. I wish I was a ninfant, thought Lovejoy, and then she saw, standing on trestles under the window, pans filled with something dense and short and green. She forgot Miss Challoner and tiptoed nearer and looked to make sure; yes, it was green and short and dense. "What is it?" she asked.

"Gracious, child, haven't you ever seen mustard and cress?" said Miss Challoner as Mr. Isbister had said about the ivy.

"It looks like very special grass," said Lovejoy.

"It's for eating."

"*Eating?*" Lovejoy was shocked.

"You buy it in twopenny packets," said Miss Challoner, "and sow it thickly; it will come up anywhere, even on flannel."

"Even on not much earth?" There was not much earth on the patch of lawn.

"Yes."

"If you sowed it now?"

"Any time, except in winter."

Perhaps Miss Challoner sensed Lovejoy's burning interest because she opened her desk and said, "I have some over. Would you like these?" and into Lovejoy's hands she put half a dozen packets. Lovejoy's thanks were so fervid that Miss Challoner asked her name.

"You have a very responsive and charming little girl in your class," Miss Challoner was to tell Lovejoy's teacher, Miss Cobb.

"Lovejoy charming?" asked Miss Cobb, who only saw Lovejoy's inscrutable small mask.

"I shall expect some cress on bread and butter in about ten days," Miss Challoner called to Lovejoy when she saw her on the stairs. After that it was strange how Lovejoy disappeared as soon as she saw Miss Challoner.

The mustard and cress was sown thickly all over the patch; the mustard seeds were like tiny dark yellow balls, the cress as fine as grass seed, but oblong, nut brown; the cat net had been lost when the gang raided the first garden; in any case it would not have been big enough to stretch over the new lawn, but Tip and Lovejoy crisscrossed black cotton from side to side; it looked professional again, and Tip was impressed. "They'll be up in five days," Lovejoy told him. She had the prospect of a lawn, but there were still only the eight little seedlings in the beds—"And they're a mistake," said Lovejoy restlessly.

"What are you thinking of *now*?" said Tip. Lovejoy did not answer but he knew. Something special.

Sid's boy had left, and the next Saturday Tip began work with Sid and Lucy. "Delivering ice," said Tip. "Ugh." On Monday he came to Lovejoy in the garden.

"Here's half a crown," he said. He might have been a husband handing over his first pay packet; he gave it proudly but resentfully.

> When I was single,
> My pockets did jingle—

Tip might have sung that. "I went round with Sid the whole blooming day, and was that ice dirty and heavy!" He grumbled but all the same he was proud that he, Tip, had earned his first real money—a huge big lot, he thought, but Lovejoy held the coin with her head bent over it. "Well?" said Tip belligerently.

"It isn't enough," said Lovejoy.

"Not *enough*! It's half a crown!" He sat down beside her, feeling suddenly tired. "What do you *want*?" he demanded.

"A box of pansies," said Lovejoy instantly.

"A box?" said Tip in alarm. "You said they were fivepence each. A whole box would be—" Words failed him.

"Ten-and-six," said Lovejoy calmly.

She said nothing more, and Tip's heart sank; then, sitting beside her, he found himself distracted from the pansies. He was noticing how she had a ridge of very fine short hairs on the back of her neck, soft as down, mouse-coloured but tipped with gold; they looked as if they were protecting the tender knobs of her spine; gently Tip put out his finger and felt those little bones. Then he sighed. It was no good; even when Lovejoy was difficult and ungrateful he found it impossible to be angry; instead he began to coax her. "Couldn't you have those little white things?" said Tip.

"Alyssum," said Lovejoy dully.

"They're pretty," urged Tip, "and only ninepence a dozen. For half a crown you could have more'n three dozen of those."

Lovejoy turned her head to look at him. "What would white look like against white stone?" she asked, like stone herself.

"But they're cheap," Tip pleaded.

Lovejoy did not want to drive Tip—she would have worked herself, the whole day with Sid, if Sid would have taken her—she did not want to be hard, but it was that or spoil the garden. "People will want to drag you down," Vincent had said. "Don't let them. *They must not.*"

It was strange how things grew, not only plants, ideas, thought Lovejoy; a little while ago—and now she conveniently shrank into little the time that had seemed so endless—a little while ago half a crown to spend, to buy the trowel and fork, or seeds, would have seemed impossible riches—but that was seeds, thought Lovejoy; she had not known about seedlings then, or pansies. There were other flowers, not only alyssum; lobelia, for instance, was a good bright blue, or there were dark red button daisies, but, "Pansies are all sorts of colours," she said yearningly. "Purple and yellow and brown and gold." They were more than that; she searched for a word, and a phrase from Mrs. Combie's Cornish past that Mrs. Combie sometimes remembered came to her. "They're handsome," she said.

"All right," said Tip. "I'll go on with Sid," and, as if he felt that gave him a right over Lovejoy, he put his hand on her neck.

"You'll only have to give me three more Saturdays," said Lovejoy under his hand. "I'll get the sixpence," she said generously. Then she stopped, her face unhappy again. "In three weeks it'll be too late," she wailed. "Mr. Isbister says pansies have to be planted *now*." Tip took away his hand.

*   *   *

"Hail Mary," said Lovejoy as she slid into the nearest kneeling-chair. "I want eight shillings, please."

It sounded like an order and she blushed. She had not even

lit a candle, and even Lovejoy knew that the Virgin Mary did not keep a store from which one could order; the candle shilling, Liz and Charles for Vincent, had been unwonted favours, unwontedly quick. "You have to pray for things for ages," said Tip, "and you don't always get them then."

"Why not?" asked Lovejoy, who wanted a quick return.

"God doesn't want you to have them, I s'pose," said Tip.

Lovejoy looked sternly into the church at the plaster figures. "Which one is God?" she asked.

Lovejoy had an idea she could circumvent God but, all the same, at the moment she was a little anxious. She had knelt down on the left of the chapel, which meant that the statue was looking away from her; was that a bad sign? Lovejoy did not know any prayers but she knew a hymn that Mrs. Combie sometimes sang, a whining little hymn with a repellent tune. "Gentle Jesus, meekanmile." Lovejoy started to whisper it; whispers seemed fitting here—lips have to make the prayers, you can't just think them, she thought. The church was always filled with that soft pattering. ". . . meekanmile, look 'pona . . ."

But, though she whispered, Lovejoy was thinking about something else; perhaps because of the small miracle of Liz and Charles—"They were near the restaurant. Why shouldn't they go there," Tip had asked, but Lovejoy insisted it was a miracle—she kept thinking, not about Gentle Jesus but about the restaurant. She could not help it. She fixed her eyes on the statue, its pink and blue, its gilt, and plaster lilies, and the restaurant came into her mind.

There was only one topic there now, the big refrigerator. Vincent said he must get one, and the harder Lovejoy tried to pray, the more she heard Mrs. Combie's perpetual words, "One hundred and forty-four pounds! Oh, George!"

"But it's hire-purchase, Ettie. Forty-four pounds down and six pounds, six-and-nine a month for eighteen months.

That's easy terms. It's such a sensible way to buy things!" said Vincent. "Look 'pona little child," prayed Lovejoy. "Only six pounds, six-and-ninepence a month."

Lovejoy was suddenly still on her knees. Then she made the sign of the cross as Tip had taught her. "Thank you," said Lovejoy earnestly to the statue and she tiptoed out.

That afternoon she went to Vincent's favourite greengrocer shop, Driscoll's in Mortimer Street off the High. Mr. Driscoll, wearing a white apron doubled round his waist, was standing in the middle of the shop talking to a man whom Lovejoy thought she knew; the man had on a long old-fashioned overcoat and a bowler hat and was pointing to vegetables and fruit with a stick; as he pointed them out Mr. Driscoll wrote on his pad and a boy, in another white apron, lifted the fruit or vegetables out and laid them on pink tissue paper in a box. After a moment Lovejoy recognized the man; it was Mr. Manley.

"Two asparagus," said Mr. Manley, pointing to the fat bluish and cream bundles. "See they're slender, none of your thick sticks, John, and is that English spinach?"

"Just in," said Mr. Driscoll.

"Put in a pound," said Mr. Manley, "and three of Jersey potatoes."

As Mr. Manley went on and Lovejoy listened she began to think that Vincent was wrong; peaches, new potatoes, asparagus—it seemed that Mr. Manley had very good meals in his house.

"That's the lot," he said at last in the abrupt way that offended Vincent. "Send them round quickly."

"The boy will take them straight away," said Mr. Driscoll.

Most people, Lovejoy knew, did not have their greengroceries sent straight away, and she knew from the battles between Mrs. Combie and Vincent that Driscoll's was expensive. Even the people from the river flats did not buy their vegetables here but in the despised High Street. Driscoll's was for the Square people, for Somebodies. Mr. Manley must be Somebody, thought Lovejoy, even if Vincent did not think so.

She knew quite well that she herself was very far from a Somebody but she had come because, for what she wanted, it was no use going to the big High Street shops or to Woolworth's; there they held on to the paper of plants until they had the money; besides there were no plants better or fresher than the ones in the boxes outside Driscoll's; she had often looked at them longingly.

"Well, little girl? What can I do for you?" Mr. Driscoll had come back from taking Mr. Manley to the door. Lovejoy was glad she had put on her checked coat even if she had to leave it open because it would not meet and it hurt under the arms. "Do you think Mother will send me a new coat soon?" she had asked Mrs. Combie.

"She should," said Mrs. Combie, "and shoes. You do need shoes."

"She should but she hasn't," said Cassie.

"Couldn't you write and ask her?" Lovejoy kept her eyes on Mrs. Combie, ignoring Cassie.

"I do write," said Mrs. Combie, later and privately to Lovejoy, "I write but she doesn't answer."

Lovejoy had done her best; she had brushed her hair until it glistened, and put on clean socks and whitened her plimsolls. "If you want a part you must look as if you didn't need it," her mother had told her often. "Look good, even if you don't feel it." Lovejoy saw Mr. Driscoll's eye take her in and felt his approval. "What can I do for you, little lady?" he asked.

"I want—" but before she had time to finish her sentence Mr. Manley had come back.

"John, I forgot. I shall want some special flowers on Thursday—" Then he paused, seeing Lovejoy. "I beg your pardon," he said to her as if she were quite grown up. "I didn't see John was serving."

"The little girl can wait," said Mr. Driscoll at once, but Mr. Manley waved his stick in his strange abrupt way and said, "Go on. Go on. Strict turns, John. No favouritism."

"Well, what *do* you want?" Mr. Driscoll said to Lovejoy.

Lovejoy was fingering the half-crown nervously, trying not to let it get sticky, but her voice was high and clear as she answered. "I want to hire-purchase a box of pansies," she said.

"Hire-*purchase*?"

"Yes, on the instalment plan," said Lovejoy and, as Mr. Driscoll did not appear to understand, "on easy terms," she said.

"She knows all the words," said Mr. Driscoll to Mr. Manley.

"I'll give you half a crown down," said Lovejoy, "and half a crown a week for three weeks and sixpence at the end." She held out the half a crown, but Mr. Driscoll, though he was laughing, shook his head.

"We don't sell plants like that," he said.

"You do if there's a guarantee," said Mr. Manley. Mr. Driscoll stopped laughing. It became suddenly serious—as it was to Lovejoy. "Do you know this child?" asked Mr. Driscoll.

"No," said Mr. Manley, which was true. Lovejoy had seen him many times but he had not seen her. "I don't know her, but I think she'll pay. Give me your pad."

Mr. Manley wrote: *Pansies, one box. Ten shillings.* He ignored the sixpence. "When you give a big order, ignore the pence," he told Lovejoy. Lovejoy nodded, and at the bottom of the small sheet Mr. Manley wrote 2/6 four times. "You cross one off a week," he said to Lovejoy. "Got your half-crown?" She nodded again. "Hand it over." She handed it to Mr. Driscoll, who crossed off the first 2/6. "See that he does it each time," said Mr. Manley gravely, "otherwise he might cheat you"; and underneath he wrote his own name. Again he wrote "Manley" without the initial.

"Haven't you a name?" asked Lovejoy. "Not a surname, a name they call you by? What is your name?"

"Reginald Marmaduke Kitchener Spot," said Mr. Manley and walked out of the shop.

The pansies went right round the beds, filling them completely. "You see," said Lovejoy to Tip, and indeed their colours against the stone were like jewels, thought Lovejoy. They were not really like jewels, they were flower colours, truthful and glowing, but they were as precious as jewels to her. "You're mad about that garden," Tip grumbled.

The mustard and cress was not as good; it was showing, the mustard in flat double leaves, the cress in tiny narrow ones like green feathers; in a short while it would be as high as grass but it had not come through exactly as Lovejoy had meant. "Those seeds must have crept about under the earth," she said, furious.

There were patches that were almost bald. "They'll thicken up," said Tip comfortingly, but there was one place about which Tip could say nothing at all, a big, bare patch, almost a ring of earth opposite the column. He looked at it in silence; it was plain he thought it very ugly, and Lovejoy's pride was stung. "I meant it to be like that," she said.

"Did you?" asked Tip doubtfully.

"Yes," said Lovejoy. Her adroitness always made Tip marvel; he knew quite well she had invented this about the patch, but, "Wait," she said now and went off among the rubble so much as if this had really been in her mind that Tip was half convinced.

Presently she came back with something round and set with shattered bits of glass.

"What is it?" asked Tip.

Neither of them knew; it had been a glass bell that held

everlasting flowers for a grave; its bottom was zinc, edged with a painted white tin frill. "Isn't it pretty?" asked Lovejoy. The glass was broken now, but, "It will make a very special sort of flowerpot," said Lovejoy. "It fits here, on the patch," and she set it down and looked at it, breaking off one or two bits of glass that were left. The bare patch was hidden. "Isn't it pretty?" asked Lovejoy again and then she said, "We must fill it with earth."

"Not more earth!" said Tip.

"More earth," said Lovejoy inexorably.

"But what will you put in it?" asked Tip. He sounded as if he were alarmed.

Lovejoy did not answer for a moment. She looked away, thoughtfully and dreamily; then, "Do you remember Mr. Isbister's summer holiday?" she asked. "Do you remember Jiminy Cricket?"

CHAPTER XVIII

THE old woman in the vinegar bottle went too far; there came a day when the little fish, tired out, said, "Go back to your vinegar bottle," and the house, furniture, new clothes, maid, and pony-carriage disappeared, but Vincent and Lovejoy had not heard any more than Tip or Mrs. Combie of that story.

With the old woman it had been a car; the pony-carriage, she complained, was too slow. With Vincent it was the big refrigerator. A duck had gone bad in the larder, and Vincent brought up, for the hundredth time, it seemed to Mrs. Combie, the question of the big refrigerator. "I tell you we must have it," said Vincent.

"We can't, George. We can't pay for it."

"Then we must borrow. Now, *now* is the moment," cried

Vincent. "At last it has happened what I said. I begin to gather my clientele, the clientele I want." If Vincent were moved he grew foreign. "No, not want," said Vincent passionately. "Not want, deserve. Without a big refrigerator—" he began.

"George, a big refrigerator costs—"

"You're always dinning figures into me," shouted Vincent. "Figures, and it hurts."

Mrs. Combie might have said that it was Vincent who dinned figures into her where they hurt much more; she had had a very painful interview with Mr. Edwards, the bank-manager, that weekend and now she had to persist. "Why not wait?" she asked in a breathless voice, twisting the overall strings tightly round her finger. "Wait till more people like the lady and gentleman come."

"And give them duck gone bad?" asked Vincent icily.

* * *

"Would you care to try something else tonight?" said Vincent to Mr. Manley. "Something more interesting. *Aiguillettes de canard sauvage?*" said Vincent smoothly. "Chicken *sauté à l'ancienne?*" That was Vincent's specialty. "Or may I suggest fillet of sole *à la Russe?*"

"You're very splendiferous," said Mr. Manley.

"Yes," said Vincent, and his smile was almost a smirk. The refrigerator had gone to his head and he had had an orgy of cooking. "At last we are equipped, almost," said Vincent. There was still the question of the dishwasher. "I'm happy to say we have installed a full-sized refrigerator."

"Umph!" said Mr. Manley. He ordered a plain rump steak.

With Vincent it was the big refrigerator; with Lovejoy it was the wreath flowerpot.

For several days after she put it in the garden Tip had not

come near her. "I won't get more earth," he had said flatly
and gone away. When Lovejoy caught him in the Street he
would not talk to her. "I've got things to do," he said.

"What things?" asked Lovejoy.

"Things with the boys," said Tip. "Boys!" he bellowed as
if he were desperate. A sudden wisdom told Lovejoy to leave
him alone.

I don't miss him, she told herself proudly and, as a matter
of fact, she did not miss him as badly as she would have done
a little time ago. These days the statue seemed to be with her
in a way that was companionable. I don't mind her now,
thought Lovejoy, I quite like her.

She's always been here, thought Lovejoy easily; why should
I mind her? She knows all about me, thought Lovejoy.

Mary was Jesus' mother, even the ignorant Lovejoy knew
that, but she was also, according to Tip, everyone's mother.
"I've got a mother of my own," Lovejoy told her jealously.

It was mysterious, but Tip seemed content to let it be
mysterious. There was the question of the baby who was
Jesus, for instance. Tip said that Jesus was God but he also
said God was so big and powerful that no one could measure
Him—Lovejoy, in her mind's eye, immediately saw the power
station—then how could He be a little baby? "How can He?"
she had asked challengingly.

"Easily," said Tip.

That was too much for Lovejoy, but Mary she could understand. "Well, that's all right," said Tip. "Perhaps it begins
with her." Mary, Lovejoy gathered, was a real mother; there
were many things that Tip must, or must not, do. I wish I
must and mustn't, thought Lovejoy yearningly, and she
thought that when her mother came back she would tell her
a thing or two; and while Mary was stern, she was—reliable
was the word Lovejoy wanted—and she had given excellent
advice about the pansies. Yes, taking all things together,

thought Lovejoy, she was glad the statue was in the garden, she had grown used to it, but, "When *my* mother comes back I won't need you," said Lovejoy; that sounded rude and perhaps ungrateful, and after a while she found a potted-meat jar and washed it so clean that it sparkled, filled it with pansies, and took it into the church. People often put bunches of flowers round the pedestal, and Lovejoy put her jar at its foot. "When these are dead I'll bring you some more," she said, kindly.

These days were peaceful. Some of them were rainy but then Lovejoy sat under the tombstone and kept dry. It was good to watch the flowers drinking, without all that work, thought Lovejoy. It was a terrible work to water even that small patch of garden.

It needed two; taking filled jam jars or bottles down the wall was difficult and dangerous, as Lovejoy had found when she tried and fell, broke a jar, and cut herself. After that Tip had fixed a piece of old waterpipe against the wall, tying it to the sharp, sticking-out bits of brick with string because he dared not make a noise knocking nails in; the pipe was shaky but it acted as a channel, and if he poured water in from an old cider bottle at the top, Lovejoy could catch it in her jam jar below. Even then it was work that took patience so that, Tip being away, it was double luck that there was rain; when it rained the garden watered itself and afterwards Lovejoy came out and smelled the earth and it was miraculously fresh. To smell it she had to get down on her hands and knees, and that brought another revelation. "If you stand up the garden's little," she told Tip. "If you get right down and look along the paths, squint and screw your eyes up, it's big."

One evening, on her way home, Lovejoy had reached the Street when she went back to the garden for the shovel.

Mr. Isbister had told her that, besides watering, she should feed her plants. "Feed them?" Lovejoy had asked astonished.

"Think you're the only one what needs to eat?" said Mr. Isbister and he told her how to make liquid food with manure and water.

It sounded complicated to Lovejoy, but she did her best. Like a real sparrow pecking at dung, she scooped a horse-dollop off the road with Tip's shovel. It was a good thing Cassie did not see her, but to a chemist nothing is unclean and, highly pleased, Lovejoy shook the dung up in a jam jar of water, kept it a few days—Mr. Isbister had said it should be old—and fed the pansies.

She made a fresh supply every few days, and that evening Lucy had been by and there were beautiful fresh dollops still smoking on the road; it was worth the trouble of going back, but Lovejoy had scooped up only one shovelful when, down the Street, came the big green car.

It came quickly but not as quickly as Lovejoy went; crimson with shame, she fled back up the steps. They would come now! she thought wrathfully; all the same she did not drop her dollop but took it safely over the wall. She did not come up until she heard Charles and Liz go into the church; then slowly, hoping they had not seen her shame, she came up the wall, climbed over, settled her clothes and hair, and waited by the bell. Charles and Liz! thought Lovejoy. Perhaps, perhaps they didn't see. Shivers of excitement and hero-worship went over her, and when they came up the crypt steps she made them the curtsy she had learned long ago for the stage; nothing less seemed to fit the occasion. "Hello!" said Charles. He had just put on his hat; he swept it off again. To me! thought Lovejoy. How she wished Cassie could see.

"It's the little saint," said Liz.

"The sinner," said Charles.

Lovejoy noticed that he held Liz's arm. That was enough for Lovejoy. They're engaged! she thought. Liz had gloves on, so that Lovejoy could not see the ring, but she knew at once what it was. A great big diamond! thought Lovejoy.

Liz was wearing—the same suit! thought Lovejoy, disappointed. She had thought Liz, like the queen, or as Lovejoy imagined the queen, would wear a new dress every day; she saw a maid, like a maid on the films in a black dress and little cap and apron, showing Liz suit after suit, dress after dress; but no, it was the same suit, same hat, gloves, and stole.

Lovejoy followed them down to the car and stayed on the pavement looking into it, at its mole-coloured leather—she knew mole, it was a fashionable colour—the plaid rug, the wood and silver and glass. There were a little clock, a radio. "Like a drive?" asked Charles.

Lovejoy had never thought that Charles and Liz might be kind to her—when Liz gave her the shilling it had seemed the work of the statue, not Liz; Lovejoy had not thought of herself in connection with them at all, except as a pair of eyes watching them perhaps, and she was startled when Charles spoke. "Like a drive?" said Charles in his lazy, offhand voice. "Just round a street or two?"

Lovejoy did not mean to be rude but she seemed to have lost her voice. Charles opened the car door for her—"As if I was a lady," she told Tip afterwards—shut her in, shut in Liz, came round to his place, and started the car. As it pulled away from the curb and down the road it felt like gliding, floating. If Vincent could see me now, thought Lovejoy as they passed the restaurant, or, better than Vincent, Cassie, or, better even than Cassie, Tip, Tip and his whole blasted gang. Lovejoy sat so stiffly erect and proud as they swept round the corner by the river that she overbalanced and fell forward against the front seat. It was then she saw what Liz held on her lap.

Liz had lifted a globe of tissue paper to look at it; Lovejoy looked too and stayed, glued where she was, her hands clutch-

ing the front seat. She did not know it but she had given a
little gasp. Charles glanced round. "Did I go too fast?" he
asked, "I'm sorry." But Lovejoy had forgotten she was in a car.

"Is it real?" she whispered.

Liz turned her head to look at Lovejoy; Lovejoy's face was
just beside her own, gazing down, and Lovejoy's hand crept
forward. "Could I—could I *touch it*?"

She had hardly dared to ask, but Liz twisted right round
and lifted it up. Lovejoy, steadying herself on her elbows,
took it into her hands. "It's a rose!" she said, stunned.

"A tiny standard rose," said Liz.

"Alive!" Lovejoy was faint with wonder.

There was cause for wonder. The rosetree was not more
than nine inches high, planted in a pot, its tiny leaves making
the correct standard bush, and on it were six deep pink-orange
roses. Each minute rose was perfectly formed, the petals
curled, each flower no bigger than a sixpence. "It even has a
scent," said Liz, "and it's hardy too."

"Would it live in a garden?"

"Yes," said Liz. "But it would have to be a very little
garden."

"Yes," breathed Lovejoy.

She was oblivious that they had come round to the church
again and the car had stopped. All she saw was the rose.

"Where did you find it?"

"Charles gave it to me. It was a special present," said Liz.

Special! and I thought I knew what special was! Lovejoy
had thought pansies were beautiful—and all the time there
was this, she thought. The garden with its joined stone edges,
its mustard and cress, seemed a child's play-garden now; I
thought I knew, thought Lovejoy sorrowfully, and all the time
there were things like this—she kept coming back to the rose.
She felt ashamed; this is what Mr. Isbister meant when he

said "something special," while I— But I never dreamed, I never thought—thought Lovejoy and gave a miserable little choke. She handed the rose back to Liz and blindly put out her hand to find the door. She felt that they were looking at her in surprise but she could not help it.

"Wait," said Charles suddenly. He got out, opened Lovejoy's door, but stood blocking it. "Have you got a garden?" he asked.

Lovejoy nodded. "We got the pot," she said huskily. "We were getting the earth." Tip had said he would not get it, but that, she knew, could have been settled. "The earth," she repeated and swallowed. "It doesn't matter now." Her voice died away and she bent her head so that the two sides of her hair swung forward and hid her face, showing her neck. Tip could have told Charles how potent that was.

"Well. Well. Well," said Charles. There was such a long silence that Lovejoy raised her head. He was looking across at Liz and Liz was looking back at him. This time it was Liz who nodded.

"First present I give you, you give away," said Charles, pretending to grumble. "I suppose I can get you another," and he reached in and took the rose from Liz and set it in Lovejoy's lap.

When the heavens open one does not say thank you. Lovejoy gazed dumbly at the rose, at Liz, at Charles, until, "You're in the car," Charles prompted gently. "You must get out now." He helped her out, closed the door, lifted his hat again, and got back in the driving seat, but before he could start the car Liz beckoned. Lovejoy ran round in the road to Liz's window.

"You'll take care of it?" said Liz. "And you must transplant it. That means put it in another pot, a bigger one; spread the roots out and press the earth down well. Do you know how?"

"Yes," said Lovejoy huskily.

"And wouldn't you like to know what it is?" asked Liz. "It has a name, you know."

"I know," said Lovejoy.

"It's a Robin Hood rose called 'Little Monarch'!" But to Lovejoy it could only have one name.

"It's called Jiminy Cricket," said Lovejoy firmly.

CHAPTER XIX

Olivia always spoke of "that morning," but it really began the evening before, the evening Jiminy Cricket came.

Lovejoy did not have to go and find Tip. He came to the garden; he had been having a strange nagging of conscience. "Why? I don't belong to her," he said, trying to convince himself, but he had been pulled all the time. He had brought Lovejoy half a bag of all-sorts but when he saw the little rose he stopped. "Where did you get that?" he asked suspiciously. When Lovejoy, still dazed by her luck, told him he said, "You shouldn't take presents from people you don't know."

That was one of Mrs. Malone's maxims but it was news to Lovejoy; she had always supposed one should take all one could get. "And I do know Charles," she said, which was an unfortunate remark.

"If you've got him, you don't want me," said Tip and turned away with his bag of sweets.

"I do want you," said Lovejoy, running round in front of him. There was no mistaking her agitation. "Oh, please! I can't do without you," said Lovejoy.

"Honest?" said Tip, and a glow began to come on his sullen face. "You're not kidding?"

"Oh no!" said Lovejoy earnestly. "You see, we must get that earth tonight.

"Why have you gone all cross again?" she asked.

"Think why," growled Tip, but Lovejoy could not think and she began to wheedle him.

"It only needs one more bucket of earth," she crooned, "one bucket and the garden's made. Tip. Help me. We must get that earth tonight. . . .

"But that evening wasn't only for us, it was for everybody," said Lovejoy. It was strange how it came together for all of them—for instance, Vincent.

Earlier that evening Vincent, coming out on the pavement to breathe a little air after the stuffiness of the kitchen, had seen the green car when it was higher up the Street, outside the Priest's House. Charles and Liz had been to see Father Lambert before they went to look at the church. For one moment Vincent had gazed at the car, then he dived back into the restaurant, calling, "Ettie. Ettie."

"What is it, George?" Mrs. Combie was alarmed.

"Quick. They're coming," said Vincent. He was moving vases and clearing the tables. "The one night I hadn't changed the cloths," he lamented. "That's you and your economy," but he did not sound cross. "Come along. Help," he said and gave her an affectionate slap. "They're coming."

"The lady and gentleman, George?"

"Who else?" said Vincent. "Now are you glad we have the refrigerator?" he said. His eyes grew wide. "I shall make them something they'll remember. They shall have *langouste*. Thank God we have *langouste*, and, yes, my chicken *sauté à l'ancienne*."

"Will you have time?" asked Mrs. Combie.

"They'll wait," said Vincent. "They'll have apéritifs."

Once again Mrs. Combie's doubt gave way to pride and awe; it was always the same when she watched Vincent cooking; this chicken sauté, to Mrs. Combie, was a queer and unappetizing dish; to her the white wine spoiled good chicken, but still she was fascinated as she watched. She was not allowed to stand and watch for long. "Put some roses on their table, Ettie," said Vincent. "They'll want the same one. Is Lovejoy in?"

"No, she's out somewhere," said Mrs. Combie.

"Then you must go, Ettie, quick as you can, go to the dairy and get some cream and to Driscoll's for mushrooms." Mrs. Combie hesitated. "Ettie, I must have cream and mushrooms. There's just enough time and I can't make this else, and, Ettie, get some raspberries."

"Have you any money, George?" asked Mrs. Combie.

"*I?*" said Vincent in astonishment; she had never asked him that before.

"They won't let us have them, George, unless we pay. We owe too much at the dairy, and Mr. Driscoll has sent a registered letter."

"Then pay for them," snapped Vincent. "There's eleven shillings in the till from those two lunches, if you could call them lunches. 'An omelette and a cup of coffee,'" he mimicked. "Go *on*, Ettie." Mrs. Combie hesitated, and Vincent stood up. "Ettie, when I am right, *proved* right, will you not do as I say?"

When Mrs. Combie came back the restaurant was filled with succulent smells. "Is the car still at the church?" asked Vincent.

"Yes," said Mrs. Combie. It had driven Lovejoy round, but Mrs. Combie had missed that and Vincent had been too busy to see.

"Good," said Vincent. "You take over the soup, Ettie, while I wash. I have to arrange the raspberries. Then everything is ready." He paused. "Last time she had a red Kauffman plate; get a blue."

Smooth and polished in his tail coat and carefully creased trousers, fresh linen, and his watch chain, Vincent went into the restaurant. When he saw the pink roses Mrs. Combie had arranged he frowned, took them out, and did them again; then he wiped the vase, put it back on the table, and gave the two cocked napkins a touch. The bread was cut, the new menus were written, two good red and white wines were out, one warming, the other cooling. Jauntily he went to the door and looked up the road.

The car was gone.

When life gives a blow it often gives another; that happened to Mrs. Combie that night.

Vincent was serving coffee in the restaurant—there were three people in, but even to Mrs. Combie they did not seem to be people now—when there came a knock at the side door. "Will you go?" said Vincent. He spoke in a stunned, respectful way as if she, or he, were dead; which of us? thought Mrs. Combie, but if Vincent died, she died too. "Will you go, Ettie?" he asked, and, leaving the littered kitchen, Mrs. Combie took her tired body to the door.

"Why haven't you people got a telephone?"

The voice was so loud and jovial that it jarred. We're unhappy here, speak softly, Mrs. Combie wanted to say. Vincent went quickly into the restaurant, but she had to stand and listen. "Had to drag all the way here," it complained. "Is Bertha in?"

"Bertha?" Mrs. Combie held the doorjamb.

"Bertha. Mrs. Mason. I'm Mr. Montague, her agent. Doesn't she live here?"

"Yes, but she's in Brighton with the Blue Moons," said Mrs. Combie, silently taking in the good blue overcoat, black hat, red face, and smell of soap and brilliantine and cigars.

"With the Blue Moons?"

"Yes, in Brighton." Mrs. Combie held the doorjamb tighter.

"So that's her line," said Mr. Montague. He spoke softly as if to himself, but Mrs. Combie heard. "Oh well!" he said and lifted his hat. "In that case, good night."

"But—wait." Mrs. Combie was collecting herself. "Isn't that all right?"

He shrugged. "Maybe, for all I know," he said. Then perhaps he saw Mrs. Combie's face more clearly, because he said, "One thing I do know. She isn't with the Blue Moons."

"Why? Why not?" said Mrs. Combie faintly. Her voice had reeled away.

"They're in Jersey, dear, be there all summer. I ought to know. I booked them there myself. Look here," he said. "Have some sense. Bertha hasn't been with the Blue Moons for years. Three years, to be exact. She's not in their class now. Right out, in fact. She's had odd jobs here and there, that's all. I can't do miracles. They will go on, you know, and nobody wants them. Won't listen," said Mr. Montague. "I had a fill-in job that might have helped for a week or two, but if she's not here—"

"If she isn't with the Blue Moons in Brighton," said Mrs. Combie slowly, "where is she?"

"Haven't the faintest," said Mr. Montague. "Well, no use my waiting. Good night."

"One moment," said Mrs. Combie, coming to life. "You're her agent."

"A theatrical agent has no responsibility," said Mr. Montague. It was as if a comfortable sleek car had suddenly become armoured and put out steel guns. "And there's no money owing to her, none. In fact the boot's on the other foot. She's been drawing on us."

"But—" Mrs. Combie caught at his sleeve. "Wait, Mr. Montague. There's Lovejoy. You remember Lovejoy."

"The kiddy?" For a moment Mr. Montague seemed troubled. "Did Bertha do that? I wouldn't have thought it of her." Then he withdrew behind his guns. "So she's made a muggins of you? Bad luck. Well, I must be off."

"But—" cried Mrs. Combie wildly.

He stepped back out of her reach. "I told you, she owes *us* money. Good night."

It was that evening too that Angela discovered that Lucas had disobeyed her and the Garden Committee, and had not slept in the shed. "Not even once," said Angela.

"No more earth has been taken," said Lucas defensively.

"That's not the point."

"We've scared them off."

"That's not the point," said Angela again. "You were given orders."

Lucas looked sullen.

"Orders that were meant to be obeyed. Perhaps you prefer to leave?" asked Angela. Lucas looked still more sullen.

"I didn't say that," said Lucas. His small eyes blinked.

"If you don't want to leave," said Angela, "you will sleep in the shed tonight."

Lucas cast an appealing glance at Olivia, who deliberately looked at the floor; at the admiral, who cleared his throat and looked out of the window; Mr. Donaldson was still at the office so there was no one else to meet Lucas's eye except Angela herself, and she was implacably stern. "Very well," said Lucas.

Tip had difficulty in getting Sparkey. "Last time I let him

go with you he was tired out," said Sparkey's mother. "You must have sat up all night talking."

"We didn't," said Tip and Sparkey truthfully.

"And he got a shocking cold," said Sparkey's mother.

"That was my *May* cold," said Sparkey.

"And if you get another that'll be your June cold, I suppose?"

"Yes," said Sparkey.

"Let him come," begged Tip.

Sparkey's mother wanted to go away for the night and did not want to take Sparkey with her; Tip's proposal suited her exactly, but she was still thinking of that talking in bed. "Promise you'll keep a blanket round him," she said.

She would not let Sparkey go until they had promised, though they knew it would be a singularly awkward promise to keep. "I don't *want* a blanket," said Sparkey miserably.

"We'll tie it round you," said Tip.

* * *

It was at half-past five the next morning that Tip put Lovejoy and Sparkey, impeded by the blanket, over the Square gardens palings. From the beginning it felt disastrous; it was raining hard; even bundled as he was, Sparkey was soaked already. "You're wet through," said Tip, worried.

"I'm wet too," said Lovejoy, but Tip took no notice of that.

Lovejoy was not popular with Tip that morning. She was never popular with Sparkey, who turned his big eyes on her with hate.

No whisper had come to Lovejoy of what had happened last night, but when she had come in Vincent had gone into the restaurant without speaking to her and Mrs. Combie had told her to go to bed in such a flat, dull way that Lovejoy thought they must have quarrelled again.

"Are you tired?" Lovejoy asked Mrs. Combie. She did not know what else to say for comfort.

"Yes, I'm tired," said Mrs. Combie. She added that the kitchen table wanted scrubbing but she did not get up and scrub it. "I'll do it," Lovejoy offered, but Mrs. Combie said, "No," and told her to go to bed. Then Mrs. Combie took down her old coat, and Lovejoy heard her open the restaurant door and say, "George, I'm going to the police."

"Tonight?" asked Vincent, coming to the door. "Wait till the morning, dear." Dear! then they haven't quarrelled, thought Lovejoy.

"I can't wait, I must know," said Mrs. Combie.

Lovejoy did not know what the trouble was—perhaps somebody's stolen something, she thought—but it filled the house and she had never been more glad to see Tip the next morning; but for Sparkey she would have snuggled against him, rubbing her head on his shoulder. In a passion of warmth and gratitude she had said, "Hello Tip," and now Tip was being unkind. "It's the last time," she told him earnestly. "I'll never bother you again."

"Don't tell lies," said Tip. He did not lift her carefully but jounced her up on top of the folded raincoat they put for a pad on the palings, as if he were glad to get rid of her. She slipped as she jumped down. "Ooh!" said Lovejoy and whimpered.

"Get on with it," said Tip.

The rain dripped off her nose as she dug; the handle of the shovel grew slimy with mud and put mud on her hands; her feet felt as if her socks and shoes were made of mud. It was cold and ugly, her misery increased, and all Sparkey did was to stand by her and sniff. "Stop it," she said sharply to Sparkey; he wiped his nose with the back of his wet hand and sniffed worse than ever; the end of his blanket trailed in the mud.

"Hurry up," hissed Tip.

"I can't. It's wet and heavy," said Lovejoy.

"Sparkey, for Pete's sake help her," said Tip impatiently.

"Lemme dig," said Sparkey.

"You can't," said Lovejoy.

"I can."

"You can't. You're only a baby."

Sparkey gave the shovel a sharp kick; it jerked up, throwing a shower of wet earth in Lovejoy's face. "It's in my eye," she screamed.

"Shh! *Shh!*" said Tip, but Lovejoy would not shh.

"He's thrown mud in my eye."

"Never mind. Get on."

"I do mind."

"Bring the bucket and I'll take it out for you," said Tip angrily. Lovejoy stood up, sobbing loudly enough for Tip to hear. Sparkey noticed that, though she was so hurt, she filled the bucket to the brim. Together they lugged it to the palings; the wet earth was very heavy and it took all their strength to lift it up. "Push, can't you?" said Lovejoy fiercely.

"I am pushing."

"Useless brat!"

" 'F you call me names I'll drop it."

"Shut up. Both of you," hissed Tip.

At last Tip's hand caught the handle and they could hoist it to the top. "Feels as if you'd got the whole blasted garden," said Tip so crossly that Lovejoy began to whimper again. "My eye hurts," she said, "my eye hurts."

"Well, come *out*," said Tip, exasperated. Lovejoy shinned up the tree that overhung the palings and began to wriggle out along the branch.

"Wait. You haven't helped me," said Sparkey.

"I can't lift you in that blanket."

"Take the blanket off. Help me," said Sparkey.

"You help yourself," said Lovejoy.

"You know I can't."

"Try," said Lovejoy lightly. Sparkey could not believe she could be so treacherous, but already she was out along the branch.

"I can't. I can't reach," said Sparkey frantically. Now he was alone in the garden all his bravado left him. "Love*joy*," he screamed.

"Jump," said Lovejoy and she dropped off the branch into the road and ran wailing to Tip.

No one can jump if he is wrapped in a blanket. Sparkey tried. He tried to get off the ground, to leap and catch the branch.

"Where's Spark?" he heard Tip say.

"Coming," said Lovejoy glibly.

Sparkey was too frightened to call; he tried to run, but he was caught, blanket and all, from behind, and a hand was clapped over his mouth.

If Lucas had known how big Tip was he would not have come round into the road but locked Sparkey in the shed and gone for Angela or the admiral. As it was, hearing Lovejoy wailing in the road, he concluded they were all small and, walking craftily on the grass, holding Sparkey under his arm, he undid the gate and came stealthily round on the outside of the pavement.

With a corner of his not very clean handkerchief, Tip was wiping out Lovejoy's eye and he had his arm round her to steady her; he was bending down so that Lucas could not see his height; Lucas saw their two heads together, and they looked small children to him; he also saw the bucket in the road. "Got the lot red-handed," he said and pulled Angela's whistle out of his pocket and blew it.

The steadiness of Tip showed at that whistle; he and Love-joy both jumped—"Out of our skins," said Lovejoy resent-

fully; it was days before she felt she was truly back in hers—
but Tip had taken almost the last grits of earth out of her
eye and he did not loose his hold. "Stand still," said Tip. "We
can run much faster than he can." He drew the last grit out,
and, "C'mon," he said, picking up the bucket. It was then he
saw that Lucas had Sparkey. "Run. Leave the bucket. Run,"
he told Lovejoy and went to meet Lucas.

At the same moment Sparkey wriggled free; while Lucas
had been carrying him, the knot where Tip had fastened the
blanket had slowly come undone, and Sparkey wriggled himself from its folds. Lucas snatched at him, but it is difficult to
find a hold on a thin small boy, slippery with rain, and
Sparkey twisted away. There was only one way to stop him
and Lucas kicked his legs. With a scream of real pain—quite
unlike Lovejoy's—Sparkey doubled up on the pavement.

It was too much for Tip. "Kick someone y'r own size y'old
b——," he shouted at Lucas.

Lucas was in a temper. The shed had been uncomfortable,
he had not slept all night, his little eyes were red, and he was
full of resentment and dislike. The new hole in his garden,
the trampled bed, drove him to fury. "Kicking's too good for
you little swine," he said. Sparkey tried to get up, and Lucas
booted him again.

Tip looked at the black boots and leather gaiters, the warm
box-cloth breeches, and at Sparkey trying to get up, rising
and falling like a hurt fledgling on the pavement. Tip's cheeks
grew red and he lowered his head and ran at Lucas; his head
hit Lucas full in his soft old stomach; Lucas gave a sound as
if a gust of air had blown out of him and, like Sparkey,
doubled up; then his knees crumpled and he sank down on
the pavement.

Is he dead? thought Tip, crouching down. As he thought
it a hand took him by the collar; he could not see whose hand
it was, but it felt authoritative; he was put smartly on his feet,

the hand still holding him, and he knew it was the police. With all the force of his lungs Tip bellowed at Sparkey and Lovejoy, "Run. Run."

Sparkey obeyed. Without looking back, hopping and limping, limping and hopping, he ran down the Square towards Motcombe Terrace, but Lovejoy would not leave the bucket. "Leave it, you little fool. Run," shouted Tip, but through all her panic and dismay she would not let it go. The bucket was too heavy for her by herself, but she lugged it along, bumping it on the pavement, her arms nearly pulled from the sockets. She heard the short blasts on another whistle; windows were pushed up in the houses, doors opened, but she kept on.

At the edge of the palings she turned to see how close the police were and knew she need not hurry. The policeman was not coming after her; still holding Tip, he was bending over Lucas, who was twisting and writhing on the pavement. Tip did that to him, knocked him down, a big man, thought Lovejoy with pride. Then round the corner came a second policeman, and a voice floated out from the steps of Number Eleven. "Constable, I am Miss Chesney of the Garden Committee. That is the gardener who is hurt. Bring him in here." Her voice was clear in the Square, high and imperious, a lady's voice—the blue-winged lady, thought Lovejoy, and shrank back against the palings. The two policemen bent to lift Lucas, though the first still kept his hold on Tip. Now's my chance, thought Lovejoy, who had to cross the road, but oddly enough she did not take the chance; she stood and looked back at Tip, left there with the policemen.

Tip. Lovejoy had a sudden feeling of his arm round her, of the way he had pressed her to him when he thought she was hurt. "Leave the earth. Go back to him," the feeling said to her. Tip. Tip! Lovejoy began to tremble; then her coolness came back. "He's caught. There's nothing you can do and you must save the earth," said the coolness, and she picked up the bucket and staggered across the road. As she reached the pavement and dumped the bucket down, there was a sound of sobbing and hobbling. It was Sparkey.

"They've got Tip," cried Sparkey, anguished. "I didn't know they'd got Tip," and he ran past her.

"Sparkey, come back," commanded Lovejoy. "Spar-key! Come back. They'll catch you too. Come back." But he went on running, still limping, and bellowing "Tip." He's doing what I wanted to do, thought Lovejoy. Half ashamed, half jealous, she hung between running back and going.

The policemen were going in at Number Eleven; one had taken Lucas, the other marched Tip, and Tip was fighting. With a sudden sinking of her selfish little stomach, Lovejoy watched. Sparkey ran full tilt into them. "Don't be silly," Lovejoy told herself and picked up the bucket again.

One person had seen her. While they were busy bringing in Lucas and the uncontrollable boy, Olivia kept out of the way; she did not like to look at the boy, the indignant way in which he fought was too genuine; she removed herself to the side of the steps and looked as far away as she could down the Square. "Olivia will never cooperate," said Angela, annoyed.

Looking away, Olivia saw a very small boy, running and hopping towards them, and, far away on the corner, a girl. She had something in a bucket and was making off with it— something heavy, thought Olivia. Was it the swag? She watched Lovejoy drag it round the corner.

"Only one of them?" Angela was saying to the policeman.

"One and a half," said the policeman as Sparkey came panting up. "But I think we've caught the one we want," said the policeman, holding Tip down in a chair.

Olivia said nothing.

CHAPTER XX

THAT journey, from the Square down Motcombe Road and Motcombe Terrace into Catford Street and to the church, was unutterably dreary. Lovejoy was soaked through, bedraggled and muddy; the bucket was so heavy that the wet rags wore and the handle hurt her hands; but all this was nothing to the desolation that filled her. She kept seeing Tip as he had been taken into that house; she seemed still to be there while her legs took her doggedly up the Street.

It had never seemed such a long way. Looking back on the times with Tip, it seemed that they had almost run with the buckets—but then he is strong, thought Lovejoy. A tear of mourning slid down her cheek.

Her breath hurt right through to her back when she carried the bucket up the church steps, and she could not lift it up onto the wall. Oh, Tip! Tip! she mourned again, pressing her head against the wall; she could not have believed she could miss anyone as much. She tried again, but the most she could do, straining and pushing and panting, was to get the rim of the bucket level with the top and tilt it so that the earth fell over the wall. If it falls with a plump, it's all right, she thought; if it falls with a shower, it's wasted; but the earth was so wet that it fell all together, making a resounding plump. It'll be there, thought Lovejoy, comforted.

Now she had to climb over with the shovel and scoop the earth up. She chanced leaving the bucket on the steps and climbed down, adding soot to the mud on her hands and knees. She had to make six journeys between the earth and the garden plot, carrying a little each time; her plimsolls were greasy, the wet marble was slippery, and twice she slipped; the second time the handle of the shovel rapped her sharply on the mouth and cut her lip. Now there was blood on her as well as mud and soot.

The earth was enough to fill the wreath pot and soon it was all ready to hold Jiminy Cricket. Lovejoy forgot the whole miserable morning, forgot Lucas, the police, Sparkey, even Tip, as she knelt down and tapped the pot and loosened the tiny rose tree; carefully she spread its roots out—they were like brown lace—stood it in the flower-wreath pot, and patted the roots down, pressing earth in among their fine threads; then she brought more and more earth in handscoops till the roots were firm and the tree standing up; with the shovel she filled the wreath pot, made the earth firm all round, and there was Jiminy Cricket blooming in the garden.

How long she knelt and looked, Lovejoy did not know; then, far over her head, from behind the houses, came the sound of the Angelus. Seven o'clock. A moment later St. Botolph's sounded it from the Square and a light snapped on here in the church; it was for the quarter-past-seven Mass.

Lovejoy glanced up at the statue; there was no light by the altar and she could see only a dim blur of blue and white but she was reminded of Tip.

What will they do to him? thought Lovejoy. Will they take him away? Will he be sent to one of those schools like Maxey? Or to prison? The skin under her hair seemed to prickle and she knew, in little, some of the fears of a wife whose husband has been arrested. Fears for him, for their name, for the home they had made together, even financial fears. They'll tell Mrs. Malone, thought Lovejoy, and quailed; all the Malones will know, the whole Street, and we haven't finished paying for the pansies. What will Mr. Driscoll do? Will he ask for them back—as Mrs. Combie was always threatening Vincent about the refrigerator? But in one thing the pansies were different from the refrigerator: Mr. Driscoll did not know where they were.

The garden was safe here, behind the church, tucked away; no one, no Driscoll or policeman, could find it. Not even Sparkey knew just where it was. No one knew. Then a thought seemed to ripple all through Lovejoy. No one, unless Tip told.

"And why shouldn't I have told?" Tip was to ask long afterwards. "I didn't, but why shouldn't I?" And he said the thought that had eaten into him all the way through that time. "Sparkey didn't run away and leave me."

"I didn't run away. I took the earth to the garden."

"All you ever think about's yourself."

"I didn't think about me, it was the garden," but for Tip it was not possible to see that. He had only made the garden for Lovejoy; though he had grown to like it, to be interested, he did not know that things were sometimes made for themselves, not for human beings.

There was no artist in Tip, and—she might have stayed with me, was all he could think or feel. That thought had filled him all the time at Number Eleven and at the station; he, a big boy, had to blink tears back from his eyes. Tears! Tip had thought, appalled; that was what girls did to you, and he said bitterly, "Girls!"

Lovejoy, in the garden, knew enough of Tip to know he would not tell lies. He never will, she thought in despair, and he'll have to say *something*. She herself was glib—but I'm not there, she thought distracted.

"Just like a girl, always wanting to interfere," Tip was to say. "Couldn't you trust me?" But Lovejoy could not.

But where'll I go? she thought. To the Square? And dare I ask? Knock and ask if Tip's there? I'm so dirty, she thought in dismay; Number Eleven seemed a very big, important house to her—and I'll have to take the bucket; I can't leave it here on the steps.

She gave a great shiver, from fright and cold; then slowly got to her feet, put out a finger and touched Jiminy Cricket, and started off across the rubble to go back.

* * *

"You needn't come," said Angela to Olivia.

In a long coat and the hat with the blue wings, the avenging-angel hat, Angela was ready to go with Lucas and the doctor to the police station. Doctor Dagleish was driving them—Olivia had thought often that it was remarkable how Angela could inveigle important people, doctors, bishops, Members of Parliament, to do small tasks for her, drive her, fetch her, collect parcels, ring up; now Doctor Dagleish, on his hospital morning, had meekly come to see Lucas; the police doctor would have done just as well, thought Olivia, but no, Angela had rung up Doctor Dagleish and he was ready to drive out of his way, to take them to the station. Angela is very, very wonderful, thought Olivia. All the same she had oppose her.

"I'm coming," said Olivia, and with unaccustomed bold-
ness she said, "I saw it all. I might have something to say
too."

"Don't be silly," said Angela. "It will only upset you."

"Yes," said Olivia.

"Then why?" Angela was tapping her foot.

"I believe I should be upset."

"I ought to have stopped her then," said Angela afterwards.
Olivia had been oddly assertive over this—"this episode,"
said Angela. In the house, while they had all been busy with
poor Lucas—when at last he got his breath he had been terribly
exhausted, but they had been able to make him swallow a little
brandy—Olivia had interrupted and asked the policeman,
"Would there be any objection to my taking these boys down
to the kitchen and giving them a hot drink?"

"A hot *drink*!" Angela had said. "After all they have done!"

"Whatever they have done they are soaking," said Olivia,
"and the little boy has a cold in the head. They must have
been out very early, and it's chilly for June. Besides, this sort
of thing is a great strain," added Olivia.

"Really, Olivia, I don't—"

"Lucas has had brandy," Olivia pointed out.

At the police station they had to wait a little—"For the
boy's father," the constable said—but at last they were shown
into a room that was so bare that it was a shock to Olivia. It
seemed to come sharply down to reality—where things are
just what they are, thought Olivia, no pretence or covering up,
stark. The waiting room had had tables and chairs, a picture
over the gas fire; there was a fireplace here, but it was swept
and empty, as was the room, with its mustard-brown walls
and high windows; there was nothing except two big old
battered desks, with a chair behind one of them, and, along
the whole side wall, a fixed bench, marked and blackened
with use—from all the people who have sat on it, thought

Olivia, been made to sit on it, lost children, pickpockets, drunks, prostitutes; now Tip and Sparkey sat there, and with them was a man, a huge man, thought Olivia.

"Sit down, please," said the constable politely. Angela looked round for chairs, but there was none except the one at the desk and the constable did not bring that forward. Olivia would have followed Lucas to the bench, but Angela stopped her with a look. "Thank you, we would rather stand," said Angela frostily.

An inspector came in; he was tall in his uniform with its row of ribbons, and bareheaded; Olivia noticed his smooth brown hair. How well groomed they are, she thought. Behind him was a younger, even bigger, policeman, who stood waiting. "What would he be?" Olivia whispered to Angela.

"He's the jailer," said Angela.

"The jailer?" Olivia shrank back.

"Don't be silly," said Angela. "He's there to do what is needed, take people into custody, control anyone who is troublesome."

"Like our boy," said Olivia and she looked apprehensive for Tip.

"People don't get brought in here for nothing," said Angela, who had seen the look. "It's serious." Olivia's heart began to beat uncomfortably.

The inspector gave her, as well as Angela, a quick look; I suppose he spends his life summing people up, thought Olivia; for some reason that did not perturb her. She sat there, listening quietly, almost from habit letting Angela handle this. Angela had already begun. "I am Miss Angela Chesney. This is Lucas, the gardener, who was hurt." She did not introduce Olivia but went on, "Now, Officer—"

"Inspector Russell," said the inspector quietly. "I'm sorry we kept you waiting. As you see, Malone's father has come now." The man with the boys stood up.

"I guessed he was a Malone," said Angela, speaking of Tip. "They wouldn't give their names," she said indignantly.

"Jack Smith, Johnny Smith, they all say that," said the inspector. "They give them fast enough when they come here." He has a real smile, thought Olivia, not one clicked on. The inspector turned to Mr. Malone. "Your wife's not back from work?"

"No, sir." Mr. Malone spoke in a thick, low, blurred voice as if he did not understand what was happening. "She does a night shift, sir."

"And the small boy's mother is away?"

"Just for the night, sir."

"He is staying with you?"

"That's right," said Mr. Malone.

The jailer motioned Tip and Sparkey to stand in front of the desk; they were dry but very, very dirty. All the bragging had gone out of Mr. Malone; he looked as big and bewildered —as an ox, thought Olivia, an ox suddenly put under a yoke, as he stood beside Tip, his cap in his hand. "Look," he said to the inspector, "couldn't we wait? The missus'll be home soon."

"These ladies have waited nearly an hour already," said the inspector. "You're the father. We must carry on." He looked at Tip and Sparkey and the constable. "Well, what is this all about?" he asked. The constable cleared his throat, but before he could speak, "We stole," said Sparkey with pride.

"We didn't steal," said Tip, red-faced.

"We stole," said Sparkey.

"We didn't," said Tip.

"My boy never stole," said Mr. Malone. "He wouldn't."

"We stole," said Sparkey firmly.

"Now wait. Wait," said the inspector and motioned to the constable to begin again.

"At five forty-five this morning," said the constable, "I was at the junction of Mortimer Street where it joins Mortimer Square—"

"It begins long, long before that!" Angela broke in. "These children . . ." and she went eloquently on.

The boys' eyes grew round with surprise as they listened to Angela. Shears? Iris plants? They began to be shocked. It looked as if the lady were telling lies; indeed, the inspector stopped her. "You mean the shears and plants disappeared?" he said. "You say the gardener caught the children taking earth. There is no evidence they took anything else."

"Evidence?" said Angela, nettled. "What evidence do you want? I think they are an organized gang of young thieves."

"Let's keep to what we can prove," said the inspector. "They took earth."

"Thirteen loads of it," said Angela.

"Thirteen?" Even the experienced Inspector Russell was amazed.

It was then that Olivia made her speech about the full marks for persistence, ending with her tribute to the bucket. Tip lifted his eyes and looked at her appreciatively.

A third policeman had come in and stood waiting by the desk. "Yes?" asked the inspector.

"There's another of them, sir. Says she belongs. A little girl."

"Does she belong?" the inspector asked Tip.

"No," said Tip.

"Yes," said Sparkey.

"She's just as wet and dirty, if that's anything to go by, sir," said the policeman.

The inspector asked Tip again, "You're sure she doesn't belong? You're sure?"

"Yes," said Tip.

"No," said Sparkey.

Then Olivia spoke. "There was a little girl. I saw her."

Tip looked at Olivia as if she were a traitor, and the inspector nodded to the policeman.

As Lovejoy came in her feet left wet marks on the floor; she might have been a bedraggled small wet sweep, except that she carried the bucket, not brushes. She had dared at last to knock at the back door at Number Eleven. "They've taken those boys to the police station," said Ellen, who had answered. "They're very naughty boys," she had added severely.

The inspector asked Lovejoy her name—"And don't say Mary Smith," but Lovejoy was too chilled and tired and alarmed to have thought of that. "Tell me your name and where you live," said the inspector.

"Lovejoy Mason. Two-hundred-and-three Catford Street." It was so small a whisper that the inspector could hardly hear.

"Did you say 'Lovejoy Mason'?"

"Yes."

He spoke in an undertone to the jailer, who went out of the room and came back with some papers. The inspector took them and nodded, then looked at Lovejoy. "I've heard of you," he said. "You live with a Mr. and Mrs. Combie?"

"Yes."

"Harris," said the inspector. It seemed odd to Olivia that a jailer could be called Harris. "Send someone down to Catford Street to see if Mrs. Combie can come."

The jailer went to the door, and the inspector told Lovejoy to sit down. "We can go on with the boys," he said to Angela, and listened while the constable finished his account. When it was over the inspector sat, thoughtfully drumming his fingers on the desk. "Let's look at the bucket," he said. Lovejoy had put it down by the desk, and he lifted it and looked at it carefully. "What made you think you weren't stealing?" he asked Tip.

"It was dirt," said Tip. His voice was husky and desperate,

and he cleared his throat loudly in an effort to explain. It was a rude sound, and Angela raised her eyebrows. "You can't steal dirt," said Tip. "It—it's—" and he remembered something he had learned about land in history lessons. "It's common," he said.

"It may be," said Angela, "but in London it's scarce and valuable." And she said again, "You can buy it at the Army and Navy Stores, two-and-six for fourteen pounds, packed in cartons."

Olivia made a sudden strangled noise, and all their eyes turned on her. Is she laughing? thought Lovejoy, shocked.

"Olivia, be quiet," said Angela. "You make me ridiculous."

"Not you, it. It's ridiculous," said Olivia.

The inspector was not laughing. He was looking at Tip.

"It looks very like stealing to me." His voice was grave. "A mean kind of stealing. The gardener said you put the smaller ones over the railings to do your work for you. That's mean, isn't it? Then you attacked an old man carrying out his duty. You winded him and kicked him."

"I didn't kick him."

"He says you did."

"He's a liar."

"He kicked Sparkey." Lovejoy had unveiled her lids and spoke straight at the inspector. "Take off your gumboot," she commanded Sparkey, "and pull down your sock. Show them." Sparkey peeled down his grey cotton sock, and on his lean little shin was a great mark. He showed it to the company and beamed, but once again Lovejoy was to know the over-riding power of grown-ups.

"Lucas kick a child!" said Angela. "Never."

"Not never. This morning," said Lovejoy.

"Never laid a hand on him," said Lucas.

"Are you sure?" asked the inspector.

"I only nabbed him," said Lucas. "Course he didn't like

that. Don't you listen to them, mister. That's a bad boy," he said vindictively, jerking his thumb at Tip.

"He's not," said Mr. Malone in a bellow.

"A young devil," said Lucas. "I've been arter him for weeks. He's a rough, bad boy."

"He isn't," cried Lovejoy, coming up like a jack-in-the-box. "You should have seen him taking the grit out of my eye," and as usual the thought of herself and Tip overwhelmed her with tears. "Its all my fault," she sobbed. "He wouldn't have been caught if I'd jumped Sparkey up, and Tip didn't put us over the railings—at least not like you said."

"Better let me be the one to go in," Tip had said the first morning. "It might be dangerous." At that time of the morning it had been only half light in the garden, night in the bushes.

"Snakes 'n tigers 'n ghosts," Sparkey had said, his teeth chattering. "There was a girl murdered in some bushes in a garden jus' like this."

"I'll go," said Tip with a reassuring pat to Lovejoy.

The plan had been to put his raincoat, folded, on the paling spikes and use it as a pad. "Suppose it gets torn?" Lovejoy had asked with the respect she gave to clothes, but as most of the Malone clothes were torn Tip did not think it mattered.

"Hold a stake with each hand," said Lovejoy, "and stand on the bucket." She turned one upside down. "Spring and kneel on the top, then you can jump down"—but Tip could not get over the railings. The Malones were big and powerful but they were not made for springing. Tip could climb, pull himself up by his arms—onto the church wall, for instance— but when Lovejoy commanded, "Jump," he could not jump; "Spring," and he could not get off the ground.

There was a pause, a long pause; then, "It will have to be me," Lovejoy had said in a little voice; her legs were as strong as a cricket's; one spring and she had been up, a second later, over, but there had been another complication. When she had filled the buckets she could not hoist them up level with the top of the railings.

" 'F I could just *get* the handle," said Tip, "I could lift them over." It was no good. She could not get them up, even with Tip pulling hard on the rope. "The rope sticks," he said. "It's the stakes. Can't you get it a little higher?"

"No," said Lovejoy, panting breathlessly.

"I'll have to put Sparkey in," said Tip.

Sparkey had been half dead with excitement and terror as Tip lifted him up and Lovejoy lifted him down; his little legs in the shining new gumboots had kicked wildly in an effort to be helpful. Frantically he helped push up the bucket; Tip managed to grasp it and haul it higher, then brought it down heavily on the other side; some of the earth spilled out, but he managed to scoop it up from the pavement with his hands. "Now the other one," he said, and, hoisting, stretching, and panting, Lovejoy and Sparkey had got it up.

"How'll you get out?" whispered Tip. "You can't get out by yourselves."

"We'll climb up that tree and drop down," said Lovejoy. "Kin Sparkey?"

"He can if I lift him." Tip had caught Sparkey as, sternly directed by Lovejoy, he dangled from the branch; and presently, light as a cricket again, or a bird, Lovejoy had dropped down beside them.

"It was all *me*," Lovejoy sobbed now, as Eve must have sobbed. "I told him what to do and he did it." She covered her face with her hands and the tears ran out between her fingers.

"What do you say to that?" the inspector asked Tip, but Tip was furious.

"I don't take orders from a girl," said Tip.

"Did he?" the inspector said suddenly to Sparkey.

"No," said Sparkey with scorn. "She wasn't in the gang. Girls can't be," he said loftily to Lovejoy.

The inspector looked thoughtfully at Sparkey. "You're too small to be in the gang, of course," he said.

Sparkey's ears went red. He looked as if he were going to cry. "I *am* in the gang, amn't I, Tip?" he asked.

"It can't be much of a gang," said Inspector Russell.

"It is!" cried Sparkey furiously. "It's the worst gang for miles." And he flung at the inspector, "Maxey Ford was in it."

"Maxey Ford." Now the inspector's face, as well as his voice, was grave. He looked at Tip. "I am sorry to hear that. You know what happened to Maxey."

"Yes," said Sparkey reverently, and he declared, in an access of loyalty, "It wasn't fair. Tip's much better at stealing than Maxey."

"Oh, shut up, Spark," said poor Tip, but Sparkey took this for modesty and went on, "Tip's *chief*; Maxey never was."

"I see," said the inspector, and he said suddenly, hardly, to Tip. "Do you always get other people to do your jobs for you?"

"I—don't," said Tip, astounded.

"He's not that kind of boy," cried Mr. Malone in anguish, and to Tip, "Oh, I wish your mum would *come*."

There was a moment's pause, then Angela's voice came, clear and imperious. "It seems quite obvious, Officer—"

"*Inspector* Russell," said the inspector.

Angela makes them angry by not thinking of them, thought Olivia. She thinks it doesn't matter, but it does.

"Inspector, then," said Angela impatiently. "It's obvious that this boy should be charged."

"But on what charge?" said the inspector.

"What charge?" said Angela. "I shall charge him with stealing the earth, of course."

"But can you?" said the inspector. "I'm not sure you can."

"Why ever not?" In Angela's astonishment the "ever"

slipped out. She isn't handling this, it's handling her, thought Olivia.

"The houses in Mortimer Square are leasehold, isn't that right?" asked the inspector.

"Yes, but what has that to do with it? Why can't I charge him?"

"I don't think you can steal earth," said the inspector, "and anyway it's not your earth," and all the faces turned to look at Angela; even the blue-winged lady, it seemed, could not have everything her own way.

"Oppose her and that's the best way to make her go on"— both Olivia and Ellen could have told them all that. "The Garden Committee's, then," said Angela more impatiently still. "Why quibble?"

"It's not even the Garden Committee's," said the inspector. "The earth belongs to the freeholders, whoever they are; I don't know much about it but I can guess that even if you started a private prosecution, on a charge like that you would end up in a good old legal tangle."

"Then I'll charge him with trespass," said Angela, but the inspector shook his head.

"Trespass isn't an offence," he said, "except on a railway."

"Well, I can charge the boy with assaulting Lucas."

"You can't," said the inspector again.

"Are you trying to be obstructive?" demanded Angela.

"I'm keeping to the law, madam," said the inspector crisply.

"Why can't I charge him with assaulting Lucas?" Angela's eyes were very blue, very frosty. She's angry, thought Olivia, but the inspector was not a Mr. Wix or a Doctor Dagleish; he was quite unperturbed. "Why can't I charge him with assaulting Lucas?"

"Only Mr. Lucas can do that," said the inspector.

"Lucas, then," said Angela, and the inspector looked at him. "Do you wish to make a charge?"

"Of course he does," said Angela.

"Miss Chesney, *will* you let him answer for himself?" And the inspector asked Lucas again, "Do you want to make this charge?"

Angela made a movement, but Lucas seemed curiously unwilling to answer. He looked at the inspector, at Angela, at his hands, and was silent.

"You heard the officer," said Angela.

"I don't want to make no trouble, be unpleasant," murmured Lucas to his boots.

"It's sometimes one's duty to be unpleasant," said Angela. "The boy hurt you, he might hurt other people."

"He never hurt *any*one," bellowed Mr. Malone to the skies.

"He hurt Lucas," said Angela. "Well, Lucas?" Another silence while Lucas fidgeted. "You are acting for the Garden Committee, remember," Angela said.

Lucas looked this way and that. How like a rat he is, thought Olivia; almost she drew her skirts aside. Angela was looking steadily at him, the cold glint still in her eyes. At last, "I'll charge him," said Lucas. It sounded like a groan.

The inspector was looking over their heads to the third policeman, who had come in again and was standing inside the door. "Mr. and Mrs. Combie are both out, sir," he said.

"Out?" Lovejoy came two steps away from the bench; in the warm room she steamed as she walked. "Out? They're never out."

"They are both out," said the policeman evenly. "They left a message on the door—for the little girl, I suppose—that they had gone to see a Mr. Montague."

"Mr. Montague?" said Lovejoy, puzzled.

The policeman went away, and the inspector turned to Tip and put the charge in words that Tip could understand. "You're charged with assaulting Mr. Lucas at approximately six o'clock this morning, the fifth of June, on the pavement of Mortimer Square. You needn't say anything if you don't want to; if you do say anything I shall take it down and tell it to the magistrates. Do you want to say anything?"

Tip stared dumbly at the inspector. "No reply," said the inspector after a moment, and he wrote that down. Then he spoke to Mr. Malone. "Will you go bail for him to appear at the Juvenile Court—let's see, it will be Chelsea Juvenile Court—next Wednesday at ten o'clock? The bail will be five pounds."

"But—I haven't got five pounds," said Mr. Malone in dismay. Olivia made a movement, but Angela caught her.

"That's all right," said the inspector to Mr. Malone. "You don't have to pay it if the boy appears. Now sign here, on the back of the charge sheet."

Breathing suspiciously, glaring at them all, with the pen held like some sort of dangerous weapon in his hand, Mr. Malone signed. Olivia noticed how the pen trembled; she did not like to see that little tremble. "Now you can take him home," said the inspector to Mr. Malone. "You too," he said to Sparkey.

"Can't I be charged?" said Sparkey. "Please. Please," he said frantically.

"You go along home," said the inspector. "In any case you're under eight."

"I'll *never* be big," wailed Sparkey in despair.

"And I must go," said Angela and gathered up her things. "Olivia, you take Lucas home," she said as she went out, but Olivia did not hear.

She was looking at Tip and Lovejoy. Mr. Malone had come to Tip and taken him by the shoulder, but Lovejoy's hand was locked in Tip's.

"Now be a good girl," said Mr. Malone. Lovejoy shook her head. He tried to prise her fingers away, but he, who seemed really as big as Olivia's ox or one of his own great dray-horses, seemed unable to loosen that small hand.

"I'll stay with him," said Lovejoy.

There was a noise outside as if a henhouse full of hens had broken loose in the police station. Mr. Malone swung round, his face happy with relief, and a second later Mrs. Malone burst into the room; as a policeman hastily caught and shut the swing door, Olivia caught a glimpse of five other Malones outside.

"Did you see the mother?" Olivia asked Angela afterwards.

"I did, and a whole tribe of Malones. I told you he was a Malone."

"Did you speak to her?"

"No. She's a real virago and I was in a hurry. Did you?"

"Yes. She called me a dirty old Judy," said Olivia. "I liked her."

"*Liked* her?"

"Yes. If I had a boy I hope I should fight for him like that."

When she had finished with Olivia, Mrs. Malone had started on Inspector Russell.

"There's no name I wouldn't put on you," she said.

The inspector nodded to the jailer, and presently he and Mr. Malone prevailed on Mrs. Malone to go. When finally she swept Tip, Mr. Malone, and Sparkey out of the room, "we were left in a sudden flat silence," said Olivia.

"Who were left?" asked Angela.

"The inspector, the little girl," said Olivia, "and I." She paused. "Then a policewoman came in."

"Lovejoy," Inspector Russell had said, "this is Woman Police Constable Mountford. She wants to talk to you."

The extreme gentleness of his voice made Lovejoy afraid. Vincent sometimes spoke to her like that when he was deeply sorry. The woman policeman made her more afraid. Last time—that time, thought Lovejoy, it was a woman policeman, asking those questions. Lovejoy could hear them still, and her own answers—baby answers, thought Lovejoy scornfully.

"Where do you live?"

"We don't live anywhere."

"You don't know where you stayed?"

"We don't stay. We can't, because of the bill. They want us to pay it so we go somewhere else."

"Somewhere else?"

"Yes. That's where we were going." That Lovejoy had been a stupid little silly, thought Lovejoy scornfully, but this Lovejoy now had the same vision of that big hole and thousands and thousands of little ant people being swept into it. "I don't want her to talk to me," said Lovejoy, looking at Woman Police Constable Mountford with horror. She looked round for Tip, but Tip had gone with his mother. His mother! thought Lovejoy and quivered.

"You're not afraid of us, are you?" said the inspector coaxingly. Lovejoy might have said, "Yes," but instead she stood glaring and breathing hard. Then, "You say it, not her," she said to Inspector Russell. He and the policewoman looked at each other. "All right, but stay," he said in an undertone.

Lovejoy darted across the room and caught Olivia's hand. "You stay too," she croaked.

"But—" Olivia was half dismayed, half touched. She was always to remember the clutch of Lovejoy's hand. "They want you alone," she said.

"Stay. Stay," begged Lovejoy.

"Perhaps it would help if you would," said the policewoman.

"I? Not my sister?" Olivia could not believe it.

"You, please," said Inspector Russell.

He beckoned Lovejoy to his desk. She advanced warily and stood in front of it. "He's going to try and make me tell," she thought and braced herself, dropping her lids, but the inspector was speaking in this same extraordinarily gentle way

"I have to talk to you," he said, "about your mother."

CHAPTER XXI

By EIGHT o'clock that evening the episode of the sparrows had been considerably overlaid in Angela's mind. For her the day had held many things: a meeting of the C. W. B.—"I've forgotten what the C. W. B. is," said Olivia; "Child Welfare Board," said Angela patiently—a luncheon party; work in the afternoon with Miss Marshall; "And I had to take a taxi to get to the lecture in time," said Angela. "You *know* what lecture, Ollie, I told you. The Contemporary Arts Society in Gower Street, of course. It's a pity you didn't come. You ought to be more interested in things." After that a publisher friend had arrived—"He came, she didn't go to him," Olivia told Ellen, marvelling again—to talk about Angela's book, *Simple Accountancy for Women;* it seemed anything but simple to Olivia, but Angela had almost finished it, and,

"I think he will do it," she said. Then she had signed her letters, changed, and had a quick dinner—quick because the Discussion Group was meeting at Number Eleven that night. "Not to discuss," said Angela, "but to lay down our programme for after the summer recess. We'll meet in the dining room, then have sandwiches and tea up here in the drawing room at half-past nine."

Olivia had spent most of the day alone. The happening— "Call it an episode if you want," she said in thought to Angela, "to me it was a happening"—was whole and extraordinarily important in her mind. After dinner her voice talking to Angela, the taste of coffee in her mouth, even her headache, seemed to be outside Olivia—on my skin, she thought—while deep, deep in her the morning's interview was still going on.

"Lovejoy, your mother has gone away for a little longer than she thought," Inspector Russell's careful voice had said. "She forgot to give Mrs. Combie an address. I wonder if there's anything you can tell us that will help us to find her quickly."

Lovejoy said nothing.

"Does she write to you when she's away?"

"She sends postcards."

"Have you any of them?"

Lovejoy put her hand in the pocket of her coat and drew out a small wad of postcards which she gave to the inspector. There were nine or ten—seaside postcards, thought Olivia. There was one of a pig with a caption, "I may be a little piguliar but I *do* like Eastbourne," some bathing-dress ones, and seaside views. They were all very dirty but Lovejoy watched them jealously as he turned them over, looking at the postmarks. "But these are two years old," he said.

"Yes," said Lovejoy and held out her hand for them.

"She hasn't written for some time?"

"No."

The inspector studied his pen. "When she was here, this time, was she any different?" he asked.

There was a pause; a thought that was evidently sharp-edged struggled to speak in Lovejoy; then, "She didn't buy me any clothes," she said in a low voice.

"Does she usually?" asked the policewoman.

"Of course," said Lovejoy as one would say, "Clothes before bread."

"Haven't you anyone she might have gone to? An aunt or uncle?" suggested the inspector. Lovejoy shook her head.

"Cousins?" asked the policewoman. "A grandmother?" Lovejoy went on shaking her head.

"No friend?" The inspector watched her narrowly. "No new friend?"

Another pause, and Lovejoy said unwillingly, "There was Uncle Francis."

"Was Uncle Francis's name—" they looked at a paper— "Colonel Baldcock?"

"Yes."

"But you called him Uncle Francis?" Lovejoy breathed disdainfully through her nose, her nostrils pinched. "Perhaps she told you to?" said the inspector.

"Yes."

"Do you know where Colonel Baldcock stayed in London?"

"No."

There was a silence; then Lovejoy had looked up and put an end to the skilful and delicate fencing. "Has Mrs. Combie been landed with me?" she asked.

Olivia put down her coffee cup with such a sudden rattle that Angela looked up and frowned.

"Angela," said Olivia suddenly, "wouldn't anything make you change your mind?"

"Change my mind about what?"

"The children. Let Lucas withdraw the charge against the boy. There is, I'm sure there is a different—complexion," said Olivia, floundering.

"Complexion? You don't mean complexion," said Angela.

"Yes, I do," said Olivia more certainly. "Something that would put a different colour and look on it."

"The charge is right," said Angela decidedly. "Tip Malone is part of a really bad gang, Olivia, and leading the others astray. You heard what the little one said."

"The little one was boasting."

"And he gave away the truth. Ollie, don't you think people as experienced as I and that inspector—Inspector—"

"His name is Inspector Russell," said Olivia. "You should remember it."

Angela disregarded that, as Olivia had known she would. "—that we know what we're doing?" finished Angela.

"I sometimes think," said Olivia, "from watching, of course, because I am not experienced, I think experience can be a— block." Again it was clumsy, but she knew what she meant.

"And why?" asked Angela, amused.

"Because if you think you know, you don't ask questions," said Olivia slowly, "or if you ask, you don't listen to the answers." Olivia had observed this often. "Everyone, every-thing, *each* thing, is different, so that it isn't safe to know. You—you have to grope."

"That would be a nice efficient way to deal with things," said Angela. She looked up again from the notes she was making. She's not even listening to me, thought Olivia. "What is it, Ellen?" asked Angela.

"There's a Father Lambert," said Ellen.

If Ellen were dubious about anyone she always said "a" before the person—"a Mr. French," "a Miss Smithers." "A Father Lambert." Ellen was rigid with disapproval. She called Catholic priests "black beetles."

"He wants to see you, Miss Angela," said Ellen as if she advised against it.

"Do you know what it's about?"

"I think it's about those children."

"If he thinks he can get at me—" said Angela.

We English, thought Olivia, always think that priests will get at us. I wonder why? That seemed to put the words in her mouth. She had not meant to take the Father's part against Ellen and Angela but she said, "You sound as if you were afraid."

Ellen frowned at Olivia. "Now I suppose you'll see him," she said to Angela.

"Why you should think I'm afraid I can't imagine," said Angela. "Ask him to come up, Ellen."

If Ellen called Catholic priests "black beetles," Angela treated this one as an unpleasant species. She asked Father Lambert to sit down, but she did not introduce him to Olivia. "I am Miss Angela Chesney," she said distantly. "You wanted to see me?"

"Yes," said Father Lambert, "about a parishioner of mine, a young Irishman, Tip Malone."

"I warn you, we're not feeling whimsical about him," said Angela.

"I wasn't being whimsical," said Father Lambert quietly. "That boy always seems to me like a young man."

"If he is manly," said Angela, "it's all the more important that he should be taught the difference between right and wrong. I feel you have come here to make some sort of an appeal. It has been decided that the boy ought to be prosecuted. I must tell you that nothing you can say will make me change my mind."

Father Lambert looked at the carpet for a moment. Then he said, "The boy's mother came to me straight from the police. It's a terrible disgrace for her and Tip, Miss Chesney."

"She looked to me as if disgrace would not mean much to her."

"You're wrong," said Father Lambert. He went on, "I have been busy investigating since, and I think I know the whole story now."

"So do we," said Angela.

"But we don't!" Olivia burst in, "and we *must*."

"Olivia, *please*," said Angela, and she whispered sharply, "Don't hold your heart like that. It looks ridiculous."

"There was talk about some tools being lost," said Father Lambert after a moment.

"Stolen," said Angela.

"The children have tools," said Father Lambert, "an old hand fork and a broken shovel. They found the shovel in the Malones' yard; the girl bought the fork at Dwight's; that's our junk shop in the High. You wouldn't know it, but most of us do a good deal of buying and selling there. She did buy the fork." His face relaxed into a smile. "She bought it with money she stole from one of our candle boxes."

"So she's a thief, too," said Angela. "I'm not surprised."

"She's a redeemed thief," said Father Lambert. "Tip made her put the money back."

"That's what he says."

"It's what I say." He was stern, then again that look of— tenderness? thought Olivia. "I watched it," he said.

"And didn't interfere?"

"Why should I? Tip had it in hand." Angela sniffed but Father Lambert went on. "Mr. Dwight also has a pair of shears; they were sold to him by a man called Lucas."

"Lucas!" Olivia sat up in her chair.

"I don't believe it," said Angela.

"We have Mr. Dwight's statement, and that of Lucas himself when he was taxed with it."

"It's impossible," said Angela.

"I'm afraid startling things are not impossible, Miss Chesney."

"I'm not startled," said Olivia in a loud voice. "I never did like Lucas."

"Olivia, please be quiet."

"I don't know about the iris plants—" Father Lambert began again.

"Lucas probably only bought half and kept the money," said Olivia.

"Olivia!" Olivia could see that Angela was very angry—not because Lucas stole, thought Olivia, but because she knows now that she was wrong. "We will deal with Lucas," said Angela.

"I'm afraid you won't be allowed to, Miss Chesney. You have made this into a police case and—"

"Are you trying to blackmail me?"

"I'm not even trying to trade." Father Lambert's voice was still good-humoured. "I only want—"

Angela cut across him. "What you tell me makes no difference to the boy's case. He is charged with hurting Lucas. What Lucas has done, or not done"—she's being deliberately insulting, thought Olivia—"doesn't alter that," said Angela. "It's not our main complaint, I know that, but it's the only way of punishing the stealing of our earth. That wasn't a little theft, Father Lambert. They took thirteen loads—".

"Buckets," said Olivia. "Buckets, but of course, those are child loads."

"They stole them," said Angela, ignoring Olivia.

"There are degrees of stealing," said Father Lambert. "To make a complete crime there must be intention, or knowledge, that it was wrong. Tip thought the earth, the actual earth, was free."

"Then why was it fenced?"

"That's what I've always wondered," said Olivia. "In the

country, where there is plenty, perhaps one can fence, but not here, in London, where there's so little. It should be open."

"Don't be silly," said Angela. "It's the other way round."

"Yes," said Olivia, "and that is wrong. It's not"—and she groped for the word—"not just. It's grasping and horrid." A strange rage flared up in her. "Tell him they should have bought it at the Army and Navy Stores," she flung at Angela and turned to the window; her shoulders were shaking.

"Tip knew they were trespassing," said Father Lambert after a moment, "but he did not mean to steal."

"He did not mean to steal our earth," said Angela bitingly. "But he knew he could get money for it, which was what he probably did."

"It's dry outside now and a fine evening after the rain," said Father Lambert. "Would you come with me? I won't keep you very long, but there is something I think you ought to see. Will you come?" He added, "Please."

"The case will come into court," said Angela. "Anything you want to show can be produced then."

Father Lambert smiled. "I couldn't produce this in court."

"Then I fail to see—"

"If you would only look!" For the first time he showed a hint of impatience.

"I am very busy this evening," said Angela. "In fact"—she looked at her watch—"in exactly ten minutes we have people coming here."

"Then you won't come?" said Father Lambert.

"I'm sorry, I can't." She went to the door and held it open, but the Father was looking at Olivia—"As if I were an identity," said Olivia afterwards, but that was not the right word.

"You mean entity," said Angela. "Isn't everyone that?" but Olivia shook her head. Up to that moment, or the moment that Lovejoy had taken her hand, she, Olivia, had been a shadow.

"You won't come?" said Father Lambert to Angela. He sounded disappointed but not disappointed as much for himself as for Angela. "You won't come?"—as if he were giving her another chance; then he looked directly at Olivia and said, "Will you?"

"Yes," said Olivia breathlessly.

*   *   *

"You're not going to walk through the Square in daylight with one of *those*!" said Ellen.

"I am," said Olivia. "I must." She sounded sure and secure but she did not feel it. Her hands shook as she put on her coat and took a scarf and her gloves.

"You are making a mountain out of a molehill," said Angela.

Olivia was suddenly inspired to answer, "A molehill can be a mountain to a sparrow," and went to join Father Lambert in the hall.

*   *   *

There was a burr of conversation in the drawing room when Olivia came in. "You mean a buzz, surely," Angela would have said, but no, Olivia meant a burr; something hard and difficult to break into, she thought. She burst in upon it. "Oh, Angela! Something after our own hearts!" she cried.

Nobody heard her. The Discussion Group was relaxing, which meant, as Olivia had often found, that they all talked together instead of separately, making a great deal of noise; Ellen, not long ago, had brought sandwiches and tea in. This light, brittle talk was more dashing to Olivia than the serious discussion would have been. Why? Because to interrupt that would have been more momentous, thought Olivia.

"Another cup, David?"

"Angela dear, these wonderful sandwiches! What *do* you put in them?"

This near the table, and, all round, fragments of talk drift-ing, floating, thrown, shreds and scraps—like confetti, thought Olivia, confused, but not like confetti, more like the rice they throw with it, hard and pelting.

"The convertibility of the pound depends . . ."

"She shouldn't have *written* it . . ."

"In the second act, when that red dress . . ."

". . . nepotism of the *worst* degree . . ."

". . . it's elementary psychology, my dear Lionel. The sim-plest reflex . . ."

And Angela, her golden head bent above the teapot, called out gaily, "Don't let Bernard start on reflexes, or we shall *not* get back to the discussion," and then to Miss Monkton, "Fresh salmon paste, a recipe of my mother's."

"*Tay* salmon. I knew it! I remember at Upton-on-Sev-ern . . ."

"Angela, something after our own hearts," cried Olivia again. It had lost its force, but to Angela it sounded far too loud. For a moment she had thought it was Miss Monkton still speaking; then she saw it was Olivia, Olivia with her dark face flushed, her hair untidy—in great wisps, thought Angela—her coat smudged with dirt—when Father Lambert had unlocked the churchyard door they had clambered over the rubble. Olivia's eyes were lit up, shining—blazing, thought Angela. "You needn't prosecute," cried Olivia, waving her gloves. "They haven't done anything wrong. They didn't sell the earth. They used it for a garden." And she cried, "Angela, wait till I tell you about the garden!"

"Olivia dear, we are in the middle of a meeting."

But Olivia blundered on; the people, the meeting, did not seem to her important, only the need to reach Angela. "A little garden almost in a church," she said, and her harsh voice was soft and full of respect. "Father Lambert watched them making it; they didn't know that he watched; it's made in the rubble that nobody wanted, where nobody saw. It's careful and—innocent," said Olivia, pleased to find the right word. "Innocent," she repeated, her eyes on Angela.

"If you bend down, about the height of a child, and look, then you can see what it is," Father Lambert had said of the garden. Olivia wanted to make Angela bend down to that. She tried. "There are paths, of marble chips," she said, "and edgings of stone, and a lawn of mustard and cress; they had a wreath-case for a flowerpot, and a little column with ivy growing up it, truly beautiful, and beds of pansies, blooming!" said Olivia. "And there, in those beds, is our earth."

Angela was making stabs with a small silver knife at the sandwich on her plate. Olivia, watching her, knew that a struggle was going on in Angela. She's going to give up, thought Olivia, give up her own way, give in, and she felt a surge of love for her sister; but someone gave a titter, quickly and politely suppressed, but a titter. Well, I suppose I am comic, thought Olivia; she was astonishingly unperturbed about it; she did not suffer her customary blushing or flinching, but Angela stiffened as if she were stung. She laid the knife down, and, "At least she admits it's our earth," said Angela humorously.

"Don't joke," said Olivia. It sounded like an injunction.

"Then don't talk as if this were a miracle," snapped Angela.

"It is, in that place, out of those children."

"Nonsense, all little guttersnipes make mudpies," said Angela. "Another cup of tea, Miss Monkton?"

For a moment Olivia stood where she was; her heart had begun its uncomfortable bumping, but she hardly noticed it; her hand holding the gloves she had waved so triumphantly tightened so that the knuckles were white; then she went out and closed the door.

She heard bursts of laughter from the drawing room. They're laughing at me, thought Olivia. Fools. It was the first time she had called anyone a fool but herself. Her heart was bumping so that she had to lean against the landing panelling and close her eyes, holding her hands to her breast. In a moment she knew the pain would come, and she stayed there, trying to will her heart to be quiet, shrinking from the pain. Then it swept over her so that she almost groaned. It's different, thought Olivia. It's worse. I wish Ellen would come, and, as it stabbed again, she did groan, "Ellen. Somebody. Please."

Somebody came out of the drawing room and closed the door behind him. Olivia immediately stood up. It was Mr. Wix. He's going to soothe me down, she thought. She was right. "Olivia dear," he said gently and earnestly, "you mustn't be so unhappy." He had come close to her; he could not bend over her, she was too tall for that, but he bent his head a little so that she could see how the light caught the burnish of his well-kept dark hair and shone on his good brow, his black silk vest. Angela often said, "He seems such a boy to be a rector!"—but boys shouldn't interfere with older people, thought Olivia disagreeably, and she scowled at Mr. Wix.

"You know," he was saying with an attractive cameraderie, "Angela's right. If you were accustomed to these cases you would know this was only one of a hundred."

"There is no case like it," said Olivia. The fight against the pain made her sound even more blunt and rude than usual.

"Of course I haven't seen the garden—"

"Then you don't know what you're talking about," said Olivia.

"You are taking this far too much to heart—"

"Isn't that where we should take it?" And mine hurts, hurts, thought Olivia, wishing that Ellen would come. Oh go *away*, she wanted to say to Mr. Wix.

Then, remembering the children, she summoned herself. It might help if he could understand. "Mr. Wix—"

"Call me David."

"David, Wix, what does it matter? What matters is that that garden is what I said, innocent."

"Then it will be proved so. We haven't to judge."

"Angela has judged all along."

"That's not fair," said Mr. Wix. He must have seen that Olivia looked ill because he began trying to soothe her again. "We must trust," he said. "It's not old-fashioned to say God is good. Remember, not one sparrow can fall to the ground—"

"But they fall all the time," said Olivia. "We knock them down. We knock them, crush them—carelessly or carefully, it doesn't matter which, and they fall. That's what humans do to humans, so don't talk to me about God." There was a pause; Mr. Wix was silent. Then Olivia spoke and she was not talking to Mr. Wix but to herself, and her voice was not loud but uncertain. "Wait," she said. "Humans to humans?" And, as if she had just found out something, she asked, "Is that how it works? Someone, one person at least, is meant to see the fall and care?" She was always to remember that moment, standing in the hall with Mr. Wix, with the pain stabbing her. "See and become the instrument. I have seen. I wish I hadn't," she said loudly, "but I have and I shall keep my eyes open, in spite of you."

"In spite of us? Isn't that a little unkind?" he asked. The accustomed easiness of his voice was as insulting to Olivia as Angela's banter. She was suddenly so angry that she trembled from head to foot and felt sick. The hall and stairs seemed to sway in as if they would fall on her; the pain went through her as she had known it presently must do, but she had the last say. "In spite of you," said Olivia firmly, and fainted.

*   *   *

"Why wasn't I sent for before?" asked Doctor Wychcliffe. Olivia had refused to have Angela's pet doctor, Doctor

Dagleish. "This is something I want of my own," she had said. She had come round before Doctor Dagleish arrived, and sent him away. "He would talk me over with Angela and I won't be talked over," she told Ellen, and sent her to telephone the old doctor who had known them as children. "I'm the eldest," she told Doctor Wychcliffe as she might have told him then. "I want you to tell me what it is. Me, not Angela."

"But you must have had this condition for years," grumbled Doctor Wychcliffe.

"By condition you mean illness, don't you?" said Olivia. "You can tell me, I'm not afraid." Nor was she, but when he had finished—Angela called him a blunt old man, but to Olivia his bluntness was truthful and not unkind—she lay still.

"I should like," she said at last, and politely as if she were speaking of some everyday thing, "I should like it if you could arrange, as much as you can, of course, to help me to go on a little longer. I have a reason," said Olivia, and it seemed to her as if she never had one before, "a reason for not wanting to die just now."

CHAPTER XXII

"Can I see Tip?"

"Holy Biddy, is that *you* again?" shouted Mrs. Malone.

"*Please* can I see Tip?" But Mrs. Malone blocked the door.

"You're not going to see Tip any more," she said. "Put that on your needles and knit it."

"But—"

"Haven't you done enough?" demanded Mrs. Malone. The Wednesday after the catching, as Mrs. Malone called it, they had had to take Tip to the Juvenile Court. To her dying day Mrs. Malone would remember the cut of that disgrace, but, "It's five pounds if we don't, Mary," Mr. Malone had said. Not that much happened. "We have considered all the circumstances," the chairman had said to Tip, "and we are not going to put you on probation; but you must realize that everything we have heard today has been written down in this court, and if you get into trouble again you will not be let off so easily."

"It was written down against him," said Mrs. Malone, trembling, "and for what? For you!" she said to Lovejoy.

For more than two weeks Tip had been kept away from Lovejoy. He was guarded on his way to school and back by a posse of Malones. In the evenings Mr. Malone kept him in, and on Saturdays he was escorted to Sid, and Sid was under contract to bring him back; as for Sundays, he was sent right away to Mrs. Malone's aunt in Streatham.

Lovejoy hung about the corners and spent long hours in the garden, waiting. She had even courted Sparkey to see if he had a message, but Sparkey's mother pounced on her and drove her away. If the Malone girls found her they set upon her. Lovejoy had a black eye from Bridgie Malone—not really black, thought Lovejoy, purple and olive green, but very unsightly. Still, she would have borne even more than that to catch a glimpse of Tip.

"Please can I see Tip?"

"I told you, no."

"*Please.*"

"No."

Then one day Lovejoy came, desperate, to the Malones' basement door. "Please, Mrs. Malone. They're going to send me away."

It is amazing how hard people can be when they have to protect someone else. Mrs. Malone was big and warm-hearted, but, "Good riddance to bad rubbish," said Mrs. Malone and shut the door.

Lovejoy had thought she knew what it was like to be shut out; she had been alone when she was lost, alone lying waiting for her mother in bed, and sitting on the stairs while the gentlemen were in the room; she had learned to manage without her mother, for a long time now she had "counted her out," thought Lovejoy, but there had always been some-one—Vincent, Mrs. Combie, then Tip. Tip! Lovejoy twisted her hands together as she looked at the closed door, gave a strangled little gulp, and fled down the Street.

Like Tip, Lovejoy had to appear in the Juvenile Court— "But not once, twice," said Lovejoy. The second time the chairman had come straight to the point.

"This is a very sad thing that has happened to you," he said, "but it has happened. Now we have to find someone kind and careful who will look after you."

"I can look after myself," said Lovejoy.

"Not at eleven years old," said the chairman gently. "Tell us, is there anyone to whom you would like to go?"

"I'll stay with Mrs. Combie," said Lovejoy.

"I can't do it," said Mrs. Combie. She had been sitting just behind Lovejoy; now she started to her feet and came to the table, the table that was covered with all those papers. Lovejoy had been frightened by the papers, the school report, the doc-tor's report, and the mysterious things that were written about her in Miss Dolben the Probation Officer's report. "They knew all about me," Tip was to say proudly; it did not make Lovejoy feel proud; she felt as if she were suddenly made public and she quailed.

"I couldn't do it, sir, madam, sir," said Mrs. Combie, look-ing from one magistrate to the other. "Not with Lovejoy, not whatever they pay." She spoke so quickly it was difficult to hear. "I don't mind for a little while till things are settled, but I couldn't take the responsibility. It's not that she's not a good child, sir," said Mrs. Combie, coming back to the chairman. "She is, but she has *ideas*." Mrs. Combie spoke as if that were a disease.

"She seems a sensible little girl," said the chairman. "She knows that things have changed."

"Still, I couldn't," said Mrs. Combie again.

The chairman picked up the typed sheets Miss Dolben had put down, and looked inquiringly at her. "Mrs. Combie has difficulties of her own at home," said Miss Dolben.

"Yes," said Mrs. Combie, breathing loudly. "Why should I take Lovejoy?" she asked. "Just because I let the room? Why me more than anybody else?"

"I know it's not your responsibility," said the chairman soothingly. "It's only that she had become fond of you."

"Because she doesn't want to go into a home," said Mrs. Combie.

Lovejoy did not want to go into a home. "They'll make you wear uniform there," Cassie had said.

"The children at the Compassion Home don't wear uniform," said Lovejoy, but the thought of walking two by two in a crocodile as she had seen them in the Street made her feel sick.

Now as Lovejoy stood in front of the bench, though Mrs. Combie was sitting down again behind her, she knew there was no one. She did not count Miss Dolben, in the tweed coat and skirt, with the red veins on her nose, though Miss Dolben was taking a great interest in her. "She's kind," Lovejoy told Vincent, "only you don't want to look at her very much." There were plenty of pretty probation officers, and Lovejoy, looking at the row of them at their desks, thought, I wish I had a pretty one. She said that afterwards to Mrs. Combie. "You think too much what people look like," said Mrs. Combie for the hundredth time, but Lovejoy could not help it; she had condemned Miss Dolben's coat and skirt the first time she saw it, and averted her eyes from the veins, though there she had tried to help Miss Dolben. "There's a clinic you can go to for that nose," she had told her.

"You're a rude, ungrateful little girl," Cassie had said.

"Isn't there anyone else?" the chairman asked Lovejoy.

"Yes, Mrs. Combie." She went on saying it while the magistrates told her to stand back a little so that they could confer together. Lovejoy stood back, but, straining her ears, she could still hear.

"Miss Angela Chesney, who was concerned in the case about the boy, is on the Committee of the Home of Compassion," she heard the chairman say. "She has told Miss Dolben she could get the child in there. There's a vacancy, and Miss Dolben thinks that a good idea—isn't that so, Miss Dolben?"

Miss Dolben came up to the table. "It wouldn't mean going right away," said Miss Dolben, "and Lovejoy could keep on at the same school, which she likes. Now I have the supervision order, I could visit her there and . . ."

So it was settled while Lovejoy stood in the middle of the court with all the heads bent round her; all the people were busily writing or looking at their watches—or their nails, thought Lovejoy, her eyes on the head of a woman policeman who was quietly buffing hers. Then Miss Dolben and Mrs. Combie and Lovejoy went outside and Miss Dolben got some money and gave it to Mrs. Combie for Lovejoy's keep—"Pending," said Miss Dolben, and Mrs. Combie took Lovejoy away.

"What's 'pending'?" Lovejoy asked Vincent in an effort to read her fate.

"Waiting till it, the thing you're waiting for, happens," said Vincent.

"Then it's going to happen?" asked Lovejoy.

"It must," said Vincent, white-faced. Lovejoy looked at him; he was not talking of her but of himself.

They had come and taken away the refrigerator, before even the first instalment was paid. "Mrs. Combie asked them to," said Vincent, but he was not angry. The restaurant kept open, but Vincent did not go to Mortimer Street any longer; he bought a few things in the High—not even Driscoll's, noticed Lovejoy—and carried them home in a netted bag.

There was only one vase of flowers in the restaurant and only little meals were cooked, for one or two of the flats people perhaps, or for Mr. Manley.

At night, when Vincent stayed late in the restaurant, he did not open his books or write menus; he sat at his desk, his chin on his hands. "What is he doing?" asked Mrs. Combie. Lovejoy knew what he was doing, waiting—"Pending," said Lovejoy.

She made one more attempt on Mrs. Combie. It was in the kitchen, when Mrs. Combie was sitting at the table having one of her cups of tea; tea was the only thing that kept her alive, Mrs. Combie said. Lovejoy came and stood by her, holding the edge of the table. "I'd work for you," said Lovejoy hoarsely. "Even when I'm grown up. I'd work and give you all the money."

"Shouldn't we think of the story of the good Samaritan?" Mrs. Combie had asked Cassie, and Cassie had said, "In the story of the good Samaritan Lovejoy would have been the thief." Mrs. Combie stirred her tea and looked firmly at the tablecloth, but in spite of Cassie a great lump came in her throat.

"Please keep me," said Lovejoy.

"We can't even keep ourselves," said Mrs. Combie incoherently and she burst into tears.

Lovejoy did not know how long this fortnight was, but it might have been twenty years. It went quickly and yet the days were long; they seemed all daylight, white and mercilessly bright. It was a hot spell and cruel as all hot spells were in the Street. The house bricks and the paving stones baked in the sun, and when the babies were put out to sleep in their perambulators they cried because the heat from the pavements burned their tender skins. The road smelled of hot tar and from the open windows, open as wide as they could go, as if the rooms were gasping for air, came a stale smell of dirt and sweat and old gas and refuse from the dustbins that smelled strong; the Street was extraordinarily noisy too, because with the open windows all the radios could be heard from top to bottom of the houses. The whole Street seemed more crowded and more hopeless. The mothers let the children do as they pleased—except Tip, thought Lovejoy bitterly—but the children were too listless to do much; only if the municipal water cart came by they rushed out to get under the sprinklers. The ones at school did better; they went to the swimming bath and would come chattering along the pavement, refreshed, with their bathing suits rolled in their towels.

On the stalls there was a smell of rotting fruit and the fish, or the horsemeat for the cats went bad before Mrs. Cleary or Miss Arnot could cook it; Istanbul had a touch of heat eczema and the children were warned not to touch him. Everyone boiled the milk as soon as it came, but it still soured, and everyone had swollen, aching feet. Mrs. Combie could hardly get on her comfortable felt slippers. "Rest your feet, Ettie," Vincent would say. "What's the use of working now?" But Mrs. Combie could not stop working. Lovejoy had foot trouble too; she had come through her plimsolls and her small toes showed through the fray; she had tried to go barefoot, but the heat hurt the soles of her feet. In the bomb-ruins, among the weeds, the earth showed great dry cracks. Everything was cracking apart. "I need Tip badly," said Lovejoy. "I can't water the garden." She had to fill a jar at a time, hide the cider bottle, climb down and empty the jar, place it in position again, climb up, unearth the cider bottle, and pour enough for another jar. She went up and down, backwards and forwards, till she ached, but she only managed to keep the pansies moist—"and Jiminy Cricket, of course, Jiminy Cricket is *first*," said Lovejoy; the mustard and cress was turning brown. It would have done this in any case, its crop was over, but Lovejoy did not know that; she thought it was the heat and the

dryness, and the absence of Tip. The absence of Tip went
on and on.

Twice she had a sign of him; on each Monday morning
Lovejoy found a piece of cotton hanging over the wall and,
tied to it, an old envelope in which was half a crown. On the
envelope was written, *From Tip.* Tip dropped them over on
Sundays when he went to Mass; on Sundays, of course, Lovejoy had no chance of getting over the wall, but when she
went on Monday the half-crown was there. I can do that
anyhow, Tip had thought. Lovejoy did not know it but he
had been fighting many battles for her.

The rumour had run round the Street that Lovejoy's mother
had gone to Australia, Canada, Africa, and no one could get
her back. "Mum, couldn't we have one more child?" asked
Tip.

For a moment Mrs. Malone thought he meant one more
after Terry, the youngest Malone, who was crawling in the
area gutter; then she knew he meant Lovejoy.

"No thank you," said Mrs. Malone promptly.

"Mum, I wish you would. I'd work for her. I'd keep on
with Sid and give you the half-crown. When I leave school
I can work all day. I'll give you every penny."

"Now listen, Tip Malone. That's not a good child, or a
nice child . . ." But Tip was deaf. In a way that was mysterious, Lovejoy seemed to be more important to him than his
family, which was staggering because, to the Malones, the
Malones were the whole world.

"He didn't want to like me but he did," Lovejoy told Father
Lambert.

"That's the best way to be liked," said the Father.

Lovejoy had Father Lambert's permission now to go in and
out over the wall, and he often stopped her and spoke.

"Tip asked me about you," he said. "He sent you his love."

"If he was seventeen or eighteen I'd say he was *in* love,"

Mrs. Malone told Father Lambert. "I can't get her out of his head."

"She'll cry, Mum," said Tip.

"Well, what if she does?" said Mrs. Malone. As she had divined, Tip was feeling a pang that was far older than himself, and he turned away from her and buried his head against the roller towel on the back door. "The soles are coming clean off my feet with worry," said Mrs. Malone.

"I wonder," said Father Lambert, "if you and his father wouldn't consider accepting the admiral's offer?"

When Tip had come up in court it had had another consequence for him. His case had been defended—Mrs. Malone had seen to that—and Angela, who had pressed the admiral into going with her to the court, had been called as a witness. As they sat waiting in a room outside the court, the admiral had had a chance to look at Tip. "He seems a manly, open boy," he said.

"He's a little liar," said Angela.

The admiral did not answer. He went on studying Tip.

As the long, slow morning dragged on—"The time one has to wait!" said Angela—the admiral got up to stretch his legs in the passage outside, and, while he was there, Tip and another boy came back from the lavatory. " 'S nothing to be afraid of," the boy was saying. He was whispering because of the policeman in the passage, but the admiral had sharp ears. "You stuff 'em up," said the boy. "I don't know what you done but tell 'em you seen it on the pictures. They'll let you off."

"They'll have to," said Tip, and he said it aloud, policeman or no policeman. "I done nothing."

When they came back into the waiting room the admiral had gone across to speak to the Malones. "Isn't there anything you would like to do?" he had asked Tip. "Learn a trade, be useful, instead of getting into trouble like this?"

"I'm goin' into the Navy," growled Tip.

"Ever since he saw the St. Vincent boys at the Tattoo," said Mrs. Malone, "he's lived and dreamed the Navy, sir."

"The Navy, heh?" The admiral was pleased. He thought for a moment and then asked, "Got his name down anywhere?" Mrs. Malone looked blank. "Is he a bright boy?" the admiral went on. "Good at lessons?"

"They've got his school report in there," said Mrs. Malone bitterly. "There's nothing they didn't poke their noses into."

The admiral spoke to the probation officer who took Tip's case, and after the hearing the officer spoke to Mr. and Mrs. Malone. "If you would like it," he said, "Admiral Sir Peter Percy-Latham has offered to nominate your boy for the *Arethusa*, the training ship. They might not accept him, of course, but on his school records and the admiral's recommendation . . ."

"But he seems such a small boy, Father," said Mrs. Malone now.

"He isn't," said Father Lambert, "and"—he smiled—"one could say this business has aged him. The usual age is thirteen. The admiral would recommend it, and I could get Mr. Whittacker Adams—the gentleman on the trust—to speak a word."

"The rich young gentleman?" The Street knew all about Charles and Liz.

It was a few days later that Mrs. Malone said to Tip, "Dad's taking you for an interview for the *Arethusa* next Friday."

"The *Arethusa*? The *Arethusa* training *ship*?" For a moment Tip was quiet and rigid; then, "I'll go," said Tip, "if I can tell Lovejoy."

"You'll *go*?" Mrs. Malone was so astonished that her voice shrilled through the whole house. "Glory defend me, isn't that what you've been aching and fighting for all this time?" ("I thought he'd whoop and rush all over the house," she told

Father Lambert, "or give me a hug at least.") "Of course you'll go, my young gentleman," she said.

"If you'll let me tell Lovejoy," said Tip.

In the end Mrs. Malone knew she was beaten. "But you'll only see her for half an hour," said Mrs. Malone, "and you're to have Father Lambert with you." As if Lovejoy were a small incarnation of the fiend she added, "I'll ask Father Lambert to stay with you and she's to have a grown-up too."

"But I haven't got a grown-up," said Lovejoy when Bridgie brought the message.

It was no good asking Mrs. Combie and Vincent anything these days; they looked at Lovejoy with strange, abstracted eyes and did not pay attention. Cassie, of course, was unthinkable; Mr. Isbister would not have moved. Kind Miss Dolben would certainly have come, but, "I couldn't tell her about Tip or the garden," said Lovejoy, shrinking. She had to say, "I haven't got a grown-up."

"Then you can't come," said Bridgie smartly. "I'll tell Tip."

"I'll come," said Lovejoy. "I'll get one." It was a blind promise. She did not know how she could.

There was one grown-up, just one, whom she would not have minded asking to take her to Tip and the garden. I wouldn't mind her seeing it, I'd even show her, thought Lovejoy, and that grown-up was the ugly dark lady, Olivia, in the Square. Could I ask her? Would I dare? thought Lovejoy. What about the one with the blue wings, the Angela one? That one would be angry, Lovejoy knew that, but she also knew that if she did not dare to ask Olivia she would not see Tip.

Olivia had been up and dressed for five days—but still going between a chair and her bed, still finding the stairs a struggle; "You don't try, Olivia," said Angela—when Angela brought her a note. "Someone pushed it through the letter box," said Angela. "It must have been a dirty someone; it's got finger-marks on it." Lovejoy had been careful to keep it clean, but Bridgie had delivered it.

It was addressed to Miss Olivia, Number Eleven, The Square. Lovejoy had taken a long time to write it; she had asked Vincent about the spelling, but, as the letter showed, he had not always been listening.

Olivia read it twice and passed it to Angela.

"She's asking you to act as a go-between," said Angela, amused.

"Yes," said Olivia.

"Abominable sauce."

Olivia was so pleased that she was silent. She, Olivia, had been asked, actually asked, to join in something by a child—something very real, thought Olivia; it was to her as wonderful as when Lovejoy had put out her hand. "It seems to me a compliment," she said shakily.

"But you'll say you're not strong enough," said Angela, and with a patient sigh she said, "I suppose I could fit it in, though I have a terribly busy day. All right, I'll go."

"*You* are not asked," said Olivia.

*   *   *

From the moment she stepped into the restaurant Olivia knew something was wrong. "It will be a horrid dingy place," Ellen had said. "Let me come with you," but, "Dingy!" said Olivia and she was standing—as Charles and Liz had done—looking round her in surprise and pleasure, when a little pale man rose from a desk and held up his hand. "Please don't," he said. "Don't look at it."

Olivia obediently tried to detach her eyes from the warm brown and apricot colours, the snow-clean linen, the glass; to ignore the scent of flowers and fruit—there were roses in a vase, a dish of peaches. Vincent had promised to stop buying but while the restaurant was still there he bought a little. The roses are the day before yesterday's, he could have told Olivia. There are only four peaches. Still, they were something. "Let's at least go down with our colours flying," Vincent had said. Olivia's response, even while he stopped it, was balm, until, "Are you Mr. Combie?" she asked.

"Yes." He said it so fiercely that Olivia blushed. She was still weak and though she had come in a taxi her heart was beating painfully. She asked if she could sit down.

Vincent—and surely he is Vincent, thought Olivia—looked at her and brought her a glass of wine. "You must let me pay for it," she said timidly.

"You needn't, it isn't mine," said Vincent.

Mr. Dwight had come to the restaurant. He had brought a boy with him, and the boy spent the day pasting pink labels on the furniture, on the tables and chairs, the big plated dish-cover, the hat stand, the mahogany desk, on everything; the labels had numbers printed on them.

"Why?" asked Lovejoy.

"The furniture's going to be sold," said Vincent. Lovejoy stood still. "Has it pended?" she asked.

"Yes," said Vincent. He put a notice in the window, CLOSED, and carried in the bay trees, and Mr. Dwight's boys put two labels on the tubs.

"This is the last dinner we can serve for you, sir," Vincent had said to Mr. Manley two nights before.

"Gone bust?" said Mr. Manley. "I'm not surprised. It was a good effort all the same," he said. He looked squarely at Vincent, and if Vincent had looked back he would have seen that Mr. Manley's eyes were very friendly. He's kind and good, Lovejoy could have told him. Look what he did about the pansies.

"George," said Mrs. Combie, "don't you think we ought to serve Mr. Manley's dessert on one of the Angelica plates?"

"On a *Kauffman* plate? Are you mad, Ettie?"

Mr. Manley called Vincent over to him before he left. "I need an under-steward for my house down in the country," said Mr. Manley. "I say steward because there are valuable things there of which he would have to help take care. If it would interest you, come and see me. I should want you to cook for me occasionally when I'm down, and there would be a place for your wife with the cleaning. Think it over," said Mr. Manley.

Vincent did not need to think it over. When Mr. Manley said "under-steward" Vincent had heard only the "under." "Surely 'steward' gave you an inkling," said Mr. Edwards at the bank afterwards, but Vincent had had no inkling at all.

"Imagine," he had said to Mrs. Combie, "*imagine* waiting on Mr. Manley every night," and, "No thank you," said Vincent in answer to Mr. Manley. "It's kind of you, sir, but I couldn't do that."

"The house is Greatorex," said Mr. Edwards. Mr. Edwards had no reason to think well of Vincent and he enjoyed being a little unkind.

"*Greatorex!*" said Vincent.

"Is that a big house?" asked Mrs. Combie.

"Very big," said Mr. Edwards. "A showplace. Talk of beauty!" and he said to Vincent, "It's open to the public; you ought to go there one day and see what you've missed. Didn't you know he was Lord Manley? One thing to comfort you," said Mr. Edwards. "He's quite a famous gourmet. If I had known he was coming to you—"

"If I had known!" said Vincent.

It was over now, the restaurant was closed, but an obstinacy in Vincent made him go on laying the tables, untying the bundles of forks and spoons and knives Mr. Dwight had counted—"I'll do them up again, Ettie"—unfolding the tablecloths, hiding the labels as well as he could. There was one that showed on the chandelier; he climbed up and peeled it off and stuck it on the back of one of the cherubs' wings. He could not help there being some strange things in the restaurant; Mrs. Combie's sewing machine, for instance, was in one lot with the big dish-cover; "We have to put rubbish with something good," Mr. Dwight had said. The dish-cover rubbish! Vincent had winced. There was a bundle of towels that went with the linen and an old birdcage on the desk; Mr. Dwight had wanted to bring the mangle in but there Vincent had rebelled. "What does it matter?" asked Cassie. Vincent, if he had answered at all, could almost have cried, "It's insulting the dead."

"But dearie, why—?" Mrs. Combie asked when she saw him setting the tables.

"I don't know why," said Vincent but he went steadily on, and when Olivia came in the restaurant looked much as it always had, though it was a little strange to find the bay trees inside.

As Olivia finished her wine, Lovejoy came down, her hair brushed, her face and hands washed, though her toes looked dirty through her shoes. "I can't help that," she said helplessly. "Let's go," she said, but Vincent fidgeted round them; he had something private to say to Olivia, something he did not want Lovejoy to hear. If he or Olivia had been Angela or Cassie, accustomed to children, they would have told Lovejoy to go outside, but neither of them liked to do that and presently Vincent, after hovering, put a little jug of parsley on the table.

"Don't you think that's good parsley?" he asked Olivia, but he did not look at the parsley, he looked at Lovejoy.

"Very good parsley," said Olivia and she put out a finger and, very gently, touched Lovejoy's cheek.

"What I admire about it is the way it keeps on," said Vincent. Now that he was not speaking about himself, his face was not strained or bitter. "It's had such stony ground but still it grows. I've grown very fond of it. It's loyal."

"It's a pity you can't keep it," said Olivia.

"The rubbish heap's no place for it," said Vincent bitterly.

"But Olivia did not know anything about him!" Angela was to say afterwards.

"I once talked to him about parsley," Olivia would have said if she had been there to say it. "That told me all I needed to know."

Vincent had called Mrs. Combie to see her. Olivia, putting out her hand, feeling the unexpected bigness and hardness of Mrs. Combie's, had looked at her with respect.

"Rubbish or not," Olivia said as she was leaving, "you have made this." She looked round the restaurant openly, and Vincent did not try to stop her. "You have tried, have made," she said.

"Yes," said Vincent, "and what have I done"—he looked at Mrs. Combie and Lovejoy—"to them, my wife, and a child?" And he cried, "You shouldn't make things on other people."

"But you said it didn't matter about other people," said Lovejoy.

"Don't be silly."

"You said it."

"Then I was silly," said Vincent, "silly and blind."

"George dear." Mrs. Combie put her hand into his.

"Don't, Ettie. You make it worse. When I think about the refrigerator—"

"Don't think about it."

"I must," said Vincent. "All my life long. I must. If ever I get another chance—" His face lit up, then was sad again, "Especially if I get another chance," he said.

"And I still think," said Olivia, "that it's better to try and fail, doing what you want to do, than not to try." She could not explain it more clearly than that but she knew it was the trying that was important; even if it fails, it goes to swell the sum total of trying, as a martyr's faith, even if he is killed for it, swells the faith of everyone. "You make me very ashamed," said Olivia. "I have been such a shameful, shameful coward."

She was a coward still. "Suppose Mrs. Malone is there?" she said tremulously to Lovejoy as they walked towards the church.

"Bridgie *said* it would be Father Lambert," said Lovejoy reassuringly. "If Mrs. Malone does come, I'll answer her back." But though she sounded brave Lovejoy was as nervous as Olivia and as they came to the church she said, "Keep watch for us."

Olivia, feeling rather like the nurse in *Romeo and Juliet*, sat down at the back of the church. The churchyard door was open, and Lovejoy went out into the garden; she wanted to meet Tip there.

"I told your mother I'd not let you out of my sight," Father Lambert said to Tip as they came. "I happen to have very long sight. Go into the garden with Lovejoy. I'll put a chair for Miss Chesney in the vestibule and talk to her there."

But nothing happens as it is planned. Tip and Lovejoy had fought for this moment, pleaded and longed for it; now Tip came slowly across the rubble—to begin with, it was disconcertingly formal to walk through the church door instead of coming down the wall—and found Lovejoy sitting by the lions on her accustomed stone. "Hello," he said.

"Hello," said Lovejoy, and there was silence.

"I'm going to the *Arethusa*," said Tip. "I'm really going." He said it for something to say; after all it was what he had come there to tell her. "At least I hope I am," he corrected himself. She made no comment, and, "It's a training ship for the Navy," he said.

"I hope you enjoy it," said Lovejoy distantly.

"It's proper," said Tip. "The school's like living in a ship, and we wear sailor dress."

"Sailors are fashionable this year," said Lovejoy.

That seemed to belittle them, and Tip began to boast. "The St. Vincent boys gave a display in the Tattoo," he said. "I don't know if we do but probably we will, and I'll be in it. You can come and watch."

"I shan't be able to," said Lovejoy coldly. "I shall be in a Home."

"My mum says you have fun in a Home," said Tip. He meant to cheer her up but it sounded quite heartless. "You go to school, like the others, and have nice frocks. Sometimes they give you ice cream." Lovejoy's lips quivered but she lifted her chin and looked silently through the window at the statue. Tip wished she would talk.

"You got the money for the pansies?" asked Tip. He knew there was trouble coming by that quivering lip.

"What's the good of pansies," said Lovejoy tensely, "if you can't water them?"

"It was your fault I couldn't come," said Tip, flaring up. "It was you who got me caught."

"You're talking like your mum," Lovejoy taunted him.

" 'S true, and you left me. You ran away."

"I *didn't run away*! It was the *garden*."

"Garden! Garden! All you think about's that blasted garden."

"I can't water it," said Lovejoy. "I've broken the cider bottle. Look, the grass has all gone brown."

" 'Tisn't grass, it's mustard and cress," said Tip cruelly. He wanted to be cruel.

"You're not to tell her," Father Lambert had said. "She should be gone before it happens. Now promise." Tip had promised and swelled protectively, but now Lovejoy seemed to him not like one of Olivia's sparrows but like a little octopus, threatening to wind round him again with her threats and tears; just as he had wanted to frighten her with the statue, to punish her, he wanted to punish her now, hurt her, thought Tip furiously; the fuss of these weeks, the being guarded and kept in, seemed clinched in this. He hated Lovejoy, his mother, his sisters, all the whole gang of them—Mary, Margaret, Clara, Bridgie, Josephine—he hated Angela, even Olivia, all women, and, "It's no use your bothering about the garden," he said. "There won't be any garden soon. Get that into your nut. No garden."

The tears stopped as if a hand had seized Lovejoy and wrung her dry. "Why not?" she asked in a frightened voice.

"Because they're going to knock it down," said Tip. "They've got the money to build the church."

"But the aeroplane's not up."

"They've got it. The Jiminy Cricket people gave it to them."

"Charles and Liz?" said Lovejoy, dazed.

"Yes. The builders are going to start at once; first they'll knock the hut down, squash, flat," said Tip.

Lovejoy winced. "Who told you?"

"Father Lambert." Tip was wound up, and the hideous words went on. "They'll bring a bulldozer. It'll go over the garden, like that." He made a flat sweep with his hand. "Over Jiminy Cricket, and the pansies and the pillar and the pot!"

"The pansies and the pillar and the pot," whispered Lovejoy after him. She did not mention Jiminy Cricket.

"Yes. A lot of good it's been, all that sweat," said Tip, disgusted.

Lovejoy turned her back on him. She had decided she would not, ever again, cry in front of Tip, but to suppress the crying hurt unbearably. Movements, small hard shudders, shook her. Above her, looking down through the window, was the statue; the windows were open wide, it was hot even in the church, but a pane of glass caught the bitter shudders from Lovejoy so that they seemed to pass from her into the statue; they seemed to shake it as bitterly.

Then, "Bloody pigs," said Lovejoy.

"Who?" asked Tip, startled.

"Grown-ups, all grown-ups!" cried Lovejoy and she picked up a piece of the stone coping—a big piece, thought Tip, horrified—and threw it through the window.

The stone hit the statue midway up the robe, just where her knees would have been, thought Tip. For a moment it rocked as if it were mortally hurt, then, in front of their eyes, it slowly overbalanced from the pedestal and fell. There was a crash as it hit the floor.

CHAPTER XXIII

"I'll take you round the house," said Sister Agnes. In her black habit with a narrow white starched coif and veil, she was just a nun to Lovejoy. As with postmen, bus conductors, policemen, her uniform made her anonymous.

"This is the dining room." Lovejoy stared at the blue and white oilcloth-covered tables, the red beakers, the small chairs.

"The playroom." A doll's house, a rocking horse, toys . . .

"Did you bring your toys?" asked the Sister.

"Do I have to have toys?" asked Lovejoy, startled.

"The playground."

"Don't we play in the Street?"

"Of course not," said Angela, and, "Our children are not allowed in the street," said Sister Agnes.

"Why not?"

"We're responsible for them," said the Sister gently. "They might get lost or into trouble." Lovejoy was too polite to say that she thought they must be little duffers, but a fearful thought struck her. "Won't I go in the Street? Will I have to stay there too?" And she pointed to the netted enclosure where the sound of balls on rackets and cricket bats rose with children's voices in the air. "You're one of our children now," said the Sister.

"This will be your bedroom."

Small beds, with white covers, a locker by each bed, more toys, dolls and teddy bears on the pillows. "Delightfully friendly," said Angela, "and only five beds. In some homes," she told Lovejoy, "you sleep in a dormitory."

"But I've always had a room to myself."

If Lovejoy had been asked how she was behaving she would have said she was being good and sensible; she did not know that to Angela it seemed she had fought all the way—"About the clothes, for instance," said Angela. One of Angela's committees had given the money for the clothes. "It will save twelve pounds out of the Poor Box," she had said.

"Are these my clothes?" Lovejoy had asked Miss Dolben when Miss Dolben had fitted her out.

"Your very own," said Miss Dolben. She was well used to the vanity of girls, the difficulty of buying clothes for them, but she had never seen anything like the silent disdain of this small Lovejoy. She was pleased to see her coming round.

"The raincoat, the gym dress, the flannel blouses, the walking shoes? And that brown—frock?" Lovejoy could not bring herself to call it a dress.

"Your very own."

It was two days later that Miss Dolben had brought Lovejoy into Angela's office. "Do you know what she has done?" Even good quiet-tempered Miss Dolben was indignant. "Do you *know* what she has done? Sold them," cried Miss Dolben.

"Sold them!" Olivia, who had seen Miss Dolben and Love-joy come in and had stolen downstairs, was shamelessly eaves-dropping. "Sold them where? Why? To whom?" Angela's voice was shrill. "To whom?"

"Mr. Dwight," said Lovejoy in surprise. Where else could she have sold them?

"For three pounds fifteen!" moaned Miss Dolben. "The raincoat alone cost four pounds."

"Then it was cheating," said Lovejoy sharply. "That rain-coat was very badly cut."

"Be quiet," said Angela even more sharply, but the next moment she asked, "What did you do with the money?"

"Bought clothes," said Lovejoy with dignity.

Olivia had no business to interfere, she had had no inten-tion of betraying herself, but now she was moved to come down the last stairs and ask, "What did you buy?"

Lovejoy's face lit up. "A little box coat like a reefer," she said, speaking to Olivia, not to Angela or Miss Dolben, "not a real reefer, of course, but quite good cloth and good turnings; it was forty-three shillings, but you have to pay quite that," said Lovejoy seriously. "Then a navy cotton skirt, not much stuff in it, but well cut; it's on a bodice and the buttons will let down; that was nine shillings. I bought two of those American woven shirts, one is white and one white with navy stripes, they were three shillings each, that makes two pounds eighteen; and two pairs of white ankle socks for three-and-six. And these plain pumps," said Lovejoy, showing them. "They'll do for winter if I'm careful to keep out of puddles. They were fourteen shillings, second-hand, at Dwight's. I think I was lucky to find them, don't you? And with the shilling over and two of the half-crowns Tip gave me—after I'd paid for the pansies—I bought this little cap. It has a touch of the sailor about it," said Lovejoy. "Sailors are fashionable this year"—but that made her think about Tip, and she was silent.

Angela had taken the clothes away. "I had to," she said when Olivia protested. "Even if we buy everything twice, that spirit must be broken." She had given the money again—"Out of her own pocket," said Miss Dolben—and the raincoat, the gym dress, the flannel blouses, walking shoes, and brown frock had been bought back.

"You must learn to do as you're told," Angela told Lovejoy. "You're far too cocksure and independent."

Angela had brought Lovejoy to the home herself. "You should do that, I know," she said to Miss Dolben, "but perhaps you will let me; as I recommended her, I feel responsible. I hope the Sisters will be able to cope."

"She needs understanding," said Miss Dolben, which was generous, for she had found Lovejoy oddly difficult. Angela was less forbearing, "She needs a firm hand," she said.

This scene in the home was proving her right. "I've always had a room to myself."

There was a pause; then, "Lovejoy, do you know why this house is called the House of Compassion?" asked Angela.

"It shouldn't be called that," Olivia had said.

"Why not? It's a beautiful name for a beautiful feeling."

"If you are outside it, not in," said Olivia. She hesitated, then said, "Angela, I should so much like to do something for that little girl. Couldn't I be her guardian? Some sort of guardian?" She stopped again, blushed darkly, then said with a defiant rush, "Angela, I want to adopt that little girl."

"*What* did you say?" Angela was so amazed that she— gaped, thought Olivia. She had not known that she could make Angela look like that. "After all she's done!" said Angela.

"Because of all she's done," said Olivia.

"*Because* of all she's done?" Angela sounded as if she were —could floundering be the word? asked Olivia, fumbling again. Floundering out of her depth? But how could anything she, Olivia, said be out of Angela's depth? It was only for a moment. Angela recovered. "It's very magnanimous of you, Ollie," she said, amused, and Olivia knew she would tell people; "Olivia's efforts with the sparrows," Olivia could hear Angela saying that to Mr. Wix.

She blushed more painfully still but she persisted. "Why not, Angela?"

"Poor old Ollie. She'd make rings round you."

"Well, why not?"

"They don't let old maids adopt children, for one thing," said Angela cuttingly, "and you'd be totally unsuitable as a foster-mother. Besides—Oh, Olivia, why are you so exaggerated?"

"I talked to that Father, Father Lambert. He approves."

"Catholics are exaggerated people."

"Angela, I'm serious."

"Then don't be," said Angela.

"I know it wouldn't be easy but Ellen understands, I'm sure Ellen would help me," said Olivia earnestly. "I've spoken to her about Lovejoy. We would take all responsibility."

"Which means I should have to take it in the end," said Angela, and Olivia knew she could not contradict her; for that one brief moment Olivia had forgotten what Doctor Wychcliffe had said.

"Compassion is pity," Angela told Lovejoy now. "This home is called that because it's a home for children who are to be pitied." The Sister made a quick movement and Angela said, "I'm afraid, Sister, this sometimes needs to be said. Lovejoy is far too opinionated. Do you know why they are to be pitied?" she asked Lovejoy.

"No," said Lovejoy.

"Because they are destitute, which means they have nothing. Nothing at all," said Angela, "except what some kind person chooses to give them. You should be grateful and not criticize," said Angela.

"But I can think?" said Lovejoy. She meant it as a question but it sounded bald and rude.

"You had better think," said Angela with an edge on her voice. "Think. If there were no kind people, what would you do?"

"I'd—" Lovejoy's face was far more expressive than Angela had thought. She looked, not masked, shut in, but eager and happy, like another child. I wonder if Olivia *could* have done something with her, thought Angela suddenly. "I'd—" said Lovejoy. Then her eyes came back to Angela and the eagerness died.

"You see," said Angela.

"Yes. I have to have kind people," said Lovejoy.

* * *

When Angela had gone Sister Agnes took Lovejoy by the hand. "I want to show you something," she said. In the passage and on the stairs they passed nuns, to whom Lovejoy was introduced—"This is our new girl, Lovejoy Mason"—and other children—"Wendy, come here and say hello to Lovejoy." In that moment Lovejoy would have given anything to see even Cassie. Then the Sister opened the door of a room off the entrance hall, a room Lovejoy had not seen before.

"This is our chapel," said Sister Agnes. "If ever you find things difficult and don't feel very happy, you can come in here."

She had expected Lovejoy would find the chapel strange, even bewildering, but Lovejoy walked past her as if it were familiar, then stood as if she had been struck still. "Hel*lo*!" It was a greeting, not an exclamation. On her papers had been written *Sunday school, church, nil,* but she slid into a pew and knelt down.

After a moment Sister Agnes came and sat beside her.

"She was in a church I knew," whispered Lovejoy.

"The statue?" Lovejoy nodded, her breath held.

Angela had thought it wiser not to tell the Sisters the story of the smashing. Angela had had to know because Olivia had been taken ill, there in the church, and Father Lambert had had to go for help, but Sister Agnes could not fathom the import of Lovejoy's words. "The statue, the very same!" breathed Lovejoy.

"Not the very same, the same," the Sister corrected. "That statue must have been made in hundreds—thousands, I expect. If you saw it somewhere else it was another one." Her brisk voice was intended to shatter all untruths, but Lovejoy continued to gaze in a tranced way. Then Sister Agnes distinctly heard her whisper, "Hail Mary."

"We don't teach you to pray to Mary," said the Sister gently.

Lovejoy did not know the difference between Anglican and Roman Catholic; even she had not fathomed all the vagaries of grown-ups; she wondered why there were no candles, she missed their warmth and the live sounds of the clicking of beads—she understood beads now—the pattering prayers.

Tip taught me and I'll do what Tip taught me forever and ever, said Lovejoy silently.

"And we don't cross ourselves."

I do, said Lovejoy silently.

"You can honour her as the mother of Our Lord but you must not give her supernatural powers."

Supernatural powers, supernatural babies, and lions with wings. A wave of such homesickness came over Lovejoy for the Street, the church, the garden, Jiminy Cricket, that she could not speak.

The last day, in the restaurant, Mrs. Combie had served ham and peaches and ice cream for midday dinner. "Well, really, Ettie!" said Cassie.

"It's Lovejoy's last day."

"It's she who ought to be giving them to you," said Cassie.

"Do you know your mother owes Mrs. Combie thirty pounds? Thirty pounds," said Cassie. She had looked at Mr. Dwight's labels. "Dad's furniture," she said with a little sob. "Dad's house!" She turned to where Vincent sat. "I'd give my soul if Ettie had never seen you," said Cassie.

Mrs. Combie sat up. "Nonsense, Cassie," she said. It was the first time she had ever said "Nonsense" to anyone. "What's all this song and dance about?" Vincent and Lovejoy sat up too. "A man like Vincent, with all he does, must be expected to fail now and then. *Next* time—" said Mrs. Combie.

"You think there'll be a next time?" asked Cassie jeeringly.

"There will be a next time," said Mrs. Combie. "You'll be hearing from us, Cassie."

When Cassie had gone Vincent got up from the table. He went into the pantry and presently came back, carrying a plate. He took it to the sink and washed it and polished it carefully; then he brought it to the table, put a helping of ice cream on it, and set it in front of Mrs. Combie. It was an Angelica Kauffman plate.

Mrs. Combie put her head down on the table and cried.

Lovejoy thought it better not to think about Vincent and Mrs. Combie. I meant to bring Jiminy Cricket, she thought. He's probably dying with no one to water him—or is he smashed up?

She shut her eyes. She had meant to bring Jiminy Cricket but—I broke the statue to bits, thought Lovejoy, and I couldn't go back into the church. It's queer, she thought, when you're kind to people you can forget them but when you're not, you can't. When she had stolen the candle money the statue had been hooded up in purple but this was evidently worse, because all these days Lovejoy had felt that it was she, Lovejoy, who was swathed. "I didn't mean it," she said, still hearing the crash. "If I didn't mean it, then it shouldn't count," she argued, but it counted and she had felt muffled, hidden in sorrow and grief, and now the statue was here again, with the sky-blue robe, white veil, pink hands and face, lilies, and gilt plate on the back of her head.

"No supernatural powers," said Sister Agnes firmly. Lovejoy dropped her lids.

A nun came to the chapel door, and Sister Agnes got up. "Wait here a moment," she said.

Outside a bell clanged, and presently Lovejoy heard a sound like school, the sound of children's feet marching. She leaned her head against the pew rail and shut her eyes. Even her sharp little brain could see no way out of it. She had to have kind people.

The feet were coming nearer, the din of voices; then there was a clap of hands and complete obedient silence.

Steps came towards the chapel—to fetch me, thought Lovejoy in a panic. In a moment someone would say, "Come along."

All the things said to children rose in her mind. "Do as you're told." "Don't answer back." "Come along." "Be quiet." Lovejoy ground her teeth. Quiet, obedient, grateful. All the detestable things children should be, and all the lovely free things, thought Lovejoy, that they must not, opinionated, cocky—she hadn't Angela's word "cocksure." Cocky, thought Lovejoy longingly.

The door opened. "Come along," said Sister Agnes, but Lovejoy was praying.

"Hail Mary," prayed Lovejoy between her teeth, "Mary, make me cocky and independent."

CHAPTER XXIV

SPARKEY sat on his folded newspaper and looked down the Street.

It was almost time to go home; his mother was selling the last batch of her evening papers. Most people were home from work, only a few got off each bus now and hardly anyone got on; there was a quiet, a relaxation in the air; far overhead the evening smoke went up from the chimneys, some of the windows were lit. The bigger children, slipping in and out of the shadows, were still playing, but the little ones had gone to bed. The very big boys and girls were parading up and down the High, and a couple or so had already come down the Street, where they disappeared in a doorway—to kiss, thought Sparkey accurately. A few women stood talking late on their doorsteps—there was time to talk now—but most of

them were indoors. Istanbul, full of herrings' heads up to his
throat, sat purring on the portico wall.

Sparkey's mother came and wrapped a paper round
Sparkey's bony little knees. The October wind was chilly and
in it was a tang of wood smoke; Sparkey knew where that came
from; Lucas, reinstated, had been burning leaves in the
Square Gardens.

"An old rating, a naval man, give him another chance,"
said the admiral. Mr. Donaldson had nodded agreement.
Angela, surprisingly, had allowed herself to be guided; she
was oddly quiet and amenable; a little later she had resigned
from the Garden Committee.

The wood smoke made Sparkey think of Guy Fawkes Day.
Tip had promised that Sparkey could help with the gang's
Guy. It was Tip's last Guy. In January he was going to the
Arethusa.

Suddenly Sparkey sat up on his step. A green car, *the* green
car, had turned into Catford Street. It drove slowly down the
length of the Street as if it were looking for something, then
stopped at the river end, where Vincent's used to be. Sparkey's
patrolling was accepted now, even by his mother. "After all,
I'm nearly big enough to be in the gang," he said hopefully.
"I'm four months nearer six," and he unwrapped the newspaper swiftly from his legs and ran down the Street.

"Where are you going?" called his mother.

"Hist!" said Sparkey over his shoulder.

Charles—Sparkey had heard Lovejoy call the gentleman
Charles—was out of the car, standing and looking; after a
moment Liz—Sparkey remembered her name too; unlike
Lovejoy he thought it pretty—got out as well. They were
looking at the restaurant. What's the good of that? thought
Sparkey. It's shut.

He knew how shut it was. Like all the other boys, he had

tried to get in, but the door was locked and the windows were covered with bolted-on grids; through their mesh the rounded glass could be seen covered in grime and cobwebs and dust; the place where the bay trees had stood was full of litter and rubbish swept into the doorway by the wind, and the paper flapped eerily; the polish had gone off the door and the brass-work was black. Even the board where VINCENT's still showed was grimed and dim. "The minute you give up cleaning a place," any woman in Catford Street could have said, "the minute you give up, it's done for and black."

After a moment Charles and Liz got back into the car, which turned and drove up to the church. Sparkey ran back to the steps and was on the pavement when Charles opened the car door and got out. "But it's gone," said Liz, looking where the church had been.

Charles laughed. "Didn't you expect it to be gone?"

Hut, steps, walls, bell, aeroplane notice had been swept away, and in their place was a big empty pit; where the rubble and marble had been was space. The steps in the Street sounded hollow in this emptiness, and the wind that Sparkey's mother had been frightened of made a howling noise as it caught the open walls. Sparkey came closer. "There were bodies here," he whispered. "They found them when they cleared away the church. They dug them up."

"Cut along," said Charles sharply to Sparkey.

"They put them all in a hole and sealed them up," said Sparkey, ignoring Charles.

"Go away, you little ghoul," said Charles.

He laughed, but Sparkey thought he, Sparkey, had fright-ened Liz.

"It's life stamped out," she said, looking round the empty pit. "Our restaurant, the funny church, and I wanted to see my little saint." She sounded almost as if she were crying.

"You're hungry," said Charles. "Come along." Lovejoy would have been surprised to know that grown-up people were sometimes told to come along. "I've seen all I need to see," said Charles. "You'll feel better when you have had some dinner, even if it's not our little man's."

"I don't want any dinner," said Liz, as Sparkey often said. Then, "Look," said Charles.

He turned her to the old back wall; on a bit of brick was a tiny spurt of copper-pink and green. It was so small that it was easy to overlook it but it was there, on its piece of brick, a plant in a strange round pot. "It's—is it?" said Liz. "But—*how* can it be?" she cried. Charles went across and brought it to her, trying to dust the wreath pot with his handkerchief. "You'll dirty your gloves," he told Liz, but she took it from him.

"What was it she called it?" she asked Charles.

"Jiminy Cricket," said Sparkey obligingly.

"That was it, Jiminy Cricket," said Charles. He looked at Sparkey. "It seems to be a famous rose."

"But how can it be Jiminy Cricket?" asked Liz.

"It must be," said Charles. "It isn't likely there would be another rose like that in Catford Street."

"It's blooming," said Liz. "Someone must have watered it." The tiny leaves were dusty but they were green, and on the little standard tree were two roses and a bud, a deep pink bud.

The watchman came out of his hut. "Do you have to have a watchman on a ruin?" asked Liz.

"It isn't a ruin," said Charles. "We're building."

The watchman looked at Jiminy Cricket. "A boy comes in and waters it," he said. "He must have put it up there, on the wall."

"A boy? Not a little girl?" asked Liz.

"I think it was a boy," said the watchman. "Of course, it may have been a girl. There are hundreds of girls. I spend my life chasing kids out of here." And he glowered at Sparkey.

"Hundreds of little girls," said Liz. "Little churches, little restaurants. What does it matter what happens to one?"

"Don't be impertinent," said Charles and he took her arm and swayed her as if he were gently shaking her. "Look at Jiminy Cricket and what he has come through. Perhaps Vincent's the new head waiter at the Savoy; perhaps he has won a football pool and opened a better restaurant somewhere else. As for the little girl," said Charles, "no one, nobody, has the faintest idea what that little girl will do."

*   *   *

Olivia had died in August. It was very inconvenient, almost another of her social lapses; everyone was away, the Miss Chesneys themselves should have been in Scotland, and Noel had to interrupt his holiday. "Though why he should interrupt it to see Olivia dead when he would never have dreamed of it to see her living," Angela had begun, then, shocked at herself, said, "Hush." Once or twice in those days she had found she was saying "Hush" to herself, as she used to say it to Olivia, but then, most oddly, she seemed to be thinking some of Olivia's thoughts. She even found herself leaving the office and coming up by herself to the schoolroom. Olivia had insisted on moving there when she was ill so that she could hear the noise of the Street. "Such an odd thing to want to hear," said Noel. "And very inconsiderate," said Angela. "It made a great deal of work for Ellen."

"I didn't mind," said Ellen. "She died so happy," but Olivia's face when she died had not looked happy as much as satisfied. "What was she so satisfied about?" asked Angela. Angela had forgotten the sparrows.

On the afternoon of the funeral Mr. Anstruther, the Chesneys' young lawyer, had come to read the will.

"It isn't much more than a month ago," he said, "that Miss Chesney came to see me."

"Mr. Anstruther," Olivia had said, "you are young, but I'm sure you have some sense. Please will you tell me? Do you think I'm in my right mind?"

"My *dear* Miss Chesney!"

"I am asking you," said Olivia, "because presently Angela will tell you I'm not. You may have trouble so I should like you to telephone my doctor, Doctor Wychcliffe—I have just come from him—who will tell you that though I'm not very well, I'm perfectly sane."

"I don't need to telephone Doctor Wychcliffe," said Mr. Anstruther.

"But please do it." Olivia spoke firmly but the hand that smoothed her gloves had trembled. "You see, I want to alter my will," she said. "Alter it in rather a monstrous way." And she smiled. "When you have telephoned the doctor I should like you to draw up a draft."

"I drew it up, there and then," said Mr. Anstruther to Noel and Angela.

"I haven't so very much to leave," Olivia had said, "not like Angela, but I think it will be enough—enough for what I want," she had added, seeing Mr. Anstruther's inquiring look. "Noel and Angela think I should leave it to Noel's children. Well, they must be disappointed. The annuity to Ellen is to stand, of course," said Olivia, "but the rest . . ."

Noel's face had had a look of complacent expectancy as Mr. Anstruther came to that, but Angela had asked, "The rest?" with sudden disquiet.

When Mr. Anstruther had finished reading there was such a dazed silence that he said, "Perhaps I had better explain it to you in non-legal terms."

Olivia had apologized for the will herself. "It seems a roundabout way of doing it," she had told Mr. Anstruther, "but it was difficult to find a way that would fulfil all requirements. *All* requirements," she had said, smoothing her gloves.

"If I had left it all to Lovejoy, she would have been separated from Tip, and that little girl needs *not* to be separated. She needs a home, and the home she wants is with Vincent and Mrs. Combie, so . . ."

"A trust is to be set up," Mr. Anstruther began to explain, "to open a restaurant in the West End—" But Angela interrupted.

"Olivia and a restaurant! I can't believe it!"

"How did she come to be mixed up with people like this?" asked Noel wrathfully. "It's you and your miserable charities, Angela."

"But she never would be mixed up in my charities," said Angela. She still sounded dazed.

Mr. Anstruther went on. "The restaurant is to be managed by this man Vincent, Mr. Combie, once of Catford Street, on condition that he and his wife provide a home for Lovejoy Mason, treating her, in all respects, as if she were their own child. If the restaurant seems profitable, Vincent is to be given a half-share after five years; the other half is to be divided between the boy Tip Malone and Lovejoy Mason. Mrs. Combie, the wife, is to be paid three pounds a week by the Trustees for the care of Lovejoy, who is to have thirty pounds a year paid to her personally for her clothes." Miss Chesney said, "Lovejoy will manage well on that." "When Lovejoy Mason is eighteen, or when she marries, she is to have two hundred pounds for a training or towards furnishing a home.

"Tip Malone is to visit Lovejoy when he and she like, or when his mother will let him. The trustees are Inspector Russell of Mortimer Street Police Station"—"That nice Inspector," Olivia had called him—"the man Vincent, Mr. Combie, Father Lambert of the Church of Our Lady of Sion in Catford Street, and you, Miss Angela, if they will serve on the trust with you."

"And if not?" asked Noel hotly.

"Then the trustees are Inspector Russell, Vincent, and Father Lambert."

Olivia had always been blunt, but, anxious for the smooth working of the trust, she had not foreseen that it would sound quite as blunt and hard as it did—it had an effect she would never have believed, for Angela began to blush. It was a blush as painful and humiliating as any of Olivia's own.

CHAPTER XXV

THE admiral was showing the new member of the Garden Committee round the gardens. "We'll have some wallflowers here," he said, pointing with his stick at the long borders.

"No, sir," said Lucas.

"What do you mean, 'No, sir'?"

"Miss Chesney asked the Committee to remember the residents don't like wallflowers, sir."

The admiral did not regain his temper until they came to the shrub beds. "This is where the trouble was," he said.

"What trouble, Admiral?"

"Street children," said the admiral with a quelling look at Lucas. "You'd never think they stole loads of earth from there? The funny thing is that the holes are closing up; we didn't do anything, they're closing themselves, making new earth. Don't ask me how," said the admiral, "because I don't know."